EXILE

ANN IRELAND

EXILE

a novel

SIMON & PIERRE FICTION
A MEMBER OF THE DUNDURN GROUP
TORONTO · OXFORD

Editor: Barry Jowett
Copy-Editor: Jennifer Bergeron
Design: Jennifer Scott
Printer: Transcontinental

National Library of Canada Cataloguing in Publication Data

Ireland, Ann
    Exile / Ann Ireland.

ISBN 1-55002-400-0

I. Title.

PS8567.R43E85 2002   C813'.54   C2002-903791-3   PR9199.3.I6825E85 2002

1   2   3   4   5   06   05   04   03   02

We acknowledge the support of the **Canada Council for the Arts** and the **Ontario Arts Council** for our publishing program. We also acknowledge the financial support of the **Government of Canada** through the **Book Publishing Industry Development Program** and **The Association for the Export of Canadian Books**, and the **Government of Ontario** through the **Ontario Book Publishers Tax Credit** program.

Care has been taken to trace the ownership of copyright material used in this book. The author and the publisher welcome any information enabling them to rectify any references or credit in subsequent editions.

J. Kirk Howard, President

Printed and bound in Canada.❀
Printed on recycled paper.
www.dundurn.com

Dundurn Press	Dundurn Press	Dundurn Press
8 Market Street	73 Lime Walk	2250 Military Road
Suite 200	Headington, Oxford,	Tonawanda NY
Toronto, Ontario, Canada	England	U.S.A. 14150
M5E 1M6	OX3 7AD	

For B and B

I

I AM THE KIND OF MAN WOMEN love. My face is seamed by time, and in each line they count a century of my country's hopeless, bungling despair. In this ordinary expression they see peasant uprisings, earthquakes, and dictators whose asses widen with each year in power. Women stare into my sad eyes and trace each day spent in prison, my sufferings barely imaginable. Yet they do imagine. Then they run a manicured nail across the skin between my eyebrows and touch my pulse, and their smiles are coated with desire.

What they don't always see is that I am afraid.

My prison was a room in the basement of my sister's colleague and her husband: Marta and Rodolfo. I was lucky to be there, hidden from enemies. This woman was a professor at the university, in the department of cultural studies. The basement room had been a wine cellar, but there was no wine anymore, just red stains on the concrete floor and a faint briny smell. There was no toilet, only a tin bucket. Each morning when I passed the bucket to Marta I could read the disgust in her eyes. I watched the way she held out her arm stiffly as she climbed the stairs, horrified that the contents might slosh onto her tailored blouse. She knew my shit intimately. The maid wasn't allowed below although sometimes I heard her singing as she cleaned, her pail scraping across my ceiling. And often at night I could hear them arguing upstairs. Rodolfo would start in a low voice, which would gradually erupt into a shout, "Get him out! It is too dangerous!"

I would huddle beneath, anticipating the worst. Because I'd lost everything, had no useful opinions, nowhere to go, my life was waiting for others to decide. If I walked out the door to buy a magazine at the kiosk next to City Hall, I would disappear forever. You do something careless, once, and everything changes, not just the world, but your insides.

Both state and national police had my case on file. My employer, the newspaper, abolished all references to my work. No one was allowed to publish my poetry or my essays, and my books had been stripped from the shelves. I had insulted a very serious man.

Marta wanted to get rid of me, too. I had made her house into a place she dreaded entering. Yet my sister, Rosario, sent food, money, and probably the goddamn shit pail and begged Marta (I can hear this, Rosario's wheedling voice) to have pity. "It is an unfortunate situation."

We all underestimated the sensitivity of our General's ear. That supreme organ had sucked up the whispered idiocy of the poor writer, and with a few muttered words, he'd caused my life to shrink to nothing. One day you are everybody's friend, cakewalking down the streets of the Old Town like the mayor, half-pissed, money sprinkling out of your pockets onto the cobble-stones, wondering only which bar to visit before returning home for supper. At first I thought — we all thought — this will blow over in a few days.

Carlos, after all, is nothing, nobody, a flea in the ear of the General.

The morning after my catastrophe I saw my face in one of the daily papers, grainy, a not particularly flattering snapshot taken back in my days with the Normal Forces, wearing fatigues and that crummy short-brimmed hat. Every male child has to endure eighteen months in the military before his real life begins. Believe me, I've made up for wasted time.

At first it was a lark being a fugitive. You could even say I felt a trifle proud at being selected, out of many, to perform this role. It would all blow over in a week or two, we thought; yet this is where we miscalculated. It turned out that I was *despised* by this malevolent official. I developed a chronic cough, as if the word had lodged in my throat and no amount of water or wine would clear it. The General's despising was notorious, and now, so was I.

In the small room I sat on the leather-backed chair and knew that given the chance again, I wouldn't have spoken so boldly. I am no hero. It is more important to be alive, to breathe the diesel-perfumed air of our city than to crouch like a mole in this tunnel.

At first, in my basement chamber I was treated like a member of the family. When Marta came home from work at the university she would scoop up chops and rice the maid had cooked, pour something to drink, add a sweet that she'd picked up from the café, and bring the tray downstairs. While I was eating she would pull up a chair and tell me about her day. I think she was lonely.

That was the first couple of weeks. Then it changed. I had become a guest who lingered too long, whose every throat-clearing and fart was an irritation. Whereas at first they would invite me upstairs late at night, after the children were put to bed, to watch television and drink coffee (Marta's coffee is like tar, with a shimmering membrane of oil floating on top), they gradually retreated into their private lives. As if they wanted to forget about this pathetic human pacing their basement room. Marta's smile, when she brought food, became strained and distant, then disappeared altogether. When your life has shrunk, and when the only human contact is the food provider and the remover of the shit pail, your heart drills in your chest at the sound of feet clattering down the stairs. You begin to sweat in anticipation. You arrange yourself in the room, first sitting, then standing propped against the wall, hands in pockets. What else could I do but receive their diminishing attentions? I knew they wished me to disappear, but I had no choice in the matter. I depended completely on their good will and it made me disgusting. To them, and to myself.

I began to stink. It was difficult to bathe. Marta and Rodolfo have two small daughters, curious, sociable girls who must not know of my existence. This caused great strain.

"No!" I heard Marta cry when one of the girls put her hand on the door to the basement. "You mustn't!"

I strained to hear more, what excuses Mama used: deadly fumes? rodent infestation? Perhaps not so far from the truth.

There was a tiny window just above my head which revealed a portion of sidewalk, but I was not, in theory, permitted to open it, not even an inch. Nor was I allowed to part the curtains.

"It is too dangerous," Marta said.

Of course. Dangerous not just for me, but for all of them. I immediately began to disobey, for without sun or air a man decays, he becomes rank, a rat dying inside the plaster of the walls.

I cheated often. On Friday nights, very late, I switched off my light, propped open the window an inch, then parted the curtain just enough to feel the outside air press in, and to hear shouts and laughter from patrons leaving the bars. Sometimes I was sure I recognized voices — Sylvan and Ana — and I would listen for the sharp click of a woman's high heels on cobblestone. What if I sneezed or hiccupped? I imagined the pair of legs stopping, followed by a grunt of discomfort, then a face peering in. My nerves fired with each sound. Still, like anyone, inside this fear, curiosity flickered. One evening a pair of stockinged ankles came so close to my window that my hand rose to seize them. I wanted to see how much worse I could make it for myself. No, I wanted to stroke her skin, make her cry out. And where were all my friends, my so-called pals from the newspaper, the writers union? "Too bad for Carlos," they were saying, as they sat for endless hours in the café gulping sugary pastry.

I began to love my own country now that I was forbidden to enter it.

Marta raced to my room in a state of excitement, forgetting even to flinch at the layers of unhygienic smells. She'd pulled her thick hair back into a ponytail and it tossed from side to side as she dropped onto the other chair and faced me. I was suddenly ashamed at my appearance, the pasty unshaven face and filthy clothes. I had refused to let her wash them, thinking of their increasing stiffness as a metaphor for what was happening to me. I was a sorry specimen.

"I have interested an organization called CAFE in your case," she said in a breathless voice.

"Café?"

"Canadian Alliance for Freedom of Expression." She spoke these words in slow, careful English. "Their group in Vancouver wishes to help you."

"Vancouver?" My mind searched for geography. "Help me? How?" I was suspicious and scared. For here, in this dank basement room, I was, at least, safe. I got up and started pacing. The sole of my shoe had come loose and flapped against the cement.

"They want to bring you to the west coast of Canada, as a refugee."

Her face shone with pleasure.

A refugee. I thought of those photos: famine-stricken Africans with distended bellies grabbing for food, Red Cross trucks.

"It's good news, Carlos. You'll be free."

I looked at her. It will be you who is free — of me.

That night I hardly slept. But then night and day had long since lost their identities. The light in my cell was a timeless glimmer, like some monk's lantern in the caves of Tibet. I woke up at what may have been dawn, with my left hand clasping a woman's ankle, which slipped away as the walls crowded in. I must have wakened the household with my cries of ecstasy.

Sunlight bruises when the eyes have been in hiding. I was swept out of the house at dawn, pressed roughly into

Rodolfo's car by an anxious Marta and my sister Rosario, who both chattered non-stop and made me crouch in the back seat so I would not be seen. I hardly had a chance to smell the dewy grass or charcoal burners from the nearby market. Rodolfo stayed home with the sleeping children while his wife took the wheel.

Marta raced through the empty early morning streets and I felt each pit in the asphalt as I lay hunched across the vinyl seat, cheek hot against plastic. The international airport was thirty kilometres out of town. Everyone except me seemed wildly happy about the unfolding adventure. Especially Marta, who would have her house back whole and would send Lucía, the maid, into the basement that very day with a pail of soapy water and wire brush.

"You are a fortunate man," Rosario called over her shoulder. "You've have been offered a new life."

I was less excited than stunned. I thought of childhood journeys in my father's old car when I would lie like this, but my body much smaller, knees folded up to my chin, head pressed against my sister's sweaty thigh. Did I even want this new life? I'd become like a hospital patient: you do what you are told and are grateful for the attention.

I was clean now, freshly scrubbed and dabbed with deodorant and hair gel, decked out in new-old clothes, nails buffed and teeth flossed. The evening before, after darkness fell, I'd been permitted to creep up the stairs and lower myself into the family bathtub, an oversized porcelain monster from the previous century. Not without a pang of regret, for I had become attached to my dirt. I swept the terry cloth between my legs then down each thigh and between each festering toe until an odd smell joined the perfumed suds: something had left my body for good.

We finally arrived at the parking lot near the ugly cement building. This example of our glorious civic architecture was built under the last administration, with the hope of enticing tourists and foreign investment to our land. When I woozily lifted my head I saw yellow light spill through the floor-to-ceiling windows onto the terrazzo floor within. Silvery jets pulsed on the tarmac, spewing diesel fuel exhaust, while gnomes in forklifts toted luggage.

As a newspaper man, this building was hardly foreign to me. I'd spent many an hour in its lounge waiting for mysterious mechanical problems to be solved. Our national airline is famous for its antique equipment and flexible schedules.

"Lock the doors!" my sister cried. The place was full of thieves, even at this hour.

"Does he have his bag?" Marta said.

I had already begun to exist in the third person.

They'd selected, after a quick argument, a spot between two delivery vans to park. These would shield us as we exited the car. I felt my body creak as it unfurled, my poor spine fused from the weeks of confinement. Hot tar bled beneath our feet as we made our way to the automatic doors of the airport entrance. My pockets bulged with precious documents: passport and birth certificate, something from the Canadian government with official signatures, and the letter from CAFE written in stilted academic Spanish. Much work had been done on my behalf. This astonished me. Who were these helpful strangers in a faraway country? The doors opened and we were sucked in by the blast of icy synthetic air. It was too much, too sudden, and I started to skid across the polished floor.

"Carlos!" My sister grabbed the back of my shirt. Then she said to Marta, "Where does he go?"

Marta pointed. "Far end. First he has to check in."
She glanced around the nearly empty building. "There
shouldn't be any trouble." This phrase hung in the air like
a command.

The two women saw me off to the Departures gate, both of
them in a state of high agitation. I saw that Marta hadn't applied
her makeup, and the neck of her blouse was open, showing a
glimpse of freckled chest. Her eyes roamed the foyer, scanning
each passenger's face, each official's badge. She couldn't wait to
get out of there.

"This is the best thing," Rosario kept saying in that high-
pitched voice, which is always too excited or too sorrowful.

"Do you have your ticket? Your passport?" Marta chimed in,
equally nervous.

I felt entirely exposed, convinced that my newly shaved
face was fluorescent, that any idiot could see what I was up to,
and who was that man with his nose in a magazine? A plainclothes member of the Special Forces, trained to sniff out
criminals like myself? The General's own agent? Even a child,
a girl of no more than ten banging the side of a vending
machine, was a possible plant. When she turned around I
would see that she wasn't a child at all, but a midget, a dwarf-
policewoman, toting not a harmless O'Henry bar but a
cocked handgun.

Goodbye dear country, goodbye dear sister, goodbye Marta,
a fast embrace then their brightly coloured dresses danced
toward the exit, leaving only a light fragrance of cologne.

The colour of the airplane was navy blue: this is a sensible and
reassuring hue, and the pilot's voice was so calm he appeared to

be on the edge of falling asleep. I'd been in airplanes before, of course, but never to penetrate the skies above northern lands. How cold would it be, and how dark?

I fiddled with the sealed package of Canadian cheddar cheese. I picked at the plastic with both fingers, sawed at it with my teeth, then gave up, pocketing it for later. I'd been drinking since takeoff; the liquor was free and plentiful and I was, I confess, nervous. Not of flying, but of arrival.

"I can never open those things, either," my seatmate said. He glanced at the pocket where I'd slid the cheese.

My face reddened, as if I'd been spotted boosting the cutlery.

"You headed for Vancouver?"

"That is so." I nodded. My mind flooded with endless English drills from preparatory school: I did see, I saw, I see, I will see, I would see...

He looked like an explorer in his tan fatigues with dozens of deep pockets and flaps. His hair was thick and orange, his face freckled, yet lined. He was a young man, and I suspected he'd stayed too long in the sun for his pale complexion.

"What kind of business are you in?" he said.

I slugged wine from the plastic cup. "I am a poet."

His mouth stayed open. "No kidding."

"And what business are you?"

"I'm a sand broker. Right now I'm working on a shipping deal from Vancouver to Hawaii."

I couldn't think of a word to say.

"Actually," he confessed. "I think I'm the only one in the world who does this."

"Alas, I am not the only poet."

I pulled out a copy of *Insomnio*.

"I don't read much Spanish," he said, politely leafing

through the pages. "Just enough to get by in the field. What brings you to B.C.?"

I should have been alerted by his inquisitiveness. Instead, giddy from the wine and the altitude, I began to tell him the story in fractured English.

"My situation is funny," I said, "and more than a little tragic."

He closed the blind over the porthole so that he could see me without the coating of sunlight.

"I am about to become a writer-in-exile," I began, using the phrase for the first time.

"Really?" His eyes scanned my face. "In exile from what?"

The question was a surprise. "From anyone who might know me."

My seatmate waited for more, feet stretching as far as possible in his heavy boots, perhaps to avert the possibility of thrombosis.

"This is all I am able to say." I enjoyed the tinge of mystery, but his stare continued, so I added with a philosophical shrug, "We are all in exile from our authentic lives: it is the state of modern man."

He gave a little laugh and said, "I can tell you are a poet." Then he pulled out a black eyeshade from one of his many pockets and slipped it over his head.

Perhaps with his eyes covered he thought he'd disappeared, like the famous ostrich. To my surprise I felt a tug of loneliness and hurt.

When, hours later, the plane began to dip towards ground, I leaned over my dozing seatmate, lifted the blind and peered down at the patchwork of buildings and highways below. The sun had disappeared and a faint drizzle coated the airplane's wing. Mountains rose in the distance, just as at home.

He pulled up his eyeshade and smiled. "There she is," he said. "Vancouver. Your new life."

Suddenly I doubted him. A sand broker? Selling sand to Hawaii? It was absurd, a transparent cover. Yes, but for what?

The wheels hit the glazed tarmac and there was a deafening screech of brakes.

"Someone will be waiting for you," Rosario had told me with full confidence that our operation would unfold according to plan. "Just look for the CAFE sign."

Yes, but first I must make my way through Customs and Immigration with my documents, and I felt that instinctive terror at the sight of agents whose job it was to sniff out liars, cheats, and anyone whose belongings didn't match his story. A blonde woman in a white shirt peered at my passport with its four-year-old photograph, then my envelope of documents, and asked a few questions which I had to ask her to repeat. I felt myself growing red with strain, but perhaps she was used to such a reaction, because suddenly she slid the papers back into the envelope and said, "That's fine. You may go."

For several seconds I stood under the lights, unable to move. It was too easy, almost a miracle. The automatic doors popped open and I arrived in Canada to see a small mob of greeters waiting on the other side. I searched for those eager well-wishers who would be holding the CAFE sign, yet all I could see was a banner reading, "Welcome Home Mormon Brothers." I made my way to a curved vinyl seat, set my bag on it, and waited to be discovered.

The Vancouver airport looked much like the one I'd left hours earlier. Its air contained the same layered perfume of disinfectant, stale coffee, and fuel, yet here a hard rain drilled the plate glass windows. Outside on the grey tarmac, the plane I'd so recently departed hummed with sweat. In an hour or so, cleaned out and refuelled, it would return to Santa Clara.

Finally I spotted her, a woman wearing a yellow rain slicker, still dripping wet, racing towards the Arrivals door, holding a soggy cardboard sign. I lifted my bag, about to rise, but then I stopped myself. My heart was hammering so hard I could barely breathe. She would think me high strung, out of control, asthmatic. So, for a moment, I just watched.

Her hair was dark and long, pasted to her skull by the rain, and yet I could see that she was pretty. A slash of lipstick coated her mouth.

She scanned the clumps of arriving passengers, men in raincoats and flustered mothers with children and toppling mounds of luggage, her eyes fastening for a moment on the so-called sand broker who heaved a leather satchel over his shoulder and marched down the hallway. One wave of passengers came and dispersed, then another. The smile on her face grew strained.

Still I waited; I was not yet ready to enter my new life. It was the last few seconds of being unseen. Whenever the double doors sprang open, she lifted her wet sign and smiled in anticipation. Over and over again she was denied her pleasure. I was being cruel, yet it was inevitable. I had to watch her without being watched myself. My knees popped up and down, a nervous rhythm. Then it was time. I gripped the satchel and began to rise again, but stopped and watched as something curious happened.

A tall, thin man had pressed through the automatic doors, wearing a sweater-vest under his dark jacket and a pair of loose corduroy pants. He looked around, brow furrowed, shifting his bag from one shoulder to the other. He was about my age and even had a thatch of dark hair, but his eyes were huge and he held himself erect. Even from a distance I could see the high cheekbones, the fine features that were almost girlish.

She smiled encouragingly and went up to him, the sign raised to her chest level.

"I am Rita," she said very clearly, then, "Welcome to Vancouver."

I felt my heart flex in excitement and for a few seconds even thought, there has been some mistake, he is the exile, the real one.

His eyes settled on her. "Not me, sweetie." He tapped the soggy sign. "I'm waiting for the wife, wherever she may be."

Rita flushed, mortified. She'd been so sure. Then, stepping back, she was faced with the question: if this man was not Carlos, then who was?

I slowly advanced, carrying the athletic bag that held all my precious belongings, and felt the oversized jacket engulf my shoulders. My sneakers, a last-minute purchase, were held together with Velcro tabs instead of laces. Rosario had bought these for me. Thank you, dear sister. I slid an unlit cigarette between my lips and let it dangle.

I spotted a tiny flash of disappointment as I held my hand out.

"I am Carlos Romero Estévez."

She could hardly speak, perhaps feeling some tumult of emotion at my arrival. She ignored my hand and rose on tiptoes to kiss me, not on both cheeks, but on one, like a mother greeting her child. I felt the shroud of wet plastic press into my chest.

"I'm so glad you're here," she said. She shook her hair, sprinkling more rain. Her skin was soft and unlined, although I could tell she was over thirty by her eyes and the leanness of her face. "I am Rita Falcon, from the CAFE board of directors."

I smiled and said, "Thank you." And when she looked puzzled, added, "Thank you for my arrival, thank you for my existence."

She laughed, perhaps embarrassed by my sincerity. "You must have more luggage."

"Just this." I hefted the nylon bag Rodolfo had given me. Rita kept staring, eyes shining with pain and perhaps approval. I thought of the other passenger, the one who was waiting for his wife. Why had she been convinced that he was the exiled poet?

"Welcome to Canada," she remembered to say, but the phrase was rushed this time, an afterthought.

"Yes," I agreed, and inhaled deeply to show her that I wanted to know this place, to feel its air swell my chest, and that I was unafraid.

We drove into the city in her old Toyota, rain sputtering against the windshield and the wipers not working properly. We passed rows of stark concrete bunkers on the outskirts of the city, their roofs cradled by fog. And Rita talked.

"I work part-time at the university," she told me. She had removed the bulky slicker, and I saw that she was a slender woman, with muscular arms and a long neck, and dark hair that brushed her shoulders.

"You are a professor?"

"Goodness no. I just work in the Grad Centre. Admin."

She sifted through traffic, changing lanes twice, and laughed. "Sorry. Graduate Centre, administration. We all talk in short forms. But you understand now?"

"Yes, thank you."

"You will have a position at the university, too."

"Yes." I had heard about this.

"Writer-in Exile. Nice office. You'll be able to work, to write." Rita rolled down her window, thrust an arm out into the drizzle, and the roar of traffic crammed into our little car.

"Over there are the mountains." She raised her voice to be heard.

I stared but saw nothing, only the deep, phlegmy greyness, steam lifting from the earth.

"Wait till the clouds clear," she said, cranking the window back up. "It's a knockout."

She didn't look at me once during the ride, as if she couldn't bear to. Instead she pointed to the rain-slurred buildings as they appeared through the fog: this was her old high school, this was the theatre, the important café, while I kept wiping the fogged-up window with my sleeve, trying to see this place where I'd landed.

We spun through downtown Vancouver and the buildings were like holograms, untouched by age or wind or neglect, apparitions of buildings that might be, shedding water from their shiny surfaces. The Toyota took a sharp turn into an area of small stucco houses and leafy trees, perhaps the famous national maples. We passed a soccer field where men and women were kicking a ball through the bog, their bodies entirely coated in brown sludge.

My own body gave a jerk.

"I am a poet," I declared suddenly, ridiculously.

Rita smiled, stroking her hand over the wheel. "I've been taking Spanish classes all month, since we knew for sure you were coming." She took a breath and recited, "Yo tengo mucho respeto para los poetas."

I sank back into the seat. The windshield wipers sliced the view, back and forth, back and forth.

"Good," I said. "I am glad."

We pulled up in front of a large brown building, six storeys high, with a green door and many small windows set into the prickly facade. Its roof was flat, like a factory, and the rust-coloured chimney belched steam. Across the street was a school, its concrete yard deserted, twin basketball nets torn from the backboards.

"This is your house?" I was puzzled. There were many buildings like this in Santa Clara, containing nondescript flats for the factory workers and maids. I had rarely set foot in one. "It is big."

"It's not just my place," Rita said, giggling. "I have a two-bedroom apartment on the third floor."

I must have hesitated, for she pressed me forward and we entered the building, passing through a modest foyer lined by mailboxes. It was the size of the anteroom to my father's office. We rode up a tiny clanking elevator and stepped off, and the first person I saw was myself, reflected in a floor-to-ceiling mirror. The man I glanced at was unfamiliar, too thin and poorly dressed, a slump to his shoulders. I touched the corner of my eye where it drooped. At home I am known for a certain style, leather jackets and slim pants, and the casual five o'clock shadow, which here, in the dim light, I noted had thickened to something more sinister.

"This way," Rita said, dangling a key. "Eight-B."

The corridor was long and narrow, carpeted in faded maroon. We passed half a dozen doors, each with a brass number and a fisheye peephole. Reaching the end of the hall, Rita unlocked the door and entered just ahead. I smelled burnt popcorn and watched as a teenaged girl rose from a couch and switched off the television set.

"He's asleep," the girl said. "In your bed, like you said."

23

"Good." Rita pulled out a couple of bills and gave them to her. "Thanks Sandy."

The girl slid a math text and notebook into her pack and left, without casting a single glance my way.

The room was small, with low furniture and a black lacquered table pushed against one wall. I could hear the clatter of the elevator outside as the doors snapped shut and it wheezed back to ground level. A vase by the door held a single yellow bloom, and another vase on the black table held a quartet of irises.

"Who is sleeping on your bed?" I said.

"Andreas, my son. He's lending you his room for a couple of nights."

"May I see him, your boy?"

She paused a second, then said, "Sure. This way."

We walked through a tiny kitchen and down a short hallway, which held a series of black and white photos. These displayed my hostess wearing a skin-tight leotard, posed in strange theatrical landscapes with oversized objects: a giant clock, a chair built for giants, and a huge toothbrush. I squinted at these as we passed, then at Rita's firm body as she marched ahead of me now, clad in T-shirt and jeans. In one photo she glared at the camera, her lips tinted bright red.

"This is you?" I touched the image, slid my finger across the posed face.

She hardly looked back. "I'm a dancer, when I get the chance." She pointed towards the end of the hall. "That's his room, where you'll sleep."

A poster of a fierce-looking Gila monster, mouth yawned open and glaring, was clipped to the door.

"He's crazy about reptiles and amphibians," she said.

"So am I."

Why did I say this? It was not true at all.

She pushed open the door on the opposite side of the hall and at first, in the dark, it was hard to see anything. Then I spotted the child lying twisted in his sheet, his arms wrapped around a stuffed toy.

"He has black hair, like mine," I whispered and moved closer.

She leaned over, kissed the boy's cheek, pushed the hair back from his forehead and kissed him again. He sighed, a warm, minty exhalation.

"Where is your husband?" I asked, when we were back in the living room.

"If you mean Andreas's father, I haven't a clue."

Embarrassed, I gazed at the blank monitor of the television screen. I am not a sentimental man, but I could think only of the sleeping child with his thick hair like mine. I wondered if he was only pretending to sleep, as I so often did as a boy.

Rita had laid out a row of snacks, some sort of pâté and crackers, smoked oysters. But I was not hungry at all. Fatigue had cloaked my whole body now, and the constant search for English words and meanings had left my mouth dry and exhausted.

I pulled out a cigarette: at last, the breath I'd been waiting for.

"Sorry," Rita said. "Not in here."

I stared at her.

"But you can take it out on the balcony."

She followed me there, showing me first how the latch on the glass door worked, how I must slide the bar across. Two chairs and a small plastic table were set up on the tiny cement shelf overlooking nothing, just an alley, the air still damp. I lit up, then sat on one of the chairs and immediately skidded forward on the damp webbing.

Rita must have imagined us sitting out here, because there was a small bowl of fresh pretzels on the table and a coaster for the drink I didn't have. Across the alley was another walk-up, a mirror of the building I was now in. The glow from the cigarette seemed significant, a tiny bright light I'd brought with me and kindled to life with my breathing.

Rita sat in the other chair and propped one leg up on the railing. "You must be tired."

"Yes," I nodded with heavy eyes. "I will sleep very soon."

Did she look disappointed? "You'll meet the others tomorrow," she said, drilling her fingers on the side of her chair. "Syd Baskin is president of CAFE. There have been so many people involved with this project."

It took me a moment to realize that "this project" was me.

I exhaled, lowered my lids, but not too much. Could I detect the smell of the sea in the air? At home the sea has a different spicing, blended with the smell of food from street venders. Why couldn't I relax after the long journey? Instead I was popping nervous energy inside the exhaustion.

"You don't look like your photograph," she said gently.

"I have not been eating well."

"Of course."

When I tilted my head and blew out the cigarette smoke, I felt her watching. This was the arrival of the exiled poet. Because of his time in jail he would tire easily, not be able to process the new sensations, and like a blind man who is suddenly given sight, he is overwhelmed. Did she not say she was a dancer? Then I was caught in her choreography, and glad of it. Even my fingers seemed important as they tugged the cigarette out of my mouth.

"Do you know any of your poetry by heart?"

I felt my ass slip down the webbed chair.

"By heart?"

"By memory."

"Yes, of course."

Perhaps she was right: the poet must play himself before he sleeps. And so I pulled out my modest volume, *Insomnio*, from the jacket pocket and handed it to her.

"Page five."

She nodded solemnly and located the work, a narrative poem about the mariners who founded Santa Clara and began the cycle of corruption. I recited the full six stanzas, my voice low and whispery, punctuated by the dripping drainpipes and passing traffic. Rita held the book in her lap but didn't look once at it: she seemed hypnotized by the motion of my lips.

Was she pondering the miracle that had brought me here to her small balcony on this rainy Vancouver evening? Maybe she'd guessed it would be like this, my voice thin and fragile, like the cheap paper of my book.

When I had finished I said in the same voice, as if we were still inside the poem, "And now I must sleep."

I lay on the small bed, an X-Men quilt pressed over my body, surrounded by the noises of Andreas's menagerie: gerbils snuffling about their cage and goldfish darting between the folds of their aquatic world. If I opened my eyes I could watch the shadowy movements of a mobile, cut-out reptiles painted a fluorescent green. If I breathed in I could smell the woody nest of the small brown desert rats. The room bristled with animal life and it seemed possible that I would never sleep again. My mind was speeding crazily. I was buckled inside this cramped apartment when I wanted to roam the city streets and find out where I was. The new life was just out of reach, a tantalizing metre or two away, while I was trapped by stucco walls. The gerbil raced crazily on the rungs of his exercise wheel, wood chips flying, his small body brimming with nocturnal energy.

Why does it matter if it's four o'clock or five o'clock to the prisoner? The cell is like a sick room, where days are measured by the arrival of a nurse to take your temperature, or the regular howl of a fellow patient as dawn breaks.

I needed to create the image of a clock, of a world which ran by time and breathed time, a world which still existed. As a child in school we used to cut out cardboard hands and pin them on our scruffy hand-drawn clocks.

"At what hour do you eat lunch?" the teacher asked, and we dutifully rotated the hands to point at the correct numbers. We could lie. We could correct time, and even shoot the hands backward. We could even, like the fat boy we all called Bimmi, crunch up the hands and stuff them in our mouths.

In Santa Clara I was lucky enough to have a cellar window that aimed onto the street. Why didn't I cry out? Because my prison was actually (as Marta never hesitated to point out) a safe house, and I dared not attract attention. A blind man went for bread every morning, tapping his cane along the cobblestone. Perhaps he was a bit mad, for he would mutter profanities and become furious if the landscape changed in any way. One time the waiter from the tiny café next door dragged his sandwich board a foot further into the walkway, and the blind man stumbled against it. What a racket! The air was blue with curses involving donkeys, children, and natural disasters. I strained to hear, half-delighted and half-appalled. Tap-tap, tap-tap. In that sad basement room I creaked off the mattress and rose, snapping at the waist of my underwear. It was the point in the morning when only the bakery was open and only the blind man was up and about. Later, it was children going to school. The little ones were first, shrieking and scampering, throwing a ball to the pavement, chewing gum and passing around sticks of licorice — a distinct smell which entered my cave. Fifteen or twenty minutes later the older children sauntered by. They didn't care if they were late. They were tired, yawning heavily, reluctantly pawing off sleep.

I became an olfactory expert and recognized women by the way they smelled. I didn't see faces, but when, against all rules, I lifted the bottom of the window an inch or so, then the curtain as if it were the hem of her skirt, I could watch those slim ankles march by. A strong rose fragrance accompanied one particular woman and I learned to wait for her. Sometimes, despite the inhospitable cobblestone, she wore high heels, red patent leather, or black. My entire erotic life was contained in that pair of feet, viewed for no more than a second or two, but imagined for the rest of the day. Sometimes, on her way home from work, she stopped by the chicken place. I recognized the succulent smell of Hugo's rotisserie-roasted Pollo Loco and could easily picture her conversation with old Hugo and how his skin would graze hers as he poured change into her waiting hand. His stand was directly across from the Avenida San Sebastián metro stop a block away. She walked quickly after her purchase, lured by the smell emanating from the bag and her own fatigue, which drew her towards home and the moment when she could slip out of her shoes (now a little spotted from the day's journey) and draw her stockinged feet up onto the sofa. She would flick on the TV to the telenovela starring that girl with hair down to her ass, and plunge her fingers into the greasy bag.

I wondered if my own image might flicker across the screen: Most Wanted Man.

Wanted, yes, but never by the right people.

On rainy days bicycle wheels splashed through puddles. Car exhaust pumped through my window, making my eyes smart, yet I sucked in the complex flavours of diesel fuel avidly. This was the world, my only world now. There was a man who had a bronchial condition, and when he passed my window he scraped his lungs with a deep, phlegmy cough. The hacked-up mucus landed with a splat, inches from the bars: it was a sound I dreaded.

I hated him, the Phlegm Man.

As I loved the woman with the red shoes. My Angel. They were all mine.

And in this boy's room in Canada, even the desert rat finally fell asleep in his nest.

2

RITA LEANED OVER TO POUR FROTHY MILK into my coffee cup and I stared down the front of her blouse. This was an unexpected gift, buoyant cleavage for the just released prisoner and I was grateful, painfully so. She licked milk off her finger and smiled.

"Enough?"

Her son was watching, his spoon dangling into a bowl of Mini Wheats, hair drooping over his smooth round face.

"Yes, thank you."

"How long's he staying?" the boy asked in a mopey voice.

"Just through the weekend," his mother replied. "Then he'll be moving to the campus." She looked at me. "Syd called about lunch later today. He asked if you were nice. I said you were."

"Do you think I am nice?" I asked the boy, who shrugged and said, "I guess so."

His mother and I laughed, a nervous clatter. I was handed soft rolls with a tub of jam to go with the dish of eggs. It was easy to be astonished by the presence of such food in my hands as I sat in this modest kitchen in this city at the edge of the continent.

The walls were decorated with copper moulds of leaping fish and Andreas's scribbled drawings. Welts showed where the plaster had been repaired and painted over. On the tiny counter were several appliances, their cords crammed into a single outlet. I hadn't eaten in a kitchen since I was a child, only in formal dining rooms with sober mahogany furniture, or in restaurants and cafés. I had expected something entirely different, that I would be sitting at this moment with a group of men wearing suits in a high-ceilinged room, stacks of documents shuffling across a table, self-important throat clearings and speeches.

Andreas ate one Mini Wheat at a time, tilting it this way and that in his teaspoon, then prying at its lacy strands with his teeth. His small body was clothed in seersucker pajamas displaying pictures of rearing horses, and he stared at me with his mouth full of cereal. When I smiled, he flushed and looked away.

The professor lived on a wide, tree-lined street.

"This area's very expensive now," Rita assured me as we parked next to a mailbox. "Sydney bought years ago, before the Hong Kong money flooded in."

To my eye, the houses were not imposing, mainly wide bungalows coated with siding, or the ubiquitous grey stucco. Yet there was a cared-for look to the lawns, which were rimmed with flowers and rows of clipped shrubs, and the cars belonging to these householders were of the understated but expensive breed. The air seemed cooler here, more perfumed.

"You'll meet the lot of us today," Rita said, reaching behind to grab the bottle of wine from the back seat. "The entire board of the Vancouver branch of the Alliance."

It was Sunday and the rain had finally let up, revealing, as promised, the shimmering backdrop of mountains pressing against a crisp blue sky. Our mountains at home are more rounded and ancient, buffeted by wind and ocean spray and the searing heat.

"They're dying to set eyes on you, Carlos, after such heroic efforts."

I scraped my shoe on the front stair to remove a clump of grass. She'd spoken lightly yet the words went directly to my heart. I could imagine these heroic efforts: who had been bought off, what layers of officialdom had been bribed or threatened, and what other worthy men had been overlooked because, I, Carlos, had been selected. If only my clothes were finer, my jacket tailored, as they would be at home. I wanted to make a good impression, but something was happening; I felt a clumsiness in my body as I arranged myself to enter the house. A smile had popped on my face, but it was too soon.

"We'll go through to the patio." Rita pushed open Sydney's front door without knocking. The foyer was dark, lined in varnished wood, and smelled of lemon polish. Directly inside was an umbrella stand holding a single canvas umbrella, alongside it a bench made of cane. The tile floor gleamed. A mirror, oval-shaped within a gold frame, held not a smudge. Above, a chandelier dangled dozens of crystal teardrops which twisted in the breeze of our arrival, speckling the walls in light.

"His place is always like this," Rita whispered.

I followed her through the front room, which was a small cube, barely containing the heavy dining table and leather-seated chairs. I wondered if all rooms in Vancouver were so cramped. How odd that in a land with so much space the rooms were meanly proportioned. Perhaps in a northern climate it was easier to keep such spaces warm.

"William Morris paper." Rita indicated the walls with their pattern of foliage.

She'd told me earlier how our host was an expert on the French Enlightenment philosophers and had named his thirteen-metre sailboat *Rameau's Nephew* after the novel by Diderot. I spotted a photograph of this craft on the cluttered surface of his fireplace mantle.

We travelled through a miniature sitting room, rimmed by glass-fronted bookcases and framed posters of Impressionist painters from the Metropolitan Museum of Art, and on toward the back of the house.

"Is he homosexual?" I said, gazing at the art nouveau lamps.

Rita touched my shoulder. "Shhhh. Of course he is, but old style, very discreet."

The kitchen was large and bright, oddly spacious in comparison to the rooms we'd just passed through, with built-in pine cupboards and terra cotta tile. Every surface was immaculate, as if this were a showroom, not a workplace. There wasn't a trace of food preparation and no encouraging smells. Where was his maid, his cook?

Rita slid open the glass door at the rear and poked her head out.

"Syd-ney?" She trilled his name. "Your guest of honour has arrived."

The chatter of the small assembly abruptly stopped and seven people rose to their feet as one.

So I entered their world, the smile now taking over my face, and with it came the realization that this smile could never be broad enough, or warm enough, that my existence was an automatic disappointment, even to myself.

"Welcome, Carlos, welcome." A handsome man of about fifty with a thatch of grey hair embraced me. "I am Sydney Baskin, president of this little cadre of radicals."

I bobbed from the waist, grinning, a parody of the grateful refugee. So alert was I to any hint of dismay that when I spotted a tightening of my host's smile I wanted to say, "Be patient, I am not yet sure where I am." Wicker chairs were set in a semicircle around a little pool made of flagstones and cement. The bottom was painted blue, and darting through the water were delicate fish, orange and black. I thought of the irises back at Rita's house, and the flaming bird of paradise. Perhaps these were official CAFE colours.

Sydney introduced me to the half-dozen people in his garden, and each shook my hand with boisterous enthusiasm.

"Welcome, my friend!" Professor Daniel Rose, a stooped man with unruly hair clapped me hard on the shoulder. "We've been waiting for this moment!"

There was a strong whiff of gin and I recognized the giddy smile of an amateur boozer.

"Daniel," a woman, surely his wife, reached for the back of his shirt and tugged.

There was an awkward pause until Syd said, "Please make yourself comfortable," his voice a fraction too loud, his gesture just a little theatrical as he pointed to the empty chair.

Obediently, I sat down on the blue cushioned chair next to the fish pond, my spine erect, an awkward pose, so I swung one leg over the other in an effort to look casual, but it still didn't feel right; there was no space with the pond in the way.

So I placed both feet flat on the flagstones, hands on my lap. I never sat like this, not since I was a child at Sunday school. The little group stared expectantly, and I thought, do they want me to sing a song now? Perhaps there will be a speech and a salute to my health. Something was anticipated, but what it was, I had no idea. I eyed the tall pitcher full of pink liquid, creaking with ice cubes.

Finally a woman with pale cheeks said, "Thank God it stopped raining. You must have gotten a terrible first impression of our city, Carlos."

"Yes," I said, then added quickly, "no." I felt myself redden. Sydney poured drinks from the pitcher into tall opaque glasses. A slice of lime plopped into my glass followed by a sweet fruity smell. Sangria? After a slug I felt instantly better.

"The patio is very beautiful."

"Thank you," Syd replied.

I felt proud of myself, this simple exchange perfectly rendered.

"You are staying at Rita's?" a woman called Sandy Peeple said. She wore a sleeveless tunic over tights, like a medieval courtier.

"Just for the weekend," Rita answered. "Then he's into the university."

"Yes," I pitched in gamely. "The Chair of Exiled Writer. At least I will have a place to sit."

Their laughter was a little forced.

"Where will he live?" Sandy continued.

"I organized a spot at the married students' housing, right on campus," said Sharon, the full-breasted woman who was the wife of the slightly bombed Daniel Rose. "He'll be sharing with Rashid."

"Good old Rashid." Syd glanced at me. "A lovely guy. Pakistani. He wrote incendiary essays that were taken to be anti-Muslim. Had to get the hell out."

"Married students?" I reached for a dish of peanuts on the low glass table. "But I am not married."

Everyone laughed again. They thought I was making another joke. My coordination was off and the peanuts tipped into the fish pond. I lunged for the dish, but it was too late.

"Oh my God," Sydney cried. "If the fish eat nuts, they'll die!" He leaped off his chair to begin the rescue.

The next five minutes we spent trolling the floor of the pond, sleeves rolled up to the elbows, plucking nuts one by one. The water was cold, yet toasted lightly on top by the sun. When a fish brushes your skin it is like an infant's sigh.

"Look out for Blackie," Syd warned. "He bites."

Rodolfo's striped shirt, the one he insisted I take with me, was spattered with water and a slowly seeping nervous sweat.

Sharon Rose touched my elbow and whispered, "Syd's very high strung. Don't worry."

I loved the way she spoke, in a slow unhurried voice, her lips cracked under scarlet lipstick. She popped one of the rescued nuts in her mouth and I knew she was doing this for me, so that I would understand that nothing was wasted.

Syd took one of his oversized linen napkins and mopped himself up, carefully dabbing his forearms and each finger in turn. When he saw me watching, he gave a quick fretful smile.

We settled back into the wicker chairs and I heard Sharon mutter, "Crisis over, thank God."

Rita was unpeeling plastic wrap from three bowls full of cold noodles and salad, and mixing their contents with a pair of tongs. There was a musty smell, some Indian spicing, and no bread to be seen. And no protein for energy and endurance. Even in my basement cell Marta would bring skewers of grilled meat along with the crusty bread my people live on.

"Excuse me," I said quietly. "There is no meat?"

"Poor Carlos," Rita laughed. "Syd's a strict vegetarian."

"Vegetarian, yes." I nodded. I had an aunt who practised this regimen, not for health reasons but because she was convinced that dead beasts continue to claim their souls.

China plates with scalloped rims were passed around, followed by the bowls of food. I helped myself, using the pair of wooden tongs while Rita held each bowl in turn. I felt my hosts' polite stares, and the quick, forgiving smiles when a noodle slopped to the ground. The plate was too little, almost a saucer, and I'd misjudged what it could hold.

"This is quite an occasion," Sydney said when we'd finished serving ourselves. "Shall we toast our guest of honour?" He lifted his glass and waited while the rest of the party mimicked the gesture.

"It's been a long and sometimes arduous journey," Daniel Rose proclaimed. "For all of us." He slipped an arm around his wife's back and I watched her smile stiffen.

"Particularly for Carlos," she said.

I lifted my own glass. "And I would like to salute all of you, to thank you sincerely, and thank you Canada."

"To your new life," Sandy said, her eyes moist with feeling.

"To my new life."

We all drank, paused, then drank again, then simultaneously placed our glasses on the table, and I wondered if this was a ritual here in Canada, that all must follow the gestures of the honoured guest.

Rita touched my forearm. "Now would be a good time…"

I remembered, yes, the poem.

"Carlos would like to read to you from one of his recent works."

"Wonderful!" Frank Peeple slapped his knee in a way you knew was foreign to him. His wife gave him a puzzled look.

Rodolfo's jacket was folded over the back of my chair and I searched through its pockets until I found the crunched up piece of paper and my eyeglasses.

The guests were quiet during this bit of activity, and stared into their drinks.

I announced that first I would read the poem in Spanish, then Rita would read it in translation: we had worked this out a few hours earlier.

I smoothed the paper on my knee, cleared my throat, and as I read they leaned forward on their chairs, intent. Plates sat on their laps, untouched, attracting wasps and flies which were discreetly waved off. As I read, sun sifted between the branches of the arbutus tree and toasted the goldfish. A couple of guests knew enough Spanish to let out little grunts of appreciation at appropriate moments. There was a regular thump in the background — the kid next door popping baskets, slamming the backboard. Such a normal, everyday sound. An orange cat prowled the length of the fence, back arched, claws reaching out and tugging the air.

I knew my poem by heart and never looked at the paper. When my gaze swept past Sharon Rose I saw that her eyes were wet and a streak of mascara had run down her cheek.

When I was finished, I bowed my head and Rita began, in English:

"The Prisoner's Song."

EXILE · ANN IRELAND

It was all about bread, the loaf that I had seen fall from the wagon outside my basement prison. It was the most ordinary kind of bread, like a French baguette, only chunkier, the kind that in my country appears at every meal, and with every cup of coffee. The bread of everyday life.

I gulped my drink as she read. I was shaking. Not just my hands but my chest and gut. I felt faintly nauseous from all the vegetables and too much sweet sangria. It had been so long since I had been with a group of people that I had to relearn the rhythm of speaking and listening. Not only in my own language, but now in English, which felt like a blanket being constantly tugged away. Rita read on and I couldn't understand a word of it, my own poem.

Sydney, the president of CAFE, refilled my glass. The fish rolled over in the pond, briefly displaying their bellies to the sun. They reminded me of sunbathers on the coast, unashamed of their bodies, seeking heat and light.

Rita's voice rose and fell, and I realized that she had finished. There was a long communal sigh as we sat back in our chairs, allowed to be comfortable again.

"Your poem is very strong, very moving," Sandy Peeple said.

"Thank you." Sweat was gluing my hair to my forehead. But this woman didn't flinch. When she uncrossed her long legs I caught a flash of blue panties.

"May I ask you some questions?" she said.

"Of course."

I was puffing. Was it possible they couldn't see?

"Please tell me to back off if you don't feel like talking about it."

I waited.

Her face tightened as she sought the correct words. "Can

you tell us more about what you've been through in recent months?"

"What do you desire to know?"

"How were you treated during your imprisonment?" Her face tensed another notch.

"Excuse me, 'treated'?"

"I've read, of course, accounts of… torture." She whispered the word, like some people whisper the word "naked" or "cancer." Her gaze fell to my hand and I realized, to my embarrassment, that she was staring at my finger. Or rather, where the tip of my finger had been. My mother, one Sunday morning, had slammed the door of a taxi and my toddler fingertip had been neatly sliced off.

"Please excuse me, Carlos. I quite understand if you don't want to talk about this."

I dug my hand in my pocket, then, realizing that this would make it even more certain to her, some unspeakable altercation forming in her fevered brain, I pulled out my hand and let it sit on my knee. It was nearly dusk and the lilacs had begun to seep their sweet scent into the air. I was used to the sounds of chaos, of sirens and honking; even in my basement, with a window inches from the sidewalk, the racket of city life filled my ears.

"It is something I cannot speak of now."

Everybody nodded. I smelled a whiff of embarrassment. They were relieved, but perhaps also disappointed. For hadn't they worked hard to bring me here? Rita had told me all about the benefit, the book sale, the barbeque, a mass poetry reading, and a special plea to members clear across the country. I was grateful for the rhythmic slap of the basketball next door.

"You can smoke if you like," Sydney said, passing an immaculate ashtray.

I felt them watch as my jittery fingers worked to light a cigarette.

Finally Sandy Peeple cleared her throat and said, "I write a little poetry, too."

"Everybody in the department of English writes poetry," Syd said. "Carlos, you have little competition. Other than you, the only genuine artist here is Rita. She scrapes by with her contracts at the Grad Centre and performs her strange theatricals for tiny but avid audiences."

"Shut up, Sydney," Rita said.

I ignored this exchange and looked only at Sandy, whose intense brown eyes peered from behind her glasses.

"I think you are a good poet," I said.

She didn't blush. "Why?"

"I can tell that you have real feeling inside you, by the way you speak."

There was another embarrassed silence. I was being too earnest, too personal. Yet at the same time I could see that I had given Sandy pleasure.

Sydney made a snorting noise then exclaimed, "All this must seem incredibly decadent to you." His arms spread, encompassing the patio with its wicker furniture, the table laden with half-eaten food, and the pristine bottle of brandy which I was waiting for him to open. "Our lives are soft," he went on. "They have the texture of futons."

"Do not feel guilty for your lives," I said. "Why should you give up anything? You are just normal people leading normal lives in a normal country. It is how it should be."

"But how many thousands are there like you?" Lucy said. She had been sitting back, watchful. She was younger than the other professors and wore a pair of overalls, like a teenager. Her hair was pulled into a no-nonsense ponytail. "Not just in your country, but all over the world. Prisoners of conscience."

"What can you do for all these people?" I was getting impatient. This was beginning to sound like the discussions I had at home with my pals in the café. We got the most sentimental and vehement when we were drunk. And the next morning we went back to the newspaper and wrote our tepid columns.

Sydney cut himself a slice of soft cheese and wrapped it around a grape.

"Who among us could endure a fraction of what Carlos has been through?"

There was a respectful silence as each pondered the question. Sharon had folded her arms over her chest and was staring at me with an odd expression. Her eyes were no longer moist.

"Excuse me." I rose to my feet. "I must go to the toilet."

Again my knees banged against the table and again the peanuts spun off, this time safely to the ground. My head was throbbing: they all had stories constructed for me, much better tales than mine. How would I avoid disappointing them?

Sydney gave me instructions, which I couldn't understand, and so I found myself lurching through his house, opening and shutting doors to closets, a laundry room, a study. Somewhere rock music was playing and its pulse vibrated through the walls.

Finally, seconds away from pissing in a corner, I raced down the hall and flipped open the last door. A young man, shirtless, lay across a narrow bed. There was the sweet smell of hashish. Music was pounding from a boom box at his feet. The room was dark, except for one flickering candle. The boy lifted his head off the pillow and said in a sleepy voice, "What d'you want?"

"The toilet."

"Other end of the hall." He squinted. "You the poet?"

"I am."

"Close the door on your way out."

Above Sydney's toilet was a framed print showing a cherub pissing into a pool of tiny red fish.

3

RITA SAT IN HER STENOGRAPHER'S CHAIR, SPINE erect. I watched as, without thinking, she tilted the gooseneck lamp so it bathed one side of her face in light, while she nodded, talking to some invisible person on the phone.

"That's possible," she said. Then, "I might." Her body coiled, as if she were mapping out the next gesture. I saw the dancer in her now. She replaced the receiver in its cradle and stared at the wall while I pretended not to notice. I was playing with Andreas on the floor. We were constructing a tower from his alphabet blocks, an elaborate enterprise with a wide base and a gradually diminishing point, like the Chrysler Building in New York City, famous for its art deco elegance. The boy was impatient at first, and always glancing towards his mother as if to ask, may he do this.

"That was your father," she said after a moment, and Andreas watched her face, waiting to hear what this meant. We were so close I could hear his breathing speed up, feel his damp body shiver with excitement.

She lifted one slim leg and swung it over the other. In another day I would have to enter my students' quarters, but today I was still inside a real family.

"He'll pick you up tonight."

"Will I spend the night at Jane's?" the boy said.

She nodded. "You will spend the night at Jane's."

When he returned to our block-building construction, I saw that his face was flushed and suddenly he wasn't tentative at all. He placed three blocks one after another to finish the peak of the tower and gave a small smile of satisfaction. I couldn't keep my eyes off his fingers, so small and beautifully formed, almost elegant, tiny chipped fingernails with half-moons.

"Thank you for playing with him," Rita said later that night. The boy had just left and she gazed out the window, watching him pull away in a shiny new car with his father and the woman called Jane. "It's been a rough year for us." Her face hollowed under the sharp cheekbones, as if something had just drained out of her.

"Anything you need before bed?" she said. "Cup of tea? Sandwich?"

No thank you, there was nothing. I could hear the distraction in her voice. Tomorrow afternoon I would be driven to the residence and she would no longer have to take care of me. I thought of her lying in bed tonight, knowing that I was in her son's bed, caught between his sheets, his reptile mobile catching each breeze from the open window. Perhaps we were both less alone than we thought.

In the morning Rita took me for a tour of the neighbourhood. She talked quickly as we roamed the winding streets of Chinatown, past the florist with its bins of fresh cut flowers, and a restaurant where heroin addicts nodded over platters of guy ding. An ancient cook stood out front in his stained apron, his forehead shiny with sweat. He flipped through a tabloid newspaper and sipped something out of a metal cup. I told Rita that there was a place like this near the old port in Santa Clara. She didn't respond to this observation. I wanted to tell her how we journalists would often stay up all night, that we prowled in a noisy throng through the old town, a dangerous area after dark, and how our presence would instantly fill a tiny restaurant such as this and transform it into the most sophisticated café in the city.

Instead Rita clipped along the uneven sidewalk swinging her arms. "I never get time to do my own work," she said. "There's always something gets in the way."

Like a refugee poet who lands on your doorstep with nothing but his ugly shoes and a single volume of verse.

"I wonder if I've lost my chance, if I'm too old." She hesitated for a moment in front of a street vendor displaying cheap jewelry.

The rain had saturated everything into darkness, the asphalt, the sidewalks, even the buildings had been drenched, leaving a pungent scent of wet cement and wood. A girl stood at the corner in her tight skirt, drawing on a cigarette while a cluster of kids in sports uniforms raced by.

"I do not think you are old," I told her. "An artist can be any age."

"Not a dancer," she said. "Our knees go."

She moved so smoothly, with such grace, like an animal who is natural in its home, unlike I, who seemed to step through this dizzy space, never sure if each foot would land correctly. I wanted to touch everything I saw, to see if it was awake or dead. Even the neon sign which jumped in its tube seemed dreamlike. It is good to travel, I told myself. Everything is new.

"I like watching you," she said with a smile. "You see so much."

"And now you see me."

We laughed and for a moment her face relaxed.

A stationer's shop was wedged between a restaurant and a post office. In its window were those mottled notebooks with firm covers, a timeless style, and an arrangement of pens and pencils.

"I would like to go in here," I said.

"Why not?" she said with a gentle smile. "You're a free man."

I selected two notebooks with ruled paper and three pens with medium-thick points and a plastic envelope to contain them.

"Excuse me," I told Rita, "but I have no money."

"No hay problemo." She rummaged in her purse and gave me my first Canadian money, a green twenty-dollar bill decorated on one side by a drawing of a handsome duck and its mate, and on the other by a middle-aged woman wearing pearls.

"The Queen," Rita said, responding to my puzzled look.

"The Queen of Canada." I smoothed the bill before passing it to the clerk. "She looks like one of my mother's sisters." When we left the shop I tucked the package under my arm and said, "Now I'm a writer again."

"Next up is a pair of decent shoes." She nodded at my sneakers fitted with Velcro tabs, the kind worn by old men who are unable to reach down and tie their laces.

"And wine," I said, grinning. "To celebrate. And Canadian cigarettes."

She frowned. "I don't know if I have enough money."

"But your CAFE friends, they will pay." I thought of Professor Syd Baskin in his well-manicured house and soft leather slip-on shoes. I had landed in the care of an important organization, one that was able to influence the government of foreign countries and circumvent the wishes of such powerful men as the General. Just thinking this gave my step a new buoyancy.

4

RASHID WAS A TIDY MAN, AND TACITURN, like a rancher.
Except he was no rancher, but a pursuer of some esoteric
branch of biology which he didn't bother to explain. We shared
a tiny two-storey house in the married students' quarters on the
edge of the campus of the university. On either side our house
was attached to other, similar houses, except these ones were full
of children and babies. Out front, plastic toys were strewn across
the lawn, and in the back a row of cotton diapers danced like
seagulls on the line. Impatient mothers howled at their children
to get off the road, except these mothers were astrophysicists and
medievalists in their spare time. Their uniform, unvarying, con-
sisted of dark leggings under long tunics, and flat, boatlike sandals. At dusk each day there was a strange procession: a dozen
heavy-breasted women wearing loose shirts and shorts jogged
by, pushing baby carriages. Skipping alongside, a slim woman

shouted instructions: "Watch your posture! Pick up the pace! Don't forget to breathe!"

In the mornings I lay in bed and listened to the lives of our neighbours, the roll of tricycle wheels across the floors, the thuds and muted crashes of family life. Standing over the bathroom sink, toothbrush in hand, I could hear, less than a metre away, another man performing the same ritual, running water, spitting, splashing his face, then pissing long and hard into the toilet bowl.

Rita showed me the small campus store, and steered me away from the frozen food section with its composed meals (too expensive) and suggested that I cook "from scratch."

I pretended to memorize her instructions as she recited recipes for egg custard pie and spaghetti, nodding with concentration as she listed ingredients, warned of possible pitfalls, suggested shortcuts.

"It's a cinch," she said, leaving me with an armload of groceries on the doorstep of my little house. "If in doubt, pasta with grated cheese."

Rashid, handy in the kitchen, concocted aromatic meatless curries that sent me reeling toward the door to find supper in the Student Union Building. Sometimes I was taken out for meals by members of the university. Just as well: my stipend was a miserly $700 a month, barely enough to cover beer and cigarettes and the odd movie. I needed to eat well when I got the chance.

Rashid had no bad habits. I would watch him chop vegetables as oil sizzled in the frying pan.

"Where did you learn to cook?"

"At home."

Home was Pakistan.

"Didn't you have a mother? Servants?"

"Of course," he said. "They showed me how."

I found something demeaning in the sight of a man chopping his own vegetables for dinner. When I tugged open the fridge door to get a beer, he winced. Rashid was a devout Muslim, despite his dissident ways. When I smoked he would make little throat-clearing noises and say, "Your money would last longer without this."

I would not learn to cook because this was something others did well, and each person has his role in life: mine was not to become a chef. I found a steakhouse just outside the campus gates and the waitress was a matronly woman who made sure I was given an extra potato with my meal. I went there often, and tipped her well, because her legs were heavy and she was tired of her life, but never bad-tempered. They kept a bottle of aged scotch for me, just like at Café de la Luna.

Rashid came strutting down the stairs of our house one morning, yawning, buckling his belt around his narrow waist, wearing, as always, a white short-sleeved shirt and dark poplin pants. It was a timeless uniform, which indicated he had his mind on higher pursuits. He looked around the living room with distaste. Early sun barely cut through the heavy curtains, and our furniture, such as it was, was shabby and too big for the room.

"Clean this shit up," he said, motioning towards one or two ashtrays and some empty beer bottles.

I was barely awake, having sat up late into the night writing in my new notebooks, composing fast verses that surprised me by their acid tone.

"You could at least try," he said, frowning after I'd reluctantly tidied up. Meaning I hadn't placed the bottles in the correct place, in the recycling box, and that the ashtrays had been emptied but not washed.

A very nervous man. We would cohabit, but we were not destined to become friends.

One evening I was invited to dinner at the house of the President of the university. This impressive building, with its circular drive and row of dormer windows, sat on a secluded crescent just off campus. Arbutus trees lined the front walk, creating an arbour, and a uniformed maid greeted guests at the door and pointed us towards the back yard.

This garden was almost a meadow, half an acre in size, and the patio area was immense, shaded by a flat green awning. Our host, a thin, almost gaunt man in a tan suit with an apron tied around his waist, stood turning meat on the grill. I was astonished, of course, to see such an eminent man prepare the meal, but I said nothing. His wife coasted around in a beige linen suit, touching here an elbow, there a shoulder.

"So you're the one!" she announced, spotting my approach. "I'll tell George." Immediately she spun around, perhaps afraid that I might start to speak in Spanish, and went off to fetch her husband.

There was a whispered exchange over the eye-searing barbeque, then the President removed himself from his post, wiped his hands down the front of his pristine apron, and made his way towards me.

"Greetings!" he said with a hearty smile, hand outstretched.

People turned to see who this new important guest was.

"You'll find we're pretty informal around here, Carlos." He slipped a hand across my back and began to guide me effortlessly through the throng of guests who parted to make way. Cordial smiles emerged on the sternest of faces. I was being propelled by the President himself, being introduced in a booming voice to "Ed Moses, associate dean of arts; Leigh Cronin, poly sci; and of course Nancy Savigneau, dominatrix of those late Romantic German philosophers."

The President laughed at his little joke and I observed the others joining in a beat later, except for Professor Savigneau, who remained stony faced. She stood very still in a boxy grey jacket and tied-back hair, high heels digging into the grass, and I was astonished by her courage. At home I would be the first to join in with an ingratiating laugh, a despicable response to authority which is, nonetheless, necessary. When the publisher of *La Voz* swanned through our offices I readied myself to admire his vulgar witticisms.

The President's booming voice was at my ear. "I insist that each guest sample my special concoction."

We strode across the fine-toothed lawn to a portable bar set up under a tree. This was tended, it turned out, by the President's own son, a gangly youth of perhaps seventeen, who didn't smile or otherwise acknowledge our approach.

"Mix our man a Virtual Pion," his father commanded.

Without a word, the boy pressed the lever on a chrome-plated, industrial-strength blender and a foamy concoction, almost phosphorescent, leapt to the sides of the machine. This was poured into a frosted glass and presented to me with the sparest of nods. I tipped it towards my nose and sniffed; a distinct smell of lime aftershave lifted into my nostrils. The President waited impatiently as I tasted the brew.

"Well?" The fuzzy eyebrows formed a chevron.

"Excellent!" I beamed.

He made a little grunt of satisfaction. "Extremely potent, I must warn you. Pions keep the stars burning and power nuclear bombs." He squinted into the crowd before lifting his arm and pointing towards the area where the lawn began to slope.

"I shall introduce you to one more person," he told me, then barked "Lu-cía!" in the direction of his pointing finger.

A buxom, small-boned woman quickly approached, wearing the native dress of some small southern country, an embroidered cassock with long tassels. Her type was instantly familiar, the academic who adopts the folklórico uniform of the countryside.

"Lucía Hammond Cruz, acting head of Latin American studies." The President's voice softened as he spoke her name, and I understood that he had feelings for this woman. "A small department, but notably active." His voice rose again. "I leave the two of you to embark on a voyage of discovery."

The President swiftly returned to his post behind the giant winged barbeque. Invisible waves of heat rose before him, turning his erect form rippled and dreamlike. I looked at him for as long as possible before returning my gaze to the newly introduced guest.

"Call me Lucía." Her small plump hand withdrew from the voluminous garment and reached for mine. She spoke in a crisp and cultivated Spanish. "I have been most eager to meet you."

I bobbed my head to acknowledge this fact. Her head, tilted upwards, reached only my chin, a welcome change amongst this race of Amazons.

"There is so much we might speak of," she said, and I felt a cramp of nausea. Perhaps it was the foul drink. "You must tell me your story." At last her hand released mine. Hers disappeared under her mantle while my own flopped uselessly to my side. I guessed that Lucía was fifty years old or more.

"Begin wherever you wish." It was the voice she might use with a shy student who was about to deliver his views on the emerging peasant movement of some barbarous country.

I eyed her but picked up no sign of mockery. Perhaps she had heard about the exile's famous stories. My gaze fell to her feet, which were encased in blue plastic sandals. What a peculiar vanity, this marketplace garb in a woman from the intellectual class.

"Your family?" she prodded.

What on earth did she want?

"My family is healthy," I assured her. "Although my father suffers from diabetes."

"He is still working?"

"At the district tax office."

"So he is, in effect, a civil servant."

I nodded to the truth of this fact.

It seemed to make her think. "He is still in this position?"

"To the best of my knowledge."

"I see."

What did she see? I sipped at the merciless drink. Why was she so interested in my father?

"He has no concern for politics," I assured her.

"Of course not."

I found myself growing anxious. In my country we are not inquisitive. It is considered rude, perhaps because most of our old and respectable families have something to hide. It is why they have succeeded in remaining old and respectable. "He is a man of the nineteenth century," I insisted. "Interested only in archaic cultural matters."

"You are sure?"

"Entirely."

She peered at me, squinting so hard in the sun that her eyes almost disappeared. "Your family knows you are here?"

"Of course."

"And they know why?"

I hesitated, trying to read her face. Instead of feeling relieved to speak my own language, I felt uneasy, transparent. "In part."

At last she smiled, a nod to my enigmatic reply. "You are being very careful with me, Carlos." She spoke with a hint of approval. Then her gaze lifted and she turned to look at the thickening crowd of guests, some of whom were glancing our way.

"You are heroic to these people," she said. "They can say what they wish in their milieu, however ill-considered, even idiotic." Was it my imagination, or did she pause at this point? "And lose nothing but prestige."

I considered this.

"They are safe, or so they believe." She turned back to me with sudden animation. Both hands appeared, one sharply pointed towards my chest. "They see you and it overwhelms them. They wonder how brave they would be."

I peered around at the professor women who posed, hands on hips in their long crepey skirts, and the men in summer suits or golfing shirts and slacks, and saw each face flush under my gaze. All these searching, intelligent faces were wondering, what has this man endured?

"Do anti-U.S. sentiments inform your work?" Lucía was suddenly speaking in English, and I realized we were being approached by a man I'd met earlier, an associate dean.

"Lucía is always on topic," he said in a high-pitched voice, his smooth brow unperturbed. "The correct answer to her question is 'yes'."

I looked at this rotund man, his short-sleeved shirt tucked into a pair of ballooning shorts, and before I had a chance to respond, he lifted the glass from my hand and began to pour its contents onto the grass.

"Our President likes to force his latest invention down our throats," he said. "One must resist."

Alarmed by this revolutionary gesture, I glanced towards the President, who was prodding a sausage with a long-handled fork. He hadn't seen a thing.

The associate dean laughed. "Don't worry, my friend, there will be no repercussions."

Lucía was watching me. "He's right, Carlos. Absolutely nothing will happen."

What a strange sensation to have your own fear snatched away, made useless.

"Now then," the associate dean said as he replaced the emptied glass in my hand. "I already know you are the most interesting man here. But what do you make of us all?"

Lucía watched as I fumbled for English words.

"It is not interesting to be me," I said after a moment. "Only frightening."

He frowned and for the first time a wrinkle creased his brow. "Yes, I suppose it is," he said gravely, then lifted his voice. "I must merge now with the members of my faculty. Play my part in the general hostilities." His hand awkwardly touched my shoulder. "It's been a rare pleasure, Carlos."

When I spotted him a moment later he was standing with two women, laughing loudly as he replaced empty glasses into their waiting hands.

"Well?" Lucía called back my attention.

"Well what?"

"What do you make of us all?"

"Tell me the answer, Lucía. I am tired."

"You'll have to do better than that. You're the poet, after all."

The poet lacked imagination in so many ways.

"Why do you ask so many questions?"

She looked amused. "One is interested in the larger world."

"An interrogation is not a conversation."

She flinched, then said coolly, "I am sorry if there has been some offense taken."

Hot-faced, I strode away, heading towards the bar where I'd spotted an insulated container full of local and imported beer. Perhaps Lucía had been flirting with me. It was so hard to know. I shouldn't have spoken sharply, yet if I had to always watch each footfall, each word, how could I exist here? My character was being flattened by self-consciousness. Partly drunk, I decided to feel sorry for myself.

The President's son reached into the cooler and pulled out a beaded bottle of lager, snapped it open, and passed it to me without a word.

Lucía was alone now, lying stretched out on a massive rock that must have been dredged from the beach a kilometre away. Her feet were bare, her eyes shut, her chest under the embroidered garment was rising and falling steadily. Clearly she was asleep, or passed out from downing too many Virtual Pions. I tiptoed past to collect my jacket. Our hostess followed me into the foyer of the house, where, touching my wrist with the tips of her cool fingers, she leaned over and kissed me lightly on the cheek.

"Hasta luego." She spoke in a low voice, and handed me my hat, a dark beret. Yet before I had a chance to pluck it from her hands she was placing it on my head, tilting it just so.

The President himself drove me home.

"Did Lucía give you the treatment?" he said as he swung the car onto my street.

"Excuse me?"

"Pepper you with questions?"

"Ah, yes."

"One of our finest teachers, but…" He stopped the car near a hydrant and peered out the windshield.

"Yes?"

"Prickly. No small talk."

"No small talk," I repeated, enjoying the phrase.

"This your place?"

I had to lean forward to check the address. All the houses looked the same. "Yes."

"Good of you to come, Carlos."

He waited while I slid out of the passenger seat and crossed the lawn to the door of the miniature house I shared with Rashid.

One evening, Rita phoned.

"How's it going? Getting some work done?" Her voice was calibrated to sound friendly and not too inquisitive. I wondered if it was her job as a board member to call at certain intervals.

"Everything is excellent," I said, because I wanted her to sleep well. "And I hope that you and your son are happy."

I could hear her breathing. "It's prime season for bookings at the Grad Centre so I'm on the phone all day. I'm not getting anything of my own done."

"Tomorrow I will take you out," I told her. "Maybe for a coffee, a drink. We will talk. And you will not work for one hour!"

"Thanks," she said, and laughed a little. "But please, let me take you."

It was part of her job to look after me: I was another segment of the world that kept her from dancing.

The work that I was supposed to be doing, which my rescuers hoped would become a book that would sell to the multitudes, was not going well. They wanted the story of my difficulties, but all I'd managed to do was draw a map of my childhood home, with diagrams of the furniture, the piano, the leather footstool, the ornate chairs inherited from various uncles and aunts. It looked like the scene of a domestic murder. All that was missing was the blood and the outline of my own body.

I had been given an office, a tiny room high up in a concrete building. A single window overlooked an unshaded parking lot. I used to capture ants when I was a child, put them in a glass jar with sand and watch to see what sort of tunnels they would carve. But they never performed for me: they would scuffle hopelessly up the glass sides and fall backwards, then, after an hour or so, they would die.

I met Rita in a Vietnamese restaurant with steamy windows and a noisy air conditioner wedged over the door. She was waiting inside, reading a magazine which she slid into her patterned bag when she spotted me. I greeted her with pleasure, despite my bewilderment at this choice of restaurant, and her smile was swift, disappearing as quickly as the magazine.

She waited until we were slurping noodles from cracked china bowls before getting to the point. She seemed uncomfortable and avoided my eyes.

"You've been going through the money too quickly," she said at last. "We simply can't afford to front you extra cash; it's been twice now."

I nearly choked. Yet she sat there calmly eating, while around us the clink of plastic chopsticks against bowls never ceased. I thought we had come together to talk of our lives as artists.

"My tooth was abscessed," I said curtly. "I was supposed to tie it to a doorknob and pull?"

"Of course not. But the clothes…"

"I left home only with what was on my back."

She stabbed at the bowl with her chopsticks. "There are second-hand places we could have taken you to."

My forehead tightened. I wondered if she and her professor friends bought used clothes. Who knows who'd been wearing them, what diseases they had.

"Daniel Rose is about your size. He'll have stuff." Finally she looked up at me. "Also, I don't see why you go to Millie's all the time."

"Millie's?" This was not a conversation: it was another interrogation.

"The steakhouse. No one I know can afford to eat there three nights a week."

I stared at her. I enjoy meat. I enjoy a few ounces of scotch with my dinner. I enjoy real food, not these damp noodles and bits of chewy pork. It was not my fault that a nutritious meal costs twenty dollars in this country. But I said none of this. Never before had a woman dared to speak to me in this way, not even when I was a small child in school with the nuns.

She saw my expression. "I'm sorry, Carlos, but we are just trying to help."

A spritz of cold air hit my backside as the air conditioner switched on. Is this what it was going to be like? I would have to ask permission before eating a potato or buying a shirt? I hated the restaurant with its tippy tables and the plastic table-cloths, which were whipped off between customers. Did she think I wouldn't know how to behave in a real restaurant with a wine list? In my country, if I met a woman for lunch there would be linen napkins, heavy wooden chairs, soft lighting, and discreet, perfectly trained waiters. And we would not be eating with sticks.

Or perhaps I should be like these Oriental people, working for two dollars an hour and all the noodles I could eat. I should be grateful, always grateful to be here, in Gold Mountain.

I slipped out a Camel and popped it in my mouth.

Rita stared.

"I smoke," I said. "It's what I do."

"Perhaps you can't afford to smoke so much, Carlos."

"I am a grown man. I do not need instructions for living."

She poured herself tea from the chipped pot. "There's one more thing."

I sucked hard on the cigarette, feeling exhausted. Perhaps it was better in Marta's basement, where no one was watching and judging.

"We've had a few complaints about your behaviour at The Hub."

This was the student pub on campus. I went there in the evenings when I was lonely.

"I understand you're there six or seven nights a week." Seeing my expression, she added quickly, "Your business, except..."

I waited.

"You've been borrowing money from the students, telling them that CAFE would pay them back. We can't keep you in booze, Carlos, and neither can these kids, most of whom bust their asses all summer for tuition money and are living on less, far less than you."

I stood up, pushing the flimsy metal chair backwards.

"Perhaps next time your group decides to rescue a writer you will conduct much research. Send out questions to all his friends and colleagues, make him sign a temperance petition. I am sorry. I am sorry to all of you."

I left, or tried to; there was something wrong with the door and it wouldn't open, though I turned the knob first to the left then the right. Goddamn Vancouver door! When I turned to look at Rita, she was sitting upright in her chair, pale and expressionless.

"Coming or going?" A young man pried open the door from outside and held it for me.

Could I trust one foot to follow the other on the pavement outside? Perhaps the sidewalk had been transformed into a carpet that would be snatched away. I stood there for a moment, dizzy, heart racing. Yet my anger was a mistake. I thought of the woman I had just left in the restaurant, how she had once held up a sign at the airport as she waited for me, her hair raked flat by the rain.

5

"Do you have whisky?"

The bartender, a stout man with an earring, slid a plastic goblet across the counter. "We got red wine, sir. Courtesy of the Okanagan Wine Producers Association. Free for performers."

I took the goblet with its fruity red wine, and a handful of pretzels from the bowl. It was the annual benefit for the Vancouver chapter of CAFE and I was a featured reader, and nervous as hell. Backstage, the Aquarius Ballroom was jammed with other performers, media types, techies, and beefy men lugging TV cameras on their shoulders. Most of us wore plastic name tags, mine misspelled, and as I wove my way through the crowd, people leaned over in an obvious attempt to read my tag. Many of the media I'd met in the preceding days, when Rita had hustled me around to radio stations and newspaper cafeterias to be interviewed. I was the prize, the example of the organization's accomplishments. She told me this with a smile, but I understood that it was true. I would be reading from my sequence of "Prison Poems."

"Doesn't he have gorgeous hair!" Not for the first time a woman reached for my head and ran her hand through my mess of dark curls. Her companion, a man in a leather vest and jeans, laughed tightly. His tag read: *Vancouver Province*.

Another woman touched my shoulder and said in a pained voice, "I'm so sorry about what's happening in your country."

The elections had been news lately. Fire bombings, a riot in the South.

Christ, I was hot. The room, though big, was crammed and I wished I could shrug off the jacket Daniel Rose had lent me. But underneath was a ratty white shirt and suddenly I felt self-con-scious about it, perhaps because I knew its frayed collar would be spied instantly and would instill sympathy and orders for husbands to peel off their own shirts and offer them to the exiled poet. I wished people would stop giving me things, that just for once I could sling my arm over someone's shoulder and say, "I'll buy you a drink." But they don't want this: as a pair of hands holds out the shirt, the extra winter coat, I see eyes shining with hope and expectation. When I take, with mumbled thanks, what is offered, they smile with pleasure. They watch as I tug on the garment, pulling at too-short sleeves, and nod happily, but they desire more — the coat which touches my back is only part of it.

"Come and meet Stan Drury." Rita pulled me through the thicket of people to the far corner, under a bleached painting of Queen Elizabeth the Second in her tiara. Wine slapped over my hand onto the cuff of Daniel's silk jacket. As we tore through the crowd she shot back the biography of the man I was about to meet.

"Stan's an important poet, not just here, but nationally. And hot to meet you since he's just come back from your part of the world. Latin America figures large in his work. Stan?" She stopped in front of a huge grizzled man with tufts of grey hair held in place by a bandana. It was his T-shirt that made me gasp: CAFE DE LA LUNA with the familiar logo of two coffee cups tilting inward. The café where every evening of the week I would sit at my corner table with my fellow writers and intellectuals, arguing, moaning about the state of the world and our own fragile psyches. I felt my hand being enclosed by his rough palm then clamped by his other in a "brotherhood" shake.

"Good to meet you, man."

Then he spoke in Spanish, in the slang of my city, with an accent so authentic that I jumped with recognition. "They making you their poster boy of the season?"

His voice was crisp and unsentimental, to show that he in no way romanticized the plight of the exile.

He dropped my hand. "You must know Gabriela Piñeda. She's from your neck of the woods."

Gabriela. Indeed I knew Gabriela with her affected high-toned voice, although she came from some hick town in the mountains where her father was a rancher. I knew about her endless manifestos and gringo pals and book contracts with a dozen countries. Yes, we all knew Gabriela. I could see her now, painted mouth curved downward as she examines my pathetic self — I who had dared to place a hand around her sainted waist.

I nodded cryptically.

"A remarkable woman," Stan continued. "And the writing is damn good."

As he spoke Stan began to move his hands expressively, in the way so many Canadians feel compelled to do when speaking to a Latino. He's slept with Gabriela, of course. Another admirer set loose in the world. Soon she will be receiving an invitation to a conference, this time in Vancouver, all expenses paid, where she will captivate yet another audience.

I felt sick. The wine, which had dyed the sides of the plastic cup, had left a maroon stain on my wrist.

"I'm afraid I don't know your work," Stan said. "So I'm especially looking forward to hearing you tonight. We get so little first-hand testimony here: we're a parochial bunch, as you've no doubt noticed."

Rita nudged my elbow. "The snacks are running low; I gotta go warn Laura."

Stan followed her exit with his eyes, not hungrily, but vaguely, as if he found it hard to focus in this crowded room, in this city, in this country. He had left his real self back in the Café de la Luna.

"I understand you were imprisoned."

"Four months."

He didn't wince like the others, just nodded in a comradely way.

"The poetry of witness is not necessarily welcome in this country," he said, pulling out cigarettes — Rojos! — and offering me one.

Gratefully I tugged one from the pack and held it a moment before slipping it between my lips. It had a familiar texture, slightly lumpy, and the smell was dank and uncompromising.

"It makes readers and listeners uncomfortable," Stan went on. "They aren't sure if it's real poetry or political tract." He smoked thoughtfully, brushed on one side by a tiny woman in a bowl haircut who was seeking to cross the crowded room. Her smile tightened as he laid a hand on her shoulder.

I spotted her name tag: "Lily Hunt; *Arts Tonight.*"

"Let me modify that," Stan said. "For you, it's fine. You have a right, in fact they expect the politics. But for me, it's pretentious. A Canadian has no right to be engaged. We write pretty, well-crafted poems about bones we find on the beach, and the landscape of our lover's skin." He spat out a shred of tobacco that had become trapped between his teeth.

I slid my hand into the pocket of Daniel Rose's navy blue jacket and clasped the folded sheets of "Prison Poems."

"And he's darn cute, to boot." A tipsy feminine voice rang out and I felt, yet again, fingers lace through my hair. Startled, I looked into a familiar face: deeply lined, the wan skin lightened by a stripe of coral lipstick. She had interviewed me earlier for the co-op radio station, but then she had been serious, almost dour, clad in black overalls.

Stan snorted. "You're the new pet. Last year they saved a Muslim biologist. But listen up…" He had to lean over to confide, being a good six inches taller than me. "Were you part of the Café de la Luna crowd?"

His paunch brushed my meager belly.

"I dropped by."

"You know Sanchez? Patricio?"

I pretended to think. "Somewhat."

"And Angel. What's his last name, writes for *El Tribunal* —"

"Zubicueta."

"That's the one. You know him?"

"Of him."

Stan looked disappointed. "Sounds like I met a different circle."

"There are many circles in my town, many cafés." How could I explain that I did not want to talk to this man about my friends and enemies? He would never understand that in my milieu there are a hundred conspiracies and alliances, old feuds and ambushes. To him we were the "Café de la Luna crowd," a group of colourful characters that he felt honoured to meet.

"How many circles of dissident writers can there be in a place the size of Santa Clara?"

Carlos Romero Estévez, dissident writer. I could just see Angel's sardonic smile as he dropped copious plugs of ash on his trousers. Luckily I was rescued by Rita, who dashed over and began fiddling with my clothes, righting the collar, brushing crumbs off the lapel, while I stood stoically as a child being prepared for Sunday Mass.

"You go on directly after Stan." She removed the wine glass from my hand and stood back. "Well, you look the part."

Stan Drury laughed.

"Break a leg, you two," Rita said, before charging off again.

The backstage was emptying. Stan cocked an ear. "The show has begun."

We listened to the sound of electric guitars tuning up.

"That'll be Tim and Harvey — two of our prominent novelists making like rock stars." Stan giggled as faltering male voices began to sing:

"Get up
Stand Up
Stand up for your rights."

"Christ, aren't they awful?"

We moved to the wings where a small crowd of performers was watching. The theatre was jammed; there were well over seven hundred people in the thirty-dollar seats, shrieking and applauding as two middle-aged white guys did their Rasta impersonation. I stared with the others, transfixed. I tried to imagine, back home, the eminent and dignified Alfredo Cruz Ascencio grabbing a mike and allowing, even encouraging, his rapt audience to laugh at him, as these people were doing, laughing until they wept. And second row centre, a black woman in dreads squealed the loudest.

I had dared to think that I was beginning to understand these Canadians, their taut friendliness and polite smiles, their helpful practical advice, their fervent lack of sensuality, but now I felt my theories unravel strand by strand.

"After this," Stan whispered beerily into my face, "we'll go out and get drunk."

I dreaded the thought. This man would quiz me, naming every bar, every newspaper, every writer he'd met until he nailed me. He would find out precisely who I was — and who I wasn't.

"You're up next."

I jumped. But Rita had touched Stan's shoulder, not mine. Immediately he straightened, and, carrying his manuscript under his arm like a score, he strode on stage to the still trickling laughter and a scatter of fresh applause.

Rita looked worried. "Whose idea was it to put him on after Tim and Harvey?"

I perched on a piece of plywood shaped like a wave. This was a dark night for the theatre's production of *Sinbad The Sailor*.

Stan knew how to work a crowd. First he took the mike from the lectern and paced with it slowly until the audience played out its silliness. Then, without speaking, he stood still, all 250 pounds of him, with just the sound of his laboured breathing filtering through the PA.

"Three prose poems from the shantytown of Milagro," Stan said in a half-whisper that managed to fill the hall.

"'Milagro' means 'miracle' in Spanish, and the survival of these people is nothing less than a miracle."

The auditorium was hushed at last.

Stan's reading was full of pauses and crisp, short phrases evoking the lives of Colonia Milagro which, I confess, I have never visited. Why should I enter that slum? It's filthy, overrun with thugs and rabid dogs; open sewers stream down its mud-baked streets. Drug dealers lurk in every doorway, jackets bulging with weapons.

Stan, it seemed, had got one of these thugs to give him a guided tour of his barrio, for each poem was full of precisely observed moments. There was the child, clad in ripped shorts, who stood knee deep in the trench, washing himself, as he had been taught by his scrupulous mother, in the typhoid-infested water. The poem ended with a final image of the boy, using his finger as a toothbrush, swabbing the inside of his mouth.

"... sores like open eyes."

His work received the kind of hushed respect he was clearly accustomed to. I'd met guys like him at la Luna, passing through on "fact-finding missions," or escapees from Capitalism, with wild hair and a well-thumbed copy of the *South American Handbook*. They despised the word "tourist" and prided themselves on their idiomatic Spanish and their ability to engage real people in conversation. They always want to be escorted into the shantytowns, as if the wretched souls who hung on there were more real than the tax-paying citizens of the cafés.

Yet I felt a stab of longing as I listened to the poet's words. He had been there, in my town, in my café, just a week ago. And why hadn't I once ventured into Colonia Milagro, out of simple curiosity if nothing else? Why did I criss-cross the plaza on the same trajectory, day after day, carving out my own trench of habit and routine? I'd thought I was so safe from it all. Suddenly I could feel the heavy china cup in my hand, the exact heft of it, the curve of the handle pressing into my thumb, and my mouth went dry with longing. Longing? More like an overwhelming cloak of despair had dropped over my shoulders. It was that dark, bitter coffee that I might never taste again, the grounds slapping against the bottom edges of the cup, the little patch of mud at the bottom of distilled caffeine. And most of all I longed for my gang of compatriots who spoke with weary contempt, in a tone I had yet to hear in Vancouver, or with a sudden brittle passion that might end in shouts, but more often with a self-mocking laugh, and an order for one of those pastries with a crust that cracks open like a volcano.

I heard my name spoken.

A tall, dark-skinned woman was standing at the lectern. Stan had disappeared. She wore a floor-length purple skirt and spoke with a slight Island accent. I'd met her backstage: Eleanor something. She'd clutched my hand with long elegant fingers and said, "I've heard so much, my dear." Her skin was seamless, as if she never laughed or wept.

"She'll be introducing you," Rita had said.

"Why not you?" I'd asked.

"I'm not important enough."

I listened as Eleanor told the audience all about me, how I'd been imprisoned for months after speaking out against a powerful general, received death threats, and how the Alliance had taken on my case and worked with multiple levels of government, procuring visas, how they'd raised money "from events like this" and finally:

"I bring you… Carlos Romero Estévez!"

I stepped onto the stage, staggering because my foot had gone to sleep during the wait. I made my way toward the lectern where the smiling Eleanor stood, arms outstretched to greet me, and when we embraced I felt her bony shoulders under the shimmering cloth of her blouse. She was shaking with nervousness, a sensation that was not in the least evident during her speech. Her back was damp. The spotlight, which stroked the stage several times before settling on me, quickly eclipsed all but the centre of the front row of the audience. Eleanor slipped away. I was alone, completely alone. I stared into the invisible crowd, hearing their avidly clapping hands and whistles, imagining rows upon rows of faces radiating goodwill and expectation.

"I will read my three 'Prison Poems,'" I said in a horribly quivering voice and clutched both sides of the lectern. Light drenched my face. As I began to read I felt my whole body quake, and if the lectern hadn't been there I would have keeled over.

I'll never make it, I thought. It is impossible.

I read the English words that Rita had so carefully rendered in consultation with Syd. My mouth formed the syllables which I had practised so many times, but I lost it. I lost the language. Meaning scuttled away from the signs on the page and all I could think was that I was speaking gibberish, and how Rita must be standing backstage, listening with a growing horror.

This poet they had worked so hard to rescue was about to topple over in a dead faint. Sounds filled the auditorium — my voice, frantic and panicky. It was a clattering of rodent's teeth. Language had gone and I was dying. I stared hopelessly into the faces of front row centre, the only visible sign of humanity in the sea of blackness. Three women and a man, and they were, each of them, weeping. They were witnessing not a poem, but a car crash, metal against metal. Their pity overwhelmed them. This was the man they had saved and who was, after all their efforts, shrinking before them, cell by cell.

I droned on. What else could I do? Sometimes in my basement, when I had no one to talk to, something similar would happen. I would be talking to myself in the chattering way the lonely have, arguments and self-deprecations and manifestos of self-pity, when suddenly I would catch myself. Who was speaking? The cold room would suddenly become hot, or the hot room would become icy. The body no longer knew where it began or ended, what was outside or inside, there is no way of knowing without touch.

I came to the end of the manuscript, unpronounceable words trailed off the last trembling sheet like exotic insects which must be killed, one by one.

For several moments I just stood there, expecting the spotlight to blink off and for silence and darkness to shroud my body so that my death could be announced. But something else happened. The audience, not all at once, but in clumps, began to rise and clap.

They were applauding my death!

"Thank you. Thank you, Carlos Romero Estévez." A female voice whispered into the microphone and I felt terse hips press against mine.

I was being ushered out of the wings, and Rita was clinging to my side, cradling my elbow between her hands. She wasn't crying but I could see that she had been, for her eyes were red and puffy. The shame was a bullet lodged in my chest. I could hardly breathe.

"I fucked up," I said. "I am sorry."

She nodded, with a strange smile, composing herself as we probed through the backstage curtains and down the corridor to the green room.

"I feel so moved, Carlos, so proud."

I stared, disbelieving, drenched in nervous sweat.

"Don't you know what happened out there! I nearly died — literally!"

"So you were a little nervous." She handed me a glass of wine, which I gulped. "That's normal. People felt for you. It added to the intensity of the reading. You aren't slick, like Stan."

"I nearly died," I repeated. But I hadn't. A dozen people were milling about the room, grinning and lifting their hands in greeting. I stood beneath the faded painting of Her Majesty the Queen.

"I didn't know what I was saying. They must have heard that I was cracking up."

"They heard your beautiful, powerful poetry." Rita stared into my face and for a moment neither of us spoke. Then she jerked her head.

"Here comes Eleanor."

Eleanor sailed over, the cloth of her skirt and blouse billowing.

"I want this man's work," she cried. "We must talk."

"I'll leave you two," Rita whispered and joined a gathering at the other end of the room, despite my furtive look of appeal.

"I understand you are working on a memoir of your experience," Eleanor said. "You must show it to me."

I thought of the notebook in my office with its pathetic scrawls, half sentences, fragments of poems. I thought of the hours I spent in that cement chamber, staring out the perfectly square window onto the causeway full of laughing and chattering students.

Perhaps I looked puzzled, for she added, "You know who I am?"

I shrugged apologetically.

"Goodness!" Her laughter had the tinkle of astonishment. "You must think I'm railing on. I am the editor in chief of Pacific Rim Press, one of the leading houses in Canada." Her hand dove into a tiny patent leather handbag and withdrew a business card. "Call me early in the week. We shall go out for lunch."

I pocketed the card, but Eleanor wasn't through yet.

"I see this as an international book: there's interest in Latin America, and it certainly looks like your country is going from bad to worse. I'm assuming the work is prose…"

She waited for my reassuring nod before continuing. "Of course there can be bits of poetry spliced in."

"Thank you." I nodded again, idiotically.

"Next week then? How about Thursday?"

"Yes. Of course."

Then Rita was at my side again. "I'll drive you home," she said. "If you're ready."

"I'm ready," I said hastily, seeing Stan make his way across the room toward us, hand raised in salute.

We rode in silence until, pulling up in front of my house she said, "May I come in?"

"Of course." Yet I felt uneasy. She'd been so subdued during the ride. What was she feeling?

We stepped inside the house, stumbling in the dark over my old sneakers. No sign of Rashid, who went to bed at a sensible hour and rose with the birds.

"Drink?"

"Just water." But she stopped me as I headed back to the kitchen. "Let's stay here a moment."

So we hovered in the dark living room, Rashid's exercise machine ghostly in one corner, until I suggested we sit down.

"Please." I indicated the couch and she lowered herself onto it while I pulled up a chair.

"You could sit here beside me, Carlos."

I frowned, alert to the teasing tone, but obeyed. My uneasiness was growing. It was clear she was seeing me in some new way, perhaps excited by my appearance on stage, however pitiable it had been. Streetlight poured across our legs, and noticing this she crossed one knee over the other, tightening her black skirt across her thighs.

"I want to help you," she said after a minute.

"Everyone helps me."

"You know what I mean, Carlos." Her hand reached out and touched mine. It was all I could do not to jerk it away.

What was wrong? It was as if I were still on that stage, scratching through line after line of impenetrable language, hoping to make it to the end.

"Please let me, Carlos." Her hand folded over my fingers and squeezed.

She was offering herself as a sacrifice, the ultimate gift for the lost poet, yet I was becoming grateful too soon, and gratitude is not erotic. I knew that I must act before she became offended by my inertia. So I reached out with my free hand and touched her hair.

That was enough. Rita took the hand she clasped and moved it to her breast. How warm it was, yet I felt this sensation objectively, as I'd read the English words an hour before, with no understanding or meaning. Something had happened to my nerve endings: instead of excitement I felt a dullness, as if my skin had gone asleep. Her face turned to me, lips parted, as my invited hand pressed against the light cloth of her blouse. I do not remember plucking open the buttons, though I heard her quickening breath. My hand knew what to do but it was an animal at the end of a leash, creating its own world that I could only watch. I also began to breathe quickly, but for entirely different reasons. I was panicking inside my numb skin.

She stopped my hand. "You're icy."

I could only nod agreement.

"You don't want to do this."

How could I protest when my hand felt like something hauled from the grave?

"I'm so sorry, Carlos." She sounded peeved. "You are tired, of course."

We both seized on the excuse. I flopped back on the couch and confessed that yes, I was tired, as fatigued as I'd ever been in my life.

"I better go." She looked at her watch, an action which was entirely unnecessary.

When I saw her to the door, the cool sea-night poured in and she gave me a peck on the cheek. "So long, Carlos. It's just as well."

It had been a mistake, she was telling me, a moment of concussion brought on by the fevered emotions of the night.

I watched her trot down the sidewalk towards her car. Not once did she glance my way. Her movements were easy as she unlocked the door, slid onto the driver's seat and swung her legs in. Each sound, from the opening car door to the sigh as she settled in, dropped into the night like coins tossed into a river. A tent of fabric rose and fell as she released the brake, wrestled with the sticky gear shift, then twisted the key in the ignition. I reached down and touched myself through my trousers, and this time there was complete understanding.

6

A S USUAL, ALMOST EVERYONE IN THE HUB was at least a decade younger than I was. The men's voices were without any thickness and the women sounded like movie stars when they laughed. Lariats of smoke coiled through the air in this Wild West tavern, a perfume which engaged every human sense. Right in the centre of the campus, we gathered here each evening to feed on darkness and possibility.

I talked to Nicky, the bartender, who was a student himself, his choppy hair made blonde at the tips, wearing a small gold hoop through his left earlobe. I straddled the stool, lifted a pint of lager, and looked around. This is when I saw the girl.

Most British Columbia girls look like they just returned from an overnight hiking trip, skin glowing with health, wearing something useful for the scratchy bushes of the trail and sensible trekking boots that navigate gravel as easily as alpine grasses. They are a vibrant clan of Girl Scouts who can hang upside down from monkey bars or lift themselves to the chin a dozen times. With one hand pushed into the backs of their jeans, they drink girlish pink drinks, their faces shining with health and well-educated possibility.

This young woman had pale skin, almost white, a delicate geisha amongst the Olympians. Her face was long and thin, her hair almost black, and she was draped in a short green sarong skirt. Her small rounded belly was visible below the tank top, and clinging to her navel was a tiny emerald jewel. She stood with a group including two other girls in baggy cutoffs, and a muscular youth wearing oversized jeans who spoke loudly, stupidly, to make them laugh.

Except this smooth-faced girl was not laughing. She was looking at me through the haze of cigarette smoke. So with my smile I indicated the empty stool next to mine. Then I waited. I would see how she walked, for a woman who approaches a man must never take her eyes off him, never show fear or uncertainty.

This girl whispered something to her friends, who gave me bored glances, then she made her way towards me, hips swaying, and there was no self-conscious giggle or foolish shyness.

I straightened, took a deep breath, and felt every muscle sharpen.

I could smell her, dusted with some sort of rose fragrance which cut through the cigarette smoke.

"You are beautiful," I said when she was close enough, for I had to honour this creature who dared step away from her clan.

She blushed, a slight pinkening of that soft, white skin. Her smile wavered only for a second.

I took a quick gulp from my beer, uncrossed my legs and stared at the whole of her, from her narrow feet clad in a pair of sandals, up the slender calves to her small rounded knees, the thighs, hips, belly, and the tight black top. She watched my watching with the easy amusement of a woman who is used to being admired.

"You're pretty old for a student," she said.

"This is because I am not a student. I am a writer, a poet-in-exile."

Her hazel eyes narrowed. "I think I heard about you. Don't you have an office in the tower?"

I nodded.

"I'm an English major so most of my profs are over there."

She eased herself onto the empty stool and crossed one leg over the other, causing her skirt to ride high over her thighs. She did not make one of those fussy gestures that insecure women make, tugging the skirt in a show of false modesty.

"I'm Patty." She held her hand out to shake mine.

Her wrist was encircled by half a dozen glass bangles, and when I shook her hand, we were not colleagues making a brisk transaction, we were a man and a woman touching for the first time. I held her hand, not shaking but gently squeezing. She didn't pull free, but allowed this gesture to linger.

"And I am Carlos." I let her hand drop, reluctantly. "Why did you come to me?"

"I thought you looked interesting." She paused, running her tongue over her lips. "Older."

Music pulsed out of the speakers, some electronic rhythm without words. Hanging from the ceiling on either end of the bar, giant TV screens played some quiz show: who is the current wife of Brad Pitt?

"Where are you from?" Patty asked.

As I told her she nodded, remembering. "I read about you in the paper." She darted a glance back at her friends. "You were in jail or something."

I shrugged. "In my country, when you create provocation against the government, they are not happy."

She leaned forward, to hear better, and I stared at her breasts swelling above her skimpy top. With only a small effort I could have touched the flesh with my tongue.

"Did you write poetry that got you in trouble?"

I hesitated. I thought of the General's nasty ear with its bitten off tip, as if in childhood a pet had lunged at him. The source of my trouble.

"My poetry is erotic, not political."

She sat back, just a little.

"I do not want to speak of my difficulties," I told her, giving a dismissive gesture with my hand. "This is just my sad, personal history. And I do not want to make you sad."

Patty hesitated. "I'd be really interested in seeing your work. I took a minor in Comparative Lit last year."

"Then I will read it to you. First in Spanish, then in English."

"That would be so cool."

"I invite you back to my house, on this perfect British Columbia evening, and I read you my verse from the lowlands of my crazy country."

"Tonight?" Her eyes narrowed.

"Another day perhaps you will have forgotten me."

I waited for Patty to gather her nerve, to be the woman I knew she was, and I hoped to hell Rashid wasn't poking around the kitchen back home frying some stinky late-night meal. I could already feel my tongue sliding down her neck, and thought of how two nights earlier Rita had patted my thigh before leaving, humiliation thickening the air.

"I should get back to my friends," she said, but her eyes didn't move from mine.

I shrugged. For of course I would not force her.

"Matt's pretty touchy."

"Matt?"

"He's my boyfriend, sort of."

"That young man who wears his hat indoors?" I lifted my eyebrows.

"He's actually pretty nice."

I didn't respond.

"Well…" She slid off the stool. "It was good meeting you." She held out her hand to shake mine again.

I stared at her. So, she would go to her sort-of boyfriend in the T-shirt which advertised some resort in Cuba, and after drinking another drink they would neck in his car, and he would release her magnificent breasts from the flimsy fabric, and because she was a polite Canadian girl she would do as he asked.

I could not let this happen to a beautiful woman who knew she was meant for much more.

Ignoring her outstretched hand, its delicate wrist circled by bangles, I said, "I am sorry, Patty."

"What's that supposed to mean?"

The arm lowered and she hooked a finger through the waistband of her skirt. Now she did not look so certain.

"When you walked towards me ten minutes ago, I saw a woman who was not afraid of her body."

Her cheeks flushed crimson.

"I hope that you are not shy of your desires." I felt like an old man saying this, giving advice. Perhaps she would laugh.

Patty's mouth opened, revealing a pink tongue and her small white teeth. Of course she had never heard one of her Vancouver boyfriends say such a thing. It took her a moment to decide how to reply.

"I have no idea who you are, Carlos, or what you might do."

"I think you know exactly what I might do."

A pause. The noise of the music pulsed between us, all around us, an animal rhythm.

"Whatever."

She was leaving, her back to me now, her friends watching, and the boy, Matt, glaring, waiting to discover if I had insulted his girlfriend.

Insulted. That's what they call it here, when you tell a woman she is attractive.

I swallowed the rest of my beer. Perhaps I had had too much to drink: I was becoming too much myself. Suddenly I couldn't stand all the innocence and young, unseamed faces. They looked like burn victims, flesh pulled tight across their cheekbones.

"Put it on my tab," I instructed my good friend the bartender, and before he had a chance to protest, I got up to leave.

I pushed through the crowded room, pressing my way between damp, sweaty bodies, perhaps the only one who wasn't laughing at some shared joke, and I felt her coming, following through the knot of people. I heard her impatient voice mutter "Excuse me," yet I didn't look back, kept moving up the short flight of stairs, pushing open the heavy door until I'd escaped into the night.

There I waited for her, lighting a cigarette while I leaned

against the concrete wall, breathing in nicotine and the rich fishy ocean smell that washed over the campus when the sun was down. It was the most familiar smell I could imagine. In my city you can still walk down to the port at night and see the nets spread out to dry and the gleaming torches of fishermen making their repairs.

"Carlos?"

I pinched the match until it was extinguished, then tossed it on the ground.

She looked almost frail now, her skin pebbled by the breeze.

"Maybe we could see each other some time, for coffee." She was panting a little from hurrying up the stairs.

"Come here." I beckoned her closer.

After a small hesitation she obeyed, and I slowly reached to touch the side of her neck where the pulse throbbed. It seemed to calm her and after a moment I lowered my hand to the neckline of her top, following the rules of gravity. Then I stopped, flicked my cigarette to the ground and tipped her chin so she was looking straight into my eyes. "Do you want this?"

I waited for an answer, our bodies barely touching, a distant thud of bass beat sounding from the cellar bar.

She would hear her own voice make its demand. I could see her surprise that this man did not dissolve before her beauty like all the others.

"I do," she said. "For sure." Her words made her electric to herself.

I began to kiss her then, nudging her soft lips open, and felt her tongue instantly alive against mine. Below, her naked belly leaned in tentatively but I didn't press back, not until she insisted by becoming bolder, scooping my ass with her hands. This was a Patty she'd only guessed at, dreamed of. My hands touched her hair, her neck, her small ears, nothing hurried, no frenzied boy's passion. Each inch of her body would be honoured. I lifted her chin and saw that her eyes were closed, her cheeks deeply flushed and I kissed her once on each eyelid. She rocked from side to side, that firm belly now locked against mine.

"What the fuck's going on here, Patty?"

The sound was grotesque, a fart in the princess' bed chamber.

We hadn't heard the door swing open. We'd missed the ten seconds of released smoke and music. And we certainly hadn't heard his steps across two metres of concrete. The boyfriend emerged from the depths, eyes wild and bewildered, pants hanging halfway down his hips.

Reluctantly I pulled away while Patty's fingers trailed up my spine.

Her voice sounded sleepy. "It's no big deal, Matt."

"What's that supposed to mean?" His long arms hung at his sides, his bow legs astride the pavement, and he still clutched a beer bottle by the neck.

She went over to him and settled one of her thin arms over his shoulder, and he stiffened to prove that she could not lessen his anger so easily.

"Who are you?" The beer bottle stuck out towards me.

I told him my name, unapologetically.

"Well Carlos whatever, get the fuck out of here."

Patty's arm moved up and down his back, reassuring, but still he refused to acknowledge her presence. She looked bored now, her chin settling on his shoulder, waiting for the performance to lose steam, and then she would take him by the hand and lead him home.

I pretended to look at my watch, though it was too dark to see the time.

"It is late," I said. And I gave the smallest bow to the woman who had almost been my lover.

Behind the boy's back she lifted a hand and returned a small wave. I believe she was laughing.

I lay on my bed in the married students' housing, where the walls are leavened with the moss of ocean air, vegetal barriers like Communion wafers, and I listened to the medievalist fuck the anthropologist on the other side of this thin wall, mimicking a position they'd learned while visiting some obscure tribe up the Amazon. And I knew that this is how I would spend endless nights in Canada, listening to mating cries from a remote kingdom.

7

I STOOD AT SYD BASKIN'S OFFICE DOORWAY, third floor of Thompson Tower, where I had been asked to appear promptly at 3:00 p.m. It was 3:20. On my arrival, all heads simultaneously swerved to look at the clock. This was an art deco object, chrome and wood with elegant curves. Sitting in the cramped office were the executive board members of CAFE: Rita, Syd, John Deeth, Lucy, Sharon and Daniel Rose. My protectors and saviours. My friends. I did not apologize for being late, because it wasn't my fault that I was intercepted by Jurgen, who insisted on ducking into the faculty club for a martini. A silly drink. But I went along with him to be polite.

"Sit down, Carlos," Rita said with a tight smile.

I unpeeled the army surplus poncho (it had been raining, as usual) and managed to sprinkle water over Syd's pile of examination papers. This time I did apologize, profusely.

Syd seemed embarrassed. "Never mind. Make yourself comfortable."

I perched on the edge of the rush-seated chair, hearing myself huff from the trip up the stairs. Months of incarceration had turned my muscles to milk and the elevator was broken.

"We have a few serious matters to discuss." Syd played with the stack of damp papers. Rita, when I glanced at her, reddened and stared at the floor.

I began to sweat. I wanted to get out of this crowded little room with its serious matters. I wished I were back with the German professor in the faculty lounge, discoursing on the poems of Goethe.

"How's it going for you here?" Syd's voice emitted an artificial lilt. I was immediately on guard.

"Fine."

"Are you happy?"

I laughed. Then stopped. No one else was laughing.

"You have all been so kind."

Sharon Rose gave a quick smile then looked down at the very interesting floor and folded one leg over the other. She wore a long dark skirt and a sleeveless blouse, and her legs were bare, her feet naked in sandals. I could see the weathered skin of her heels and soles and guessed that this was a woman who liked to work outdoors, planting and using her large capable hands to snip off dead flowers and tamp down the earth. She would do this while contemplating the complex structuralism of Dr. Lévi-Strauss.

Sydney glanced at his scrawled notes. "A couple of issues have come up." He turned to the other board members for support, then cleared his throat. "I believe Rita has spoken to you about some of this."

"Ah, Rita." I smiled broadly at my friend, and reached over and clasped her hand. She gave me a quick smile, and removed her hand from mine. I shouldn't have had the second martini but the grey-bearded German professor insisted. He wanted to tell me about his mistress in Salzburg, how he was going to spend a sabbatical year with her in some Alpine village.

I loosened my belt.

"We understand how difficult it is for you to adjust to this new life." Syd looked distressed. "And God knows we have never been tested as you have, yet we have certain obligations to our membership, and to you."

"Of course," I agreed.

"There is the problem of money," he continued. "You've been racing through it. At this rate there won't be enough to last the year."

"I just do normal things," I protested, and searched in my pocket for cigarettes. All eyes watched this gesture.

"For instance," Sharon said softly. "Perhaps you can't afford to smoke."

There was a pause, then someone muttered, "Or drink."

"Your position at the university is only part-time, as we've explained," Syd said. "The stipend is not large."

"But adequate," Rita added.

"The university, like universities everywhere in this country, is strapped." Syd frowned. "The Alliance has been topping you off each week, but we can't continue this. Frankly, we had budgeted for considerably less."

God, I wanted a cigarette. I felt the cotton of my shirt stick to my sides.

"The thing is," Rita began, leaning forward with a smile that seemed genuine. "You have a way to earn money: it's been handed to you. Eleanor is dying to publish your memoirs. All she wants is to see a sample and she'll sign you."

"Exactly how far along is the project?" Daniel Rose said. He was a slight man with a deep voice.

They waited, expectant. When I didn't reply, Syd said, "Give her fifty pages and an outline; that might be enough. We'll be happy to help you put together a package."

"Delighted to help," Rita pitched in.

"Absolutely," Daniel chimed.

I looked out the streaked window at the parking lot below. It had stopped raining and people were closing their umbrellas and stopping to chat in clusters on the asphalt. Hemingway said that to get started each day he would write one true sentence. The rest would follow. Yes, but how did he know what was true?

"Thank you," I said, and began to rise from the chair. My mouth was dry: I was desperately thirsty. I'd left Doktor Bruckner in the faculty club lounge, scooping goldfish crackers from a bowl, his voice growing louder with each drink, nattering about "Marlena." Perhaps he would still be there.

"Hold on, Carlos," Syd said. "We have not dealt with the final item on our agenda."

I sank back.

"This is difficult for me, and disturbing for all of us, your friends." His face worked through a variety of expressions. I remembered the gracious smile, as, on his impeccable patio, he had once passed around a tray of stuffed mushroom caps. And how he wouldn't let my drink fall below a certain level.

"We are responsible, as legal sponsors, for your behaviour, insofar as it infringes on the rights of others."

The other members of the board had selected frozen, grim expressions.

"A certain young lady has filed a complaint with the sexual harassment officer. Apparently there was an incident outside The Hub last Thursday."

Syd stared at me, expecting what? A nod of recognition, or perhaps a blurted confession?

Thursday. Today was Monday. How am I supposed to remember last Thursday? And who was this sexual officer? I felt like I was running a motorcycle off a cliff.

"We realize that in such situations there can be misunderstandings…" Syd trailed off.

"Don't you remember?" Rita said.

"Remember what, please?"

For a moment, no one spoke.

"Allegedly, and correct us if we are wrong…" Syd cleared his throat. "You forced your attentions on a student named —" He squinted at his papers. "Miss Fry."

"For Heaven's sake, Syd," Rita interrupted. "You're so nineteenth century. He felt her up." She paused. "Allegedly."

Syd flinched. And so did I, for I understood that Rita was speaking as one who has been wounded. Perhaps she had notified this officer.

"We want to give you every opportunity to counter this allegation," Syd said, and when I looked puzzled, he added in what he thought was clear English, "Did this, or did this not happen?"

He was the director of my school and I was the student hauled in to explain his misdeeds. We will phone your father, Carlos.

Sharon flattened her hands on the desk. Her husband, Daniel, gave a sharp laugh then turned the sound into a cough. I felt their embarrassment saturate the air. Rita looked so disappointed that I couldn't bear to be in the room a second longer.

"What is this, secret police following me wherever I go?" None had the nerve to meet my stare. "Tell me, do you count how many times I shit? Record my telephone conversations?" I stood up. "Send me home, please, back to my country. At least in jail there is no pretense of freedom. The bars are visible."

They are trying to deny me my body but I won't let them. Without sex I am not a poet, not even a shitty verse-maker, because I will not live without desire. I can do nothing but shrink from their smooth faces and careful clothes and sexless cordiality. I am screaming with it every moment of the day, screaming with loneliness.

The Sexual Harassment Office was in the lower floor of the chemistry building at the edge of the campus. I had received a memo notifying me that my attendance was "mandatory." I anticipated a roomful of dour men and women poring over files, deciding my fate. My roommate, Rashid, that very morning when I most needed an understanding friend, tugged the coffee tin from my hand and snapped, "Buy your own." I stared at him. What had he allowed himself to be turned into?

"You just don't get it, do you?" He looked at me, his gold tooth gleaming, hair neatly combed back. A bowl of nutritious Special K cereal waited for him on the counter.

"Excuse me, sir," I said, and retied the damp towel around my waist. I had just showered upstairs, borrowing Rashid's apple-scented shampoo so that I would make a good impression at the meeting. "What is it that I do not understand?"

He replaced the coffee tin on the shelf above the stove and grabbed his cereal bowl. "You are spoiling it for the rest of us."

He perched on the straight-backed chair at the table and began to eat soundlessly.

"I am spoiling what, my friend?"

He set down his spoon and looked pained. "By your foolish behaviour you are tainting us all."

He was telling the truth, I realized with a cringe. By my idiot gestures I would fold up the Alliance like a tent. These good people would lose heart, and the next man trapped in his barbaric kingdom would hear the key to his cell drop into the sewer. Like it or not, I was a character in a much larger narrative than my own sorry life.

The sexual harassment officer was Ms. Coffey, an almost attractive middle-aged woman who stood by the door of the basement classroom in the chemistry building, wearing a blue pantsuit and silver earrings to greet the criminal.

"Take the chair by the window, Carlos," she instructed with a quick smile.

I obeyed. To my surprise there were no other officials in the room and no easel set up containing maps of the suspect's activity. The room appeared to be an old laboratory. The equipment was removed but there were still high counters fitted with sinks and water faucets, and a faint chemical smell lingered. We sat on a raised dais from which the lecturer must have proclaimed his thesis years ago.

Patty was already there, seated away from the window, so demure in pressed jeans and white blouse buttoned to the neck that I hardly recognized her. The boyfriend stood behind her, face as serious as a banker's, his hands pressing into her shoulders. Then, to my surprise, Rita entered the room.

"Good luck," she mouthed, and eyed the girl with passing interest. She drew up a chair and planted herself on it.

"This is an informal meeting to determine the sequence of events," Ms. Coffey said briskly, and flipped open her laptop computer. Already a tape machine was resting on the desk, its button punched to "record." "We'll hear from Patty first."

I sucked in deeply and felt the rank aged chemicals pour into my chest. What experiments did the the young chemists perform here? Did they dunk rats in acid and note the rate of decay? Were small white mice trapped in cages and fed strictly controlled diets? Perhaps no living things were used at all, only compounds mixed in precise amounts and viewed through glass. I unbuttoned my jacket and smiled at Patty, who dodged my glance as if it were toxic.

"I went outside The Hub for some air," she said, raising her voice at the end as if it were a question. "I'd talked to him," a wince of recognition, "Carlos, earlier. He seemed nice."

She paused.

"Go on," Ms. Coffey prodded, her fingers flying over the keyboard.

Rita was sitting forward on her chair, a hand clasped over each knee. Her purse had slid onto the floor.

"So I saw that he was out there too."

"Were you surprised?"

"Not exactly. I mean I sort of saw him go up the stairs ahead of me."

Another pause. The boyfriend's hands left Patty's shoulders and she seemed to float, her hair spilling over her back.

"Take your time."

"Well, I said 'hi.'"

"And then?"

She didn't speak.

"Did he reply?" Ms. Coffey glanced at the clock on wall and frowned.

"I think so. Yeah, he did."

This was very interesting, to hear the story of your life from another perspective. As she spoke I saw it all unfold, the way Patty had appeared from the door of The Hub, breathing hard, eyes scouting the darkness for me, and how I stood smoking in the coolness of the evening, waiting.

The boyfriend chewed his lower lip, and I suddenly saw how very young this couple was. Patty had not intended to meet me in this interrogation room: it was the boy's doing. He could not stand that she had been touched. Fear tracked across his face, not anger. Two emotions that tangle in every man.

"Then he just lunged at me. It was pretty weird."

"Would you say Mr. Estévez was drunk at the time?"

"I guess."

"How many drinks had you consumed, Patty?"

The girl looked startled, and her boyfriend opened his mouth as if he were about to speak. Sir, you must defend the honour of your woman. But he didn't. Ms. Coffey gave him a warning glance and like a child he kicked at the chair rung. The recording machine purred gently, sending magnetic tape spinning between its spools.

"Two drinks at most. I was pretty broke, plus I had an eighty-thirty Modern Lit class the next morning."

"Where exactly did Mr. Estévez touch you when he 'lunged'?"

There was a long silence while Patty twisted her head to look at her boyfriend, as if checking that she might proceed. I sat upright and tugged at the sleeves of my shirt. Frankly, I couldn't imagine touching this timid, ordinary girl, and I have never "lunged" in my life. I glanced at Rita, who nodded, her face absent of expression.

"Uh, here." She placed her fingers on her neck, then dropped them to her lap. "And on my left boob." Then Patty giggled.

"She's nervous," the boyfriend informed us, his voice much deeper than I remembered.

"Thank you, Patty," the sexual harassment officer said. "Now I have to ask you one final question. Is there any way that you might have led Mr. Estévez to believe that you wished to be touched? Did you, for instance, touch him?"

"No way!" She dug her hands into the snug front pockets of her jeans.

"He was all over her," the boyfriend said. "He was jumping her, like some animal."

I wondered which animal, bear or chimpanzee, or perhaps the mythical unicorn. I felt sorry for both of these young people, doomed to their ordinary lives.

It was my turn to testify and I didn't hesitate.

"Yes, it is entirely as the young lady has said."

Patty squeezed her eyes shut and I heard her soft relieved sigh. The ghost of some rodent circled his invisible cage. Ancient acids wafted through the stuffy classroom and clung to our nostrils. I would not argue or defend myself. It was demeaning. Rita sat back on the chair, her lips parted with the hint of a smile. Ms. Coffey seemed startled, as if this had never happened before in the history of the Sexual Harassment Office, that a man concurred with the lady's tale. She was used to their snivelling denials and transparent lies.

"Well then," Ms. Coffey said after a moment, and reached for a sheet of paper from her file folder and began to write on it. The room was silent except for the swish of her marker.

Moments later, I walked with Rita out of the basement office clutching an official "first warning" notice, which I immediately tossed into the recycling bin at the end of the hall. My name had entered the university's black list of rapists and predators. I pushed open the glass doors of the building where chemical interactions are pursued with grave consciousness. There wasn't a sound in the larger world, not even bird noise. Is it possible to contain a man's secret life?

"I thought you did very well." Rita squinted through the hovering sun. "That was brave."

When you achieve praise, you must nod silently.

"That girl was a flake," she said.

"A flake?"

She laughed, and didn't explain. "I have to go to work now. You'll be okay?"

I assured her that I was completely well, and she brushed my cheek with her lips.

There are people who cannot bear the reality that we must live several lives concurrently. Rita understood this, I believed. She is an artist too, and there is always both inner and outer life, sometimes twinned, but more often not. When I was a small boy I kept a diary for a brief period. A girlish pastime, turquoise ink in a hardcover leather-bound book. It stopped when I discovered my mother searching through the drawer of my desk one day. She slipped the book out, its pages filled with my tender thoughts and inscriptions, and began to read. This is when I charged into the room, bristling with fury and indignation. How dare she! My mother, calm and implacable, simply held the open book up to the light and said, "There should be no thoughts you need to hide from me."

Of course she was desperate to know whatever she could. The other male in her life demanded his secret life, and there was nothing she could do to contain him. There were no sexual officers in Santa Clara.

Our father left the house every Wednesday evening. There was a ritual to this disappearance. First he would steam up the bathroom with his shower and shaving, then enter his dressing room where the maid had laid out a fresh shirt and underwear, and where his suit would have been hung, brushed, and pressed. A painting hung next to his suits, an amateur landscape evoking his childhood home in the dry rolling hills of Santa Clara. The forests were long gone by the time I was a child, slashed to make room for the endless suburbs.

He was not a handsome man, round-faced and bald, with thin lips, and he was not tall. Yet I doubt that he ever worried about it for a minute, for he was a man of respectable family, if not lavish means.

Twenty minutes later he would emerge from the dressing room, lime cologne splashed on his rosy cheeks, decked out in a white shirt, single-breasted dark suit with cuffs, a blue or green tie, polished shoes.

On Wednesdays, my mother did not adjust his collar or brush imaginary lint off his shoulder before he left. On Wednesday evenings she did not kiss him goodbye, or tuck a handkerchief in his pocket or wish him luck on some business transaction.

Instead she sat in the dark in the parlour, drinking iced tea while he stole out, neither of them saying a word. Her deep sigh would be accompanied by the chink of ice in her glass. Then she would rise to her feet in the dark and cross the room to the old German-made piano.

Only when I was eleven years old did I discover the reason for this mysterious behaviour.

I'd gone to bed, as usual, around ten o'clock, long after Father had left. Rosario, by then, was at boarding school, away from us all. Lying there in my room I listened as my mother played the piano, which is what she did, for hours, every Wednesday evening until his return.

My mother's piano playing was excruciating. It is torture to hear the truly unmusical plow their way through beloved sonatas and preludes. She played everything, from Chopin to the great Spaniard Albéniz, with enormous feeling and intense romantic surges, crescendos that leapt towards all corners of the room, and diminuendos that burrowed like snails into the baseboards. Yet everything sounded like a military march. The notes were correct, the timing precise, and above the racket you could always hear the tick-tick of the metronome, her precious timepiece which perched on the piano next to the wedding photographs.

I lay stiffly in bed, fingers stuffed into my ears. It was worse than listening to my half-wit classmate, Stefano, recite a Wordsworth poem in his phonetic English.

Suddenly the sound stopped. Gracias a Dios! Perhaps she was fetching herself another drink. How long would the peace last?

Then she was standing at my bedroom door, backlit by the hall light, wearing what she always wore in the evening, a long midnight-blue satin dressing gown. Her hair was hanging freely, a tangle of dark curls, and I caught a whiff of that coffee-flavoured liqueur she liked to sip as she played.

"May I come in?"

My mother sat on the edge of my bed and began to stroke my hair. This was something she did only when I was feverish, or at the end of summer when I was fretting about the first day of school. Perhaps she was going to sing to me. I hoped not; her singing was even more wretched than her playing.

"Do you understand what a mistress is, Carlito?" The fingers caressed the side of my neck.

I held my breath, then said, "I think so."

This wasn't altogether true: it was a word I'd heard, and associated with other whispered words like puta, whore.

"Didn't you wonder where Father goes on Wednesdays?" Her voice was soothing in the dark.

I said nothing.

Her hand travelled slowly over my forehead. "Her name is Madame Hélène, your father's mistress," she said. "A French woman."

I was sure she could feel my pulse thud against my skin. Her distress seemed to flow from her body into mine.

"I am so sad, Carlito." She sighed deeply, a terrifying sound to a small boy.

"He must stop," I pulled myself up to a sitting position. "You must make him."

She laughed and kissed me on the lips. "I love you so much; you are one of the angels."

Somewhere far out in the ocean, a freighter bleated its foghorn as it navigated around the peninsula.

I didn't like knowing. Before I had only the sound of her overwrought playing to contend with, and my own imaginings. If I had felt sadness those nights, before her visit to my room, it was as much my own as hers. But now I'd been enlisted as confidante, and each sound of the razor scraping my father's chin as he made his preparations for his mistress made me wince. Of course we could never ask him to stop. We didn't dare.

And now it is him that I feel sorry for, his dutiful returns to the grieving wife who swept through the house like Ophelia. And what did he make of his son, squinting across the table at breakfast with a worried child's frown, wondering where this mistress had touched him, what she'd said to his familiar face, and why he liked it so much.

8

WE DROVE TO THE GULF ISLAND IN DANIEL Rose's
navy blue minivan. This was an annual trip for his
graduate student seminar and I had been invited as a special
guest. It was, I believed, part of my rehabilitation. Would
I have the self-discipline to behave myself amongst these
young women?

"I hope you don't mind," Daniel said, slinging the door back
and motioning me in, "sitting with the groceries."

The rapist was stashed in the rear of the vehicle, safely away
from temptation.

Daniel Rose's wife sat beside him in the front of the van,
then slid on a pair of oversized sunglasses, peeled back the lid
of her takeout coffee, and we began the journey. Rita was
in another car with one of the graduate students. It had all
been arranged.

"The day is beautiful." I had to strain forward in my seat so they could hear me.

"Very beautiful," they chimed in agreement.

"It could not be better," I added with confidence.

"Couldn't be better."

Perhaps I could say anything at all and they would repeat it. I leaned an elbow on one of the bags of food and felt it shift. There was a strong smell of onions.

"We always buy our groceries in the city," Daniel called over his shoulder as we merged into the highway. He cranked up the window a notch so we could hear each other speak. "Much less expensive."

"Ah," I nodded, face blasted by wind.

"Everything costs more on the Island," his wife added.

"Normally we buy only organic," Daniel shouted, "but with this gang it would cost the earth."

"Prohibitive," Sharon Rose confirmed.

"See that bag by your elbow?" Daniel nodded.

I did. Half a dozen fat cauliflowers were crammed in. A bland, gassy vegetable I am not fond of.

"Picked up the lot in Chinatown for three bucks."

"Ah," I said.

"Just because there were some brown bits."

I remembered the day, while I was still staying in Rita's apartment, that she had taken me around to the outdoor bargain bins of groceries. This was what I should buy, she told me, picking up a cellophane-packed carton of rotting eggplant. "Or this." She pointed to some unnamed straggle of vegetable. "So much cheaper." And then she immediately went inside to the stall of fresh beans to scoop up a bagful for her own dinner.

Traffic sped past on both sides. Daniel was a careful driver, hands clamped to the wheel, his back very erect. This was not an interesting conversation, I was thinking. Sharon taught anthropology at the university and Daniel was in the department of geophysics. Why did we not discuss theories of cultural determinism, or the disputed age of the Earth?

"We used to get by on fifty bucks a week for food," Daniel said as the van pitched over a seam in the highway.

"Over twenty years ago," his wife reminded him. "Before the kids were born."

I had seen photographs of their sons on Daniel's desk: handsome blonde boys, very healthy. One was a champion in the rowboat, or perhaps it was kayak, and he had been on the Olympic team in Sydney.

When someone announces that a landscape is "just like a painting" you think he is an idiot. But when the massive car ferry crosses the Strait, leaving the mainland behind until it is a forgotten shape, and when the mist shimmers over water like a gauze canopy, then you understand that the world of the artist may collide with the world of nature, and that only great works of art bring this explosion of joy. This is what I scribbled in my notebook while the others crowded the cafeteria.

The sky was a startling blue in the east, and heavy and dark in the west. You could spot exactly where the shadow began; the water was sliced in two, dark and icy near the bow of the ferry and beyond, sparkling grey-blue off the stern. I wrote a poem in the notebook Rita had bought me. The Gulf Islands ferry cut from one world to the next, its deck doused first with light then darkness. Most of our group stayed in the cafeteria for the entire journey, chattering over coffee and muffins, but I made my way to the deck to be buffeted by wind and spray and the whining of gulls, and to feel the engine vibrate beneath my feet.

In the distance a grey mammal's back humped through the waves, dolphin or whale, and I thought of the universe of ocean beneath us, those unseen creatures who flash through silence all their lives.

I wouldn't mind if we never arrived at the Island. This ferry was the perfect capsule for the exiled poet: a complete world that travelled over the watery skin of another hidden world, between land forms and still places.

After two hours, the engines cut and we coasted towards the dock of Daniel's island.

"Where were you?" Sharon met me in the narrow staircase leading to the carport.

I told her, but my description of what I saw was somehow offensive.

"We were all in the café," she said, and paused. "Wondering where you'd gone."

We walked together, threading through the vehicles until we reached the van, where Daniel waited, key in ignition.

"So, you found our wandering man," he said, leaning out the window.

Chastened, I stepped inside, into the back seat beside the bag of cauliflower.

The students had brought sleeping bags and tents, which they set up outside. The cabin was very simple, aged cedar with a screened-in verandah, musty furniture. I wanted only to stand

and breathe this country air, but all around people scurried, heaving groceries and gear, rucksacks full of clothes, bottles of wine, and coolers of ale. Sharon had tied back her hair and was wearing some sort of cut-off trousers and a big shirt that must have belonged to her husband. She barked orders like a drill sergeant: "Take it to the back room! That stays outside. Wipe your shoes!"

Around her neck hung a beaded necklace dripping with fierce-looking porcupine quills. Everyone seemed to know exactly what to do so I stayed out of the way, gazing at the scruffy fields and, in the distance, a ridge brushed with dark fir trees. There were even a dozen cows from a neighbouring farm moving slowly through the tall grasses, munching, barely looking up at our commotion. I've discovered, since leaving home, that each shift in locale is a shift in universe, and that I must catch up, find myself in the new place. This island was beautiful, my eyes told me, yet my body was scrambled. Inside, the cabin was dark and stuffy and I heard a low fervent buzzing. When my eyes became accustomed to the lack of light I could see hundreds of flies clustered around the windows, beating their translucent wings against the glass. One of the students had grabbed a copy of *The Journal of Physical Sciences* and was thwacking the insects as fast as he could.

"Die!" he chanted with each massacre. "Die!" No one but me seemed to notice.

"It is beautiful here," I said to my hostess when she paused for a moment in her order-giving. "Very simple."

"We like it." Her face was red from all the carrying and heaving and her voice had an edge.

Just stand here a few seconds, I wanted to tell her. Breathe in. Feel where you are. And there was Rita, wrenching her back as she worked to jigger open the windows, knocking them with the palm of her hand, struggling until she broke her nails.

"Why do you not relax?" I suggested.

"Because," she said in an icy voice, "there is a ton of work to be done."

I understood that she was tense, and that she was thinking of her son back home who had been taken to stay with his father. It is hard for a woman to be separated from her child.

"Why don't you help Daniel with the fire?"

I smiled gently. "But this man is an expert." Of course I've lit many fires in my day, but always in an open stone fireplace.

Daniel demonstrated the use of the oil lamps, propane fridge, and the wood stove, which was necessary both for heat and cooking. He pointed to the outside toilet, which they call an "outhouse," a term I found both sensible and amusing. It reminded me of the laundry shack back home where the maids used to wash our clothes and sheets by hand. Someone filled an immense iron kettle with water from the pump, brought it indoors, and placed it on the stove. The students had already dropped gear in carefully selected spots on the field and began to raise their tents expertly, pounding stakes in the ground, heaving the aluminum poles skyward. Before long the fields on either side of the cabin were littered with multi-coloured peaks of nylon. We looked like a small occupying army.

Sharon organized a kitchen crew to peel and chop potatoes while Daniel wedged logs into the stove and tried to get the thing lit, cursing the dampness.

By the westward window there was an ancient straw chair, which I sank into, snapping open one of the cans of beer. Late afternoon heat shimmered over the horizon and the trees on the ridge cast long shadows over the fields. The tops of their branches combed the sky and I decided that this is where I would go. I would enter into the dusk, alone.

But first, a guest has an obligation to entertain his hosts and fellow guests, especially the penniless poet who had brought no groceries or liquor, only his hungry, parched self. Whenever a student drifted in from his labours, I told him a story from my life or made an observation about this place, its smells and tastes, and I felt their earnest attentiveness as I spoke. The poet, from earliest childhood, sees and feels what others may forget.

Rita, red-faced, flitted by complaining about mouse shit in the cutlery drawer.

I talked to a beautiful girl named Maria who had thick eyebrows and was dressed in a green halter top and white shorts. I also spoke to her boyfriend, Marlon (like the great movie star from *The Godfather*), and finally to their friends in the graduate seminar. They were all so young and clever and polite.

"Maria, bellísima," I told her, seriously, for beauty is never a joke.

Her boyfriend laughed, but she didn't. Instead she looked hard at my face, her cheekbones tight against her olive skin, and she knew that I had seen something in her that these Canadian boys had missed.

When they began their first teaching session around the table in the screened-in verandah, I set out for my walk. I grabbed another beer, and an extra for the trip home. It was still hot under the low-slung sky.

The ridge looked about a mile west and it was in this direction that I hiked, squinting against the falling light, making my way slowly through the hay and grasses and spindly wildflowers, a bee buzzing around my head, the scent of camomile clinging to my nostrils while far off the cows lowed and clanged their bells. As I walked I thought of the Indians who must once have roamed these lands. Could I ever do it, live in the bush, planting simple crops, eating berries, writing my poems for no eyes and ears but my own? Perhaps that was complete freedom for a writer: to have no audience. Does a bird need applause for its flight?

The ridge drew no closer. If anything, it stretched further into the distance as the evening clouds thickened overhead. It was of no consequence if I reached my destination; it was only an ordinary idea to have this goal, which perhaps limited imagination. I drank both beers and tossed the cans into the field where I imagined they would seed and grow tender crops of Budweiser Light.

I stretched my arms towards the sky and was broadsided by a wave of vertigo, and in slow motion I collapsed to the ground. There I lay, spread-eagled on my back, and watched a distant jet tear a seam through the sky. Birds I'd never heard before peeped and chittered, and when I listened very hard I could hear the flap of their wings. I was pitching into deep sleep, a sleep uncluttered by the racket of Rashid's infernal keyboard clacking as he worked till dawn. It was quite unlike those moments of uneasy silence in the city where I was born, where one lies in fretful insomnia in the hours before dawn hoping for some hint of the life of a fellow human. The grinding wheels of the garbage truck becomes a welcome intrusion.

Hours later, when I opened my eyes I could see only grass, and my eyes and nose were full of it. I sneezed violently then sat up, squinting, hair matted, and realized where I was. But not immediately. First I was a small boy alone in my bed, and in the room beneath a Chopin polonaise lurched forward then suddenly stopped. My father's footsteps clinked up the stone stairs, his key fitted into the door. We were a family again, and the noise would stop.

"Where on God's green earth have you been?" It was Rita who jumped to her feet, relief tracking across her face.

They were all frowning up at me through gaslight, and I realized that I was still covered in grass and dirt from my little adventure. My lips were parched and I searched for a cold beer in the propane fridge. When I looked back out the window to where I'd just been, I realized from the waning light that I'd been gone for hours.

"I was listening to the ground," I said, and looked at Maria, the beautiful Italian girl, because I knew she would understand. "To hear its heartbeat."

Maria smiled, then stared into her lap.

The seminar had wrapped up and the students were sprawled about the cabin, reading or making notes.

Professor Daniel Rose pinched his reading glasses over his nose. "Never do that again, Carlos. Go off without telling anyone. You can get seriously lost out there."

Lost? You can only get lost when there is somewhere to get lost from.

I looked at Sharon, who was clearing the table and setting it with dinner things. She glanced up, but catching my eye, went back to her work. There was a tension in her movements; she was pretending to be interested in adjusting the cutlery and napkins, but it was not true. She was angry. At me? I wasn't sure.

"Anyone want more of this?" Daniel held up the ladle for the stew pot and I waited for someone to say "yes" but no one did. Before I had a chance to utter a word, he'd dropped the lid on the earthenware pot and rushed it back to the kitchen.

"Excellent!" he pronounced with pleasure. "There will be enough for tomorrow."

At home we never remove the pot before the guests have gone. His wife sat back in her chair with a strange vacant smile. She'd changed her shirt and wore a light jersey blouse, pale green. Daniel spoke to her as he spoke to his students, in this elevated teacherish tone, as if he hadn't left the lecture hall.

"Sharon, excellent stew!"

She nodded once in response, smile intact.

One of the graduate students began to talk of his trip to Paris.

"Of course the Left Bank isn't what it used to be in Sartre's day," he said, locking his thumb into his belt. He was a sharp-featured boy, perhaps twenty-two, with narrow eyes and hair swept off to one side. "So jammed with tourists," he sighed. "Deux Magots, just another clip joint."

"You kids with your European voyages," Daniel interrupted. "I wish to hell we could afford to go overseas."

"But you have this lovely island cabin," I reminded him.

"Half of it. My brother and his brood own the rest."

"And we must leave everything spanking clean," Sharon said. "Who's on dish duty tonight?"

Three of the boys jumped up, two grabbed checked drying cloths, the other an ancient sponge. It was as if they'd been doing this all their lives, hunched over the sink chattering away like old women as they cleaned.

I poured another drink while the girls burrowed deep into their chairs and sipped coffee, and I thought of the tiny state in the eastern part of my country, where the women still ride wooden carts which are pulled by their stoop-shouldered husbands.

After the work was done and the boys had joined us, reeking of detergent, I told my fellow guests of childhood vacations at my grandfather's finca, a huge ranch in the highlands where longhorned cattle roamed the forbidding landscape. "He was a gaucho," I explained. "A formidable horseman."

"Still alive?" Marlon asked, his eyes half-shut and puffy.

"I fear not." So I told them of his strange death, how he was struck by lightning one winter evening as he stood outside, flooded by the dramatic moonlight of the high country, one hand leaning against the tall metal flagpole as he took a leak. There hadn't even been a storm; it was one of those electrical short-circuits that sometimes travel between mountain peaks. The flagpole was hit, the fabric of our national banner instantly fried, and my grandfather fused to the metal.

"After a lifetime of breaking horses, murdered by patriotism!"

While I told my stories, Daniel poured rough red wine from a cask. This homemade wine contained a thick sediment that swam around our glasses like chips of paint. In the distance, some animal wailed to the darkness.

We finally left the table for the comfort of the main room. Someone passed around a marijuana cigarette and I was amazed to watch Daniel as he held it between his thumb and index finger and drew it to his lips, then took a long experienced inhalation. This was followed by a series of snorts and coughs as he wrestled to hold the smoke inside his chest.

Rita didn't smoke. She sat curled like a cat on the old sofa, gazing at nothing. Perhaps she was thinking of Andreas in his father's girlfriend's townhouse, lying on the pull-out bed, snoring softly through his open mouth. Above her, attached by a hook to the wall, was an old scythe, badly rusted. Daniel had told us earlier that it had been found in the lower field, dropped by some careless harvester and left to rust in the coastal rains. Daniel liked to tell small historical anecdotes about the cabin. He himself had placed a newspaper in the wall for future generations to find. The drainage system for the fields had been worked out according to some medieval principal that he was experimenting with. He would, in fact, draw us a diagram.

The floor of the cabin was made of unvarnished particle board, partly covered by a worn carpet. The stairs rose from the centre of the room and led to the upper floor, where none of us had been invited.

Daniel examined the immense flask of wine and frowned. "At this rate we won't last the weekend."

"What about in town," I said, remembering the village we'd driven through. A kilometre or two from the dock, I'd spotted a market. "There is a place to buy wine?"

"If you want to pay Island prices."

I watched his wife's face. I thought she looked annoyed. Perhaps she was bored by his endless talk of money. I imagined this man in bed: would he monitor his pulse, his rate of ejaculation?

"One of the boys is at Oxford," Daniel was saying. "A great honour, of course, but Sharon and I are in the poorhouse for the duration." He looked to his wife for agreement but she just yawned.

He thinks he knows her, I realized. He was sure that he understood what she was thinking and feeling at any moment, and when they climbed the staircase soon to the attic bedroom, he would tell her this, what she had been feeling.

Of course he would be wrong. But she wouldn't admit this, for it was her great power, his misplaced confidence.

The young women of the graduate seminar were long limbed and slender and I watched their earnest faces as they followed the gestures of the esteemed professor. He was a man whose voice was too low and deep for his body, for he was no taller than I, with small sloping shoulders and a drooping gut. His hands and feet were small and plump, almost embryonic in their lack of detail. Yet these girls wanted him, because he knew more about plate tectonics and the physics of soil erosion than anyone in the province.

I thought they were not beautiful in the way Sharon Rose was. They assumed that any man would prefer their lithe, unseamed bodies to hers, and perhaps there are men who do. Perhaps Daniel was one of them.

Sharon moved slowly in her womanly trance, with those sure hands that could equally cut vegetables or model some complex theory in the air. I had no doubt that those lined freckled hands also knew how to caress a man in the same unhurried manner. Her waist was soft after bearing two children, and there was no vanity in the way she pushed back her hair with restless impatience, and she never giggled as the students did. Occasionally her deep-throated laugh filled the room.

Her husband ignored her when he was speaking. The young men of the graduate seminar mimicked the professor's voice and they competed with each other to ask penetrating questions, or to make some witticism that would cause him to chuckle. Daniel was the holder of knowledge and the dispenser of praise. The girls lifted their chins and said, "Professor Rose, is it possible to devise a system which…"

Sharon watched all this with an experienced eye. She would not compete. She was beyond such games. Yet, as the evening wore on, I saw that she was tired, that she wished the students would leave the cabin and unroll the sleeping bags in their tents, but instead they lingered while the professor slugged homemade wine and held forth.

To Daniel, everything was an "interesting conceit" or "a marvellous paradox."

The wood stove crackled with its fire, and the sweet smell of marijuana hovered in the air. Almost none of the kids smoked; they found it amusing to see their teacher suck on a joint, roll his shoulders with pleasure, and ramble on. I was becoming terribly sleepy, my head so heavy I felt the great effort of keeping it up. Rita was still perched on the couch, legs tucked under her bottom, her face expressionless. When I looked around the room I realized that I didn't know which form was a girl and which was a boy. They sat coiled together, wearing the same padded vests and flannel shirts, their hair tousled. Maria's boyfriend propped an elbow on her shoulder, as if she were a piece of sturdy furniture.

"Excuse me," I leaned forward and whispered to her. "Is this man your lover?"

Maria giggled and reached up to touch the boy's hand. "Are we, Marlon?"

"Something like that," he said, yawning broadly.

But Maria wasn't yawning. She looked at me hard, those full lips not assured now, but questioning. She'd pulled away, just a notch, from her boyfriend's weight. The boy's touch was repulsive to her now, a dead thing. Her gaze dropped to my hand, which was resting on my thigh, and I knew that she had spotted my small scar, the poor abbreviated finger. Her mouth tightened and I recognized this expression: she was weaving a story of unimaginable pain and peril. When she looked up again, I saw that her eyes were moist, her lips parted.

No Maria, not tonight.

Sharon passed close by on her way to the kitchen and I stared at her bare arm with its canopy of wrinkles that surrounded the elbow. Without thinking, I reached up and touched her there.

She stopped. No one had noticed, certainly not her husband, who tilted his wine glass to the side, demonstrating some aspect of relative viscosity.

"I have been watching you," I said in a low voice.

"I know."

"Do you mind?"

"No, I don't mind." And she made that gesture again, of pushing her hair back from her face.

"The students are very young."

She laughed. "You noticed."

"Young, but not so interesting."

She pulled away and a moment later she was back sitting on her chair with a glass of water in her hand, not even pretending to keep her eyes open. The room had clogged with wood smoke. Shirts were unbuttoned, collars loosened, and a sleepy stupidity fell over the party. Our host poured himself another glass of his rustic wine and continued talking, to himself now, and the glow of gaslight made us look like nineteenth-century bandits.

"It is our duty," Daniel was proclaiming in a slurred voice, "to be intelligent. A moral imperative, as Professor Trilling would say. Not only in theory but in action. We are citizens of the world, and those of us who live in safety must help those in peril. Witness our friend right here in our midst, Carlos."

Each groggy face in the room turned to look at me.

"Observe him sitting in my cabin, smoking his cigarettes." Daniel raised one arm and gestured towards me. "Free."

I waved back and flashed a grateful smile, eyes smarting from the wood smoke.

"And should you succumb to lung cancer, it is B.C. taxpayers who will foot the bill, as they will pay to medicate my own spongy liver."

I smiled again. Yes, thank you B.C. taxpayers. Thank you everyone.

"For God's sakes, shut up Daniel!"

Eyes snapped open, the wood shifted in the stove and sent out a shower of sparks.

Sharon had leaned forward on her chair, blouse open at the neck. "Stop nickel and diming every minute of the goddamn day," she went on. "Just stop it." Her voice trembled.

There was a ghastly silence, and no one dared look at Daniel. When the wood shifted again we stared gratefully into the crackle of the dying fire.

It was he who finally spoke, with a bemused smile on his face. "May I ask who insisted we buy that oversized house in Kitsilano then tear out its entrails?" He looked around the room before settling his gaze back on his wife. "Who chose the fanciest contractor in the city?" Another pause. "So that now we're lucky to scrape together enough rupees for a dinner out?" The mouth was smiling but his voice was hard.

Sharon squeezed her eyes shut, in obvious fatigue, and like Rita, she had drawn her knees up to her chin. If we were in Santa Clara and I heard a man speak to his wife this way, I would take her hand and lead her outside. Not to make love, but to stare at the night sky with its infinite constellations named for us by the ancients, and to remember that men are small and wearisome.

"She's not going to engage," Daniel plowed on. "For the topic is vulgar." One hand reached down and tipped the giant flask in its metal harness and splashed more wine into his glass. His mouth was bruised red, his teeth dyed crimson. He looked as if he'd just ravaged some animal in the field. "I see our estimable friend, Carlos, and I believe that I would willingly exchange places."

I tittered. He was making some sort of joke, so we must laugh.

"To be in exile is the ideal state, to be cut off from the bindings of one's society is to be floating free." Daniel demonstrated this, by letting his hand rise and flutter through the air.

"I disagree." It was Marlon who ventured this opinion. "You romanticize the situation. How is it possible to be free yet dependent on others?" The young man fell back against his girl-friend's shoulder.

Daniel seemed amused by the interjection. "Because dependence is freedom. One loses the need to be responsible."

That's when Sharon got up, dusting imaginary crumbs off her lap, picked her rucksack off the floor and began to climb the stair-case. We all watched this, her heavy thighs tightening with each step. How I yearned to accompany her to that hot attic room.

No one spoke until the creaking ascent was over.

"I fear I have offended my wife," Daniel announced. "So I will take my leave now, and appease her." He pushed himself out of the deep chair and staggered until he found one of the wooden posts to cling to. "To appease such a woman," he said, "I am obliged to fuck her senseless."

The silence which greeted this pronouncement was thick with embarrassment. The only consolation was knowing that this drunken fool was incapable of violating anyone.

I stood at the window looking out into the darkness. We can be sucked into landscape and we must hold on, especially at night. For once, I wished I was not drunk. I felt my skin sag, the weight of my hair on my head. How long would I be in this strange country? I thought of the poems I had written since my arrival and I knew they were all shit. I was marking time, but this was not just something that would pass, it was my life.

"You look so sad."

Startled, I looked around to see Rita, clad in a yellow nightgown, holding her toothbrush. I forced myself to smile.

"Don't worry about Daniel. He's always like that," she said.

Was it our host's cruelty that had seeped into us all? The fire had died and the cabin was chilly. Rita shivered.

"I will find you a blanket," I said, but didn't move.

"Don't. I'm fine."

Then she went to her bed, which was a couch by the fire. I was to unroll a mat on the floor and slither into one of the sleeping bags, zip up, and lie like a corpse through the long night. The fire was dead now, its coals barely pink in their memory of heat. Instead I dragged a chair next to the window where moonlight spilled in and this is where I sat, in terrible commotion, for hours. All these people around, in the house, out on the field, and the deep-scented air pressed through the rusted screen, and I had never felt so alone. Was this nostalgia, this deluge of memories, a small boy crouching on the bandstand with his licorice candy, and later, stealing a sugary pastry from the market stall?

The more I remembered, image chasing image, the more it seemed I wouldn't be able to stop remembering. Yet these new people could see none of it, none of the ordinary moments in a boy's day: they had to invent their own drama for me. Chewing that thieved sweet roll would be an insult to their imaginations. There could be no long days of dull childhood, only the important tale mattered.

All senses were weary from translating the smells, sounds, and words, and even my hand which clenched the arm of this antique chair couldn't take in another bite. The country air was perfumed with vegetation I couldn't name. The traveller with his eager smile and field guide, if he'd ever existed, longs in the end for the smell of his own stove.

The man upstairs stirred in his bed, and I waited for him to settle, chips of dust floating down between the floor boards. I understood that I would never sleep again, not in the way of these people tethered neatly between past and present.

She stepped cautiously down the staircase, feeling with her hands for the wall. Trying to be quiet, she only succeeded in making each stair creak before setting foot on the next. Despite the moonlight, Sharon hadn't seen me yet. Her white nightgown wrapped about her knees and her hair was wild. When she reached the bottom step she dared look up, and I made a small throat-clearing noise.

"Carlos?" Sharon whispered. "That you?"

"Yes," I whispered and rose to my feet.

"Water." She made a gesture of drinking and headed to the back of the cabin, past the sleeping Rita, the kitchen a series of dark shapes she knew by heart. She snapped open a cupboard door, reached for a glass, then tipped the pitcher of pump water. All of this I watched from a standing position. She drank, and I want to say that she was bathed in moonlight, but this was not so: she was, in fact, merely a moving shape in the darkness. Upstairs the man rolled over and grunted, and I could imagine his appalling breath fill that attic chamber.

"Come here," she whispered.

She pulled up a chair next to the table and motioned for me to sit. I obeyed, while she perched on a low stool a metre away. She smelled of wood smoke. We all did.

"Have you slept?" She glanced at my clothes.

I nodded "no."

"Neither have I."

I waited.

"To tell the truth, Carlos, I've been thinking of you."

This should have pleased me, but instead I felt a surge of fear. What had she seen when she'd been thinking of me?

"Want me to go on?"

"Yes," I said.

"Okay." She hesitated before finishing her drink, setting the empty glass on the counter, then pulled her stool up a fraction closer to me. "We are all feeling immensely frustrated. You make it so hard for yourself, Carlos, by not meeting us halfway."

It was as if I'd just been told I had a terminal disease.

"Want to hear more?"

Of course not. Yet I must, and so I nodded.

"You act above us, as if we were your servants."

I stared. Her nightgown had a series of buttons which led up to the neckline and all were fastened this cool evening.

"Didn't you notice there's tons of work to do at the cabin, that everyone was busy? Yet you sat on your backside drinking beer, or buzzed off on some solo hike. Daniel expected you to sit in on his seminar: he was hurt."

I was too stunned to speak. As she said all this, of course I understood. I could see everything through her point of view. I even saw myself sitting in the corner, holding forth with some ridiculous story about my uncle to the bored students. They had been polite, pretending to listen.

"At supper you didn't lift a finger to cook or clean up. Just sat there expecting to be waited on. It's infuriating!" This last word rose above a whisper and I glanced over at Rita, appalled that she might hear. "You have no concept of how to be a guest."

A guest. Not a guest here, in this cabin; this was nothing. She meant a guest in her country. For that is what an exile must always be, a guest who stays too long.

"Around here everyone pitches in. There are no passengers." Her voice had softened, but I could see, even in the dim light, that she was shaking. I began to shiver too.

She noticed and for a minute didn't speak. "Are you afraid, Carlos?"

"Of course I'm afraid!" Of you, especially, I wanted to say.

To my amazement, Sharon reached for my hand. "Rita said something interesting today: 'We can never make him happy.'"

Her eyes didn't leave mine. "Perhaps she's right. We've all been expecting too much."

There was a thump from above as if the beast had fallen out of bed. I watched Sharon's face as her eyes closed for a second, and I knew she was praying that he wouldn't awaken.

Something inside me unknotted. It was her loneliness that I felt, even more strongly than my own. Her hand slipped away and returned to her lap.

"This husband does not make you happy," I said.

"Daniel?" She feigned surprise. "Don't take his rants too seriously. We get on fine."

"Yes, of course."

She wasn't fooled. "You don't believe me."

I shrugged.

"Anyhow, what's 'happy'?" She smiled, remembering what she'd said a moment earlier. "Sometimes it's a matter of being used to someone. Not being able to imagine any other life."

"I was used to my old life. It has been a great surprise," I said. "A great surprise, every day, to be here."

She pulled her nightgown over her knees like a little girl. "You must think about going back some day."

"All the time."

She waited for me to finish.

"But it is not possible."

She tugged at her nightgown again. "I've thought of leaving Daniel."

I hesitated. "Maybe you are afraid, too."

This was a mistake. A good guest does not enter into judgment of his host's life. Sharon rose to her feet and I feared that I had offended her. But perhaps not. As she passed by on her way to the staircase, her hand touched my shoulder and squeezed me there.

She lay for the rest of the night in her attic bed as I huddled below inside the sleeping bag which smelled of dampness, and it was as if we were reading the same page in the same book. Even her breathing was audible through the drafty floorboards, and listening so hard, I fell asleep.

Was it a rooster or a mooing cow that announced the next day? Perhaps a low-flying seaplane making its way to the mainland in time for work. I was pissing off the porch into the dewy grass when I heard Daniel coming, tripping over rucksacks in the dark cabin, swearing. The door was open and it was just before dawn, the sky soaked with early light. This was what morning should always be like, cold, damp, and promising. Daniel pulled his cock out of his undershorts before he spotted me. Then he said in a completely sober voice, "Too much goddamn wine."

I nodded agreement, as we shared the relief of emptying bladders. Half of the tents were in shadow, others gleamed with dew. Above, a hawk plunged after its prey then swooped in wide circles over a grove of fir trees. The air was so crisp that my nostrils had gone numb.

We didn't go back inside right away. There was a magic to the wakening land, the arc of new sky that began to clear our heads. My uncle's ranch held this same timeless unravelling, and I remembered his work boots, the heels worn down, soles clogged with grass. There were no books in his house except the well-thumbed manual on *Diseases of Common Livestock*, published in 1952. I loved the careful drawings of hoof and mouth disease, and limb splints, and the oddly formal language chosen by the authors.

The books in this island dacha were paperback mysteries, all composed by women authors. Daniel Rose righted himself with one hand then leaned over the wooden railing, staring into the field. The tang of sweat and earthy wine emanated from his pores. He spoke in a soft voice. "I know I was a prick last night. I hear myself, and I hate it, but I keep going."

His shorts hung below his belly, but he wasn't fat, just fleshy, with short legs and a long torso. "I rattle on, Carlos, because I haven't figured anything else to do."

He spoke as if he were releasing himself of a great burden, and that I, Carlos, had caused the moment of revelation.

"Perhaps you are a vain man," I said.

He looked shocked, for wasn't I supposed to listen to his confession without remark?

"Is that what you think?" He clapped me once on the back. But he wasn't ready to go back inside. "Is vanity such a bad thing?" Spikes of greying beard coated his chin and cheeks. He waited for me to answer and when I didn't he went on. "Nothing I do or say can compete with your experience."

One of the tents began to wake up. First there was quivering within its nylon flank, then moans and shivers, followed by a high-pitched wail. Maria, I knew instantly.

Daniel watched this, scowling. "What a performance," he said, then disappeared back inside the cabin.

I knew that I had disappointed this man. He'd opened up like a plant which blooms but once a year, and I had forgotten to applaud.

All that day Sharon moved in a deliberate slow dance that her husband couldn't understand. She organized, cooked, then went for a walk and returned an hour later, knees grass-stained. All of this made Daniel curious, and his eyes followed her. But she ignored him, and I could tell that this made him anxious. Later, I sprayed detergent into the sink and began to wash my plates while Sharon and Rita looked on with approval. There was a window over the sink and I could watch Daniel crouched near a fossil bed with his coterie of students, all of whom were scribbling in their notebooks as he spoke.

9

RITA CAME TO MY HOUSE, HER HAIR tied back, looking fretful. Rashid was upstairs: the click of his computer keyboard barely hesitated when she arrived.

"May I come in?"

I said nothing, but indicated, with my arm, that she might pass. Rita entered my living room, cast a glance over the couch where I had been lying, and at the ashtray where my cheap cigar still burned, and, inevitably, at the tumbler of flat beer. Her looking was a fine-toothed comb raking through each strand of my life. I do not apologize for anything.

Above, Rashid switched his tape machine to some mournful East Asian tune.

I made my guest coffee, using my roommate's tin of Nabob, and I wondered if he'd measured the levels of the grounds. It was more important to be accurate than generous. When I'd first moved here Rita had been so helpful. Did I need a can opener? How about a new razor? And there was the history department's old computer — she'd have it upgraded by tech services and on my desk in a week.

She sipped cautiously.

"Too strong?"

"A bit," she confessed, adding more milk until her drink was a blonde soup. Finally she placed the mug on the table and continued to stare, not at the room but at me. I am not a nervous man but this woman, with her deep brown eyes, made me edgy. If I made a joke she might not laugh, wouldn't even realize I was joking. If I told her she was beautiful she wouldn't, like the women back home, reach over laughing and pat my cheek. Here, if you say this to a woman she reddens; she does not expect it. She isn't sure if you are mocking her, or if she should be displeased. You see the mouth tense up and, in one stroke, the beauty you have commented on disappears.

"What are we going to do, Carlos?"

I wished I had whisky but I was too poor, so instead I paced around the room, threading between its oppressively male furniture. The TV perched on a packing case, the couch was covered in a revolting shade of brown, and there was my roommate's stationary bicycle lurking next to the wall, ornate with dials to measure pulse, speed, and distance travelled. You can go a hundred kilometres without leaving this room. A tire company's calendar tacked to the wall displayed an extravagant sunset shooting across the windshield of a sports car.

"What are we going to do?" I repeated. I was smiling that foolish smile I put on when I don't understand. It had been two weeks since the trip to the island cabin and I hadn't seen Sharon or any of them since, except in passing, in campus pathways, rushing from one rain-drenched building to another.

She set her coffee down on the miserable carpet. "Those books the department lent you to study English?"

I stopped pacing and looked out the window. My neighbour aimed a hose at his van while his toddler son danced around in his diaper.

"They've turned up at the Text Exchange. Did you sell them, Carlos?"

"Perhaps." Faint memory of Hemingway and a Canadian text by Mrs. Atwood. "I must eat." I lifted my palms and gave a woeful smile. "I must fix my shoes, buy underwear, eat bread with my morning coffee." The familiar rage gripped my body, yet even I was tired of it. I must smoke, Rita, and drink. Yes, I must do these things. My shoulders straightened.

"They weren't yours to sell, Carlos. They were on loan."

"I forgot." This was a child's recalcitrant voice, and I hated it. Yet what else could I do, confess that one day, without thinking more than a moment, I'd decided cigarettes were more important than literature?

"You forgot?" Frustration careened through the two words. Suddenly I knew why she'd been sent here by the board of directors of the human rights organization. Too bad, Carlos, but we have to mail you home. You have not met expectations; your behaviour leaves something to be desired. You have become an embarrassment to the Canadian Alliance for Freedom of Expression. She probably held, in her tiny red purse, an airline ticket, one way, to Santa Clara.

And didn't I want to go home?

Yes! To get out of these dull grey streets and polite smiles, the sky which opens and closes like an eye, back to where I am known, where my body sinks into the chair with a wheeze of recognition, where the skin is alive, the women aren't afraid to touch you or be touched.

Where General Rafael Mariano de Sanchez decreed, "I don't want this piece of shit to live a minute longer," his thin lips parting just enough to emit the words. In my country such men do not speak metaphorically. Their opinions become orders the moment they hit the air. The familiar gut twist made me gasp.

"The problem is that you want everything, right away. It's not possible, Carlos." Rita folded one leg over the other and unconsciously picked at the material of the sofa. "You may not realize it but there's a waiting list as long as your arm for these campus housing placements. You've got this cushy job as writer-in-residence with your own office and a stipend. Any local writer would kill for this gig." She plunged her free hand into her hair and scratched, a parody of bewilderment. "I get the impression you're comparing this place to Syd's, as if you should have a stone patio and a pond full of fish and all that reproduction furniture. Well, guess what, Carlos, I wouldn't mind having that stuff too."

"So…" I pulled up a chair. "We should both have it, no?" I was smiling.

She wagged her head. "You still don't get it, do you?"

What Rashid had said just a few days earlier. Had they been talking to each other, comparing notes? I reached and grabbed the handlebar of his stationary bicycle. He watches the news each evening, legs pumping, a trickle of sweat running down his forehead. The muffled sound of his grunts, discreetly curbed for my benefit, is as familiar as my own farts. I turned the dial to its highest tension. It would be like riding up Grouse Mountain.

"I never killed or injured anyone," I said in a low voice, though she had asked me nothing. I made it sound as if I had been flooded by an old memory, which was almost the case. She stared at my hand, my famous finger, and the frown began to leave her face.

"Others did, when it was necessary," I went on, encouraged by her attention. I knew, at once, that she must be drawn back to see me as she had that evening on stage: a man crumpled by his past yet brave enough to continue. "We were nothing more than pests, mosquitoes in the ear of the regime. We go out in the hours before dawn, I and my compañeros from The Front, and steal the food trucks coming in from the coast. Before they can fill the rich peoples' supermarket." I plucked the smouldering cigar from its ashtray and stuck it in my mouth. She was watching my every move.

"We were a bunch of crazy guys, idealistas, like Robin Hood feeding the poor. The driver, this cannot be avoided, has to be tied up, a cloth placed over his mouth, and left by the side of the road. A normal man, could be one of us, but to his employers he must be seen to suffer, to be overcome. It was for his own good."

Rita had edged toward the corner of the sofa, uncrossing her legs.

"José took the wheel, the rest crammed in, clinging to the sides of the truck, and we rode to the shantytowns. They always knew by the sound of the gears that we were coming: their own wrecked trucks didn't sound like that. And out they streamed from their hovels, waving pails and baskets and plastic bags. Grannies in ragged pajamas, little kids, naked except for T-shirts, and still-drunk men pulling on shorts… they lined up, and we filled their containers."

"Were you ever caught?" Rita's hand pressed between her bare knees. Her skirt had risen over her thighs but I let myself cast only the briefest of glances there.

"The police, of course, chased us. They shoot sometimes. Some of us came home with a slug in the arm, a bloodied ass."

"And you?"

"Not yet."

"I didn't realize…"

"That your friend Carlos was a bandit."

"I'd hardly call it that."

"Then what would you call it?"

"Brave," she said simply.

Her hands fell open, showing their pure, uncreased whiteness. Her voice changed timbre and became low and brittle. As I slid my hands over hers my eyes watered to think of that brave youth roaring up the hill as dawn light cracked the sky. I imagined the fear tugging his belly so that, despite the boxes of cereal and rice and beans inside the truck, he thought he would never eat again. My hand slid inside her open blouse.

The body forgets. Skin has to be awakened.

Rashid lowered the volume on his music. The house was listening. There was no click of fingers on keyboard. My other hand drifted under her skirt. Rashid wears a white shirt, short- or long-sleeved, and shiny dark pants. His face is very thin, but his lips are full and never quite closed, showing the white of his teeth. I pushed my tongue deep into her mouth as, at the same time, my fingers reached inside her. This time I was not too tired. Above, the tapping resumed, the keening East Indian voices swam on toward their homeland.

The days rolled by: one, two, three, then suddenly it was six. Each day has a night and this is a different kind of time, so much like prison that there were moments when I sat up in bed, convinced I was still there, aching for dawn and the life of the street. I left messages on her answering machine.

The machine said the same thing every day: "I'm sorry we are unable to take your call now but if you leave your name and number..." I left nothing but the sound of my own breathing. I would phone every hour, just to listen to the message and to try and detect any change in its tenor. I paced around my Poet-in-Exile office, sifting my big ugly feet through the beige carpet, staring out the sealed window into the parking lot where students leaned on the hoods of their cars: girls with tiny halter tops and perfect round bellies. Had she lost my number? I knew that was impossible. Perhaps Rita's machine was on the blink, or she'd been called out of town to help a sick relative. I shook every excuse out of memory and possibility, but of course I knew what was going on.

It rang when I had stopped waiting, when I'd convinced myself I didn't care and it was time to continue with my so-called life. I'd made an appointment with Dr. Sachs, professor of Joseph Conrad, the great exile, who offered to take me out for lunch if I would meet with his graduate seminar. I was just tucking in my shirt when the black phone on my desk rang. It was her ring, a distinct tonality which matched her voice and I thought, for an instant, of not answering. Why not simply enjoy my meal with Dr. Sachs, who had, I suspected, a keen nose for vintage wine. Why did she choose this moment when I was almost alive again?

"Is that you, Carlos?"

"Yes," I confessed.

"Listen," she said, as if I could do anything else. "About the other day." She took a breath. "I feel badly. We shouldn't be involved this way. It's a mistake."

"You did not like it? I did not make you feel happy?"

"It isn't good for me or for you."

"It was good for me," I interrupted. "It was very good."

She persevered. "We shouldn't mix it up personally, not while we have a professional relationship."

And how, I wondered, will I ever have any other kind of relationship here?

10

MY ASS WAS PRESSED AGAINST THE EDGE of a cardboard box marked "Doritos: Extra Spicy." My knees were pressed against my chin as the truck heaved over potholes and moaned up the hill toward Barrio de Concepción. There was a stink of rotting meat. The truck must have had an earlier life, running from the slaughterhouses before being commandeered for the Liberation. The liberation, it turned out, of fifty boxes of assorted corn chips and something called Tosties.

Our destination was the shantytown where my mother's maid lived, with its rutted dirt roads, open sewers, and ragged children with festering eyes.

"Fucking Rafael, steer the fucking vehicle around the fucking holes!" someone whispered.

The amateur guerrillas had filthy mouths. With each lurch my stomach curled another notch into itself, a caterpillar prodded by a stick. I drew the cuff of my shirt over my nose to filter out the godawful stench. What smell was outside, and what was inside the truck, our own nervous sweat blending with rotting cow. Night, especially the night which slinks into dawn, was dark and treacherous. My sister and father and mother were fast asleep in their beds, aware only of the silent progress of images across their eyelids.

None of the men spoke, except to utter casual profanities. Yet no one was still for more than a few seconds at a time: we drummed on the boxes with our fingertips, stretched our legs to create little surges of circulation. And as we lumbered along up the hill we were waking up the dogs, ownerless, of no fixed address, who lingered in fitful sleep wherever a doorway could be found. Their yelps were sickly and half-hearted, nicking some memory of lost dog passion.

Our leader and fellow student, A, crouched opposite me. He held his arm out, bracing himself against the panel so he wouldn't be pitched forward. He was so skinny that the top of his arm was the same thickness as his forearm. He wore a striped shirt with a boat neck, a reference to the Resistance fighters of the Second World War. A red bandanna, not a beret, covered his head. His lean hips propped up a pair of faded American jeans. When he saw me looking, he allowed a brief smile and showed his crooked teeth. I tried to hold that smile with my own, but he was too intent on our progress, on the changing noises outside and the groan of the vehicle as it climbed.

To be here I had forsaken my family. It suddenly hit me that it was too late to return, that this heroic episode had scooped me up and no one would care why I was here, only that I was here, that I had followed A without question. My fingers were clasped with white knuckles tight over the box, knuckles which would have to be painfully unbent in just a few moments so that I could do my work, so that I could toss these boxes out the rear door to waiting hands.

A called it, "the Work."

It was nothing like our usual work, sprawled in lecture halls taking notes while our professors drone on, or drinking rum in someone's apartment. The truck stopped, farting out pebbles of undigested gas. There was a pause when I listened so hard my ears ached, then there was a tap on the back panel. Guardedly we rose, six young men, flexing our hands, not sure what would be on the other side of that sound.

Three stout women appeared out of the darkness, unsmiling, whispering, "Dése prisa! You are late!"

I heaved the first box to a pair of waiting arms.

Luckily corn chips were not heavy. It could have been sacks of flour or beans.

She took one, two, three boxes and piled them in a tower. Behind her was a cinderblock building, half completed, rusted iron support bars stretching out its sides. Under her feet was parched dirt with ancient rivulets carved through it, remnants of a dozen rainy seasons. This hillside, only twenty years ago, was filled with trees and pasture. We had to lift the boxes quickly to keep up with these women. All of us were anxious to be done. I listened for the sound of a siren, or any vehicle noise, or the hard thud of a man's boots.

"What is this shit?" The woman I had been working with stopped suddenly. She was studying the label on the outside of a box.

"Chips?" she read. She turned to A. "You brought Doritos to us? This is what you have risked all our lives for — Doritos Extra Spicy?"

The apron tied around her middle was decorated with a picture of Mickey Mouse lifting his paddle hands in the air.

I felt myself shrink into my clothes, at the same time as I was awed by the depth of her contempt. A, sweating hard, pitched another box to the ground then stood, balanced on the edge of the truck-floor, and cleared his throat. To my surprise, he didn't answer her immediately.

"You expect us to feed our children corn chips for breakfast?" The woman waited, hands on hips, while the other two women stopped working and matched her pose.

A stiffened. "We got the wrong truck," he mumbled at last.

"Como?"

"We got the wrong truck," A repeated and made himself look at her. "It was supposed to be like the last one, full of meat." He tilted his head and sniffed. "You can smell it."

"He smells the meat." The woman turned to her friends. "Smells don't fill our stomachs."

"If they did we would be very fat!" another laughed.

The first woman did not laugh. Instead, she drew nearer to A and began to talk in a low whisper, forcing him to crouch so he could hear.

"Listen to me, University Boy, this is not a game. For us it is life or death. And quite often it is death."

"I know this."

"So next time..."

"We will succeed."

"Good." She spoke to her partners. "Let's haul this stuff into the building. Maybe we can sell it at the market on Sunday." She turned back. "Next time, University Boys, make sure you steal the right truck. If I am going to be shot, I want it to be for something more noble than this." She slapped a carton.

A grunted then signaled to the rest of us. "Vámonos."

I was starting to shiver. "What do we do with the truck now?"

A ignored my question, as he'd ignored all my questions since picking me up on the back of his scooter an hour earlier, though two days ago he'd been my instant best friend, thumping me on the back. "Hey man, we'll have a coffee, talk things over."

There was no place to turn the beast around so we backed down the hill at an infuriatingly slow creep. This time everyone was jabbering in the cavernous interior, not about what we'd just done, our humiliation, nor about the possibility of being picked up by the police and tossed into jail or pitched into the river, but about last night's soccer game.

"If it wasn't for Ortiz…" A said, shaking his head.

"The goal was shit," another interrupted, drumming on his knees.

I crouched stiffly on the floor, waiting for the brutal stupid faces of the Special Task Force to pull up in front of us.

Suddenly the truck stopped.

"Get out!" A hissed. "Scram!"

And we were off like a shot, leaping into the darkness with no idea where or what the ground was until we hit it, a sigh of dry grass and braced flesh. Riderless, our truck sailed into the dawn, its wheels cleaving through weeds and crushed pop cans.

I didn't put any of this in my memoir. I had almost stopped writing, and every time I tried, it made me sick. They thought that they wanted my story, but it was not true. They wanted their own story of me, in their own words. When I touched Rita I made her sick. And later, when I touched myself, I made myself sick.

I crossed the campus to visit The Hub because I couldn't stand to spend the night in my cramped house with Rashid's disapproving glances. Ever since that evening with Rita it was all he could do to wish me "good morning." He'd heard us, of course. Lovemaking was an activity on an order with pig-eating: both were wet and noisy. My friend The Hub bartender with the earring acted oddly when he spotted me entering that basement chamber. Instead of raising a hand in greeting, he began to vigorously towel down the counter. I waited on my usual stool for a long time before he uttered a word.

"Sorry friend, you're cut off." He whipped the towel in the air. "Not my call. It's the highers up."

So it is God who speaks to him? I stared at him hard. "A beer, please."

He began to slide glasses one by one from the overhead rack and polish away imaginary dust. "Don't make it hard for me, man."

Why should I not make it hard? "One beer, please."

"You want me to lose my job?"

"What I want, my friend, is a beer."

Finally he stopped his invented work and set his elbows on the bar so that his earring, tonight a tiny silver airplane, dangled and caught the light. Behind him the television played a music video with the sound turned off, and I watched a woman dance through a garbage-strewn alley, her mouth gaping in silent song.

"You've been running a sky-high tab and hassling the girls. Maybe this isn't the best place for you, Carlos, my man."

I nodded, contemplating his wise words, then rose from my stool, walked behind the bar, reached into the cooler and plucked two beaded bottles of Labatts from the icy interior. I slipped these into my pockets and left the establishment, forever.

I I

WAITED IN OUR STUDENT CAFÉ IN the centre of Santa Clara, a famous building where philosophy majors crammed in the far corner with their bulging knapsacks and corduroy jackets. In another corner, near the Star Wars video game, were the literature students, affecting this semester a beatnik look, the boys with goatees and the girls dressed in black. Music was jumping out of the speakers: some Caribbean mix, frenzied drums and marimba.

I sat apart, despite the usual hails of greeting, and eagerly scanned the newspaper, searching for some reference to our daring escapade: "...driver was found bound and gagged in a ditch..." but there was nothing. Only stories about some asshole who was running around bombing gas stations — el Bombadero Loco.

A would be in soon. His class finished at eleven o'clock and even if he had to drop by the library, he would need his hit of caffeine to propel him through the rest of the day. Perhaps he would sit with me at my table near the espresso machine. Of course I had it all plotted out that he would sit with me, keen to review the mission and discuss future strategy. I had some ideas on that score. He would be impressed by my willingness and subtle courage. Unlike A, I had a lot to lose. My father worked in the government tax office; in fact, he was the regional director. If my participation in A's mission was revealed, Father would be out on his ear and my entire family would be plunged into disgrace and poverty.

The thought made me tug my collar and shiver, but not without a certain delight.

For A was already there, living in the shadow of his own father's disgrace. Or heroism, depending on which side of the valley you camp.

He entered the café, as always, tilted forward as if fighting a wind, his threadbare clothes flapping in the breeze of his hurrying. His hair was an unruly mess, and he hadn't shaved.

I was gripped by an attack of nervousness and started slurping my coffee so fast it dribbled down my chin, but I didn't feel it. A raced past my table without a second's pause. His hip brushed the plastic menu, which coasted to the floor. My coffee congealed into thick tar at the bottom of the cup. I watched him from behind my raised newspaper, like some secret operative. A aimed for the philosophers' corner, where he pulled up a chair and dropped onto it, already speaking. They watched his approach, their own talk suspended in anticipation, for A always bears news. He posed, with his legs tightly crossed and twisted to one side, in a slightly effeminate manner. Soon they were laughing, smoke displacing air in a dense grey cloud.

I flushed a deep red. Why had he not spoken to me? And more to the point, why had he not seen me? I was so sure he would be drawn by the heat of my longing, and now here it was, that same heat turned inward, a furnace of humiliation.

Smoking furiously, I read the latest soccer scores: the goaltender from Ecuador had been injured by a spectator's hurled bottle. The backup, a boy called Mateo, had been brought in, an untested youngster from some nowhere town, and he'd blocked every shot. His ecstatic toothy grin covered the front page of the sports section.

Of course. I let out a gasp. A was being astute and careful. After all, if he were to hail me as if we were old chums and compañeros, everyone would notice. The student cafés were known to be laced with government agents. We always joked that Old Lucas worked not for our lousy tips, but for the Secret Police, and probably lived in one of the fancy new apartments in the north of town.

I had been so vain and self-absorbed, when I should have been grateful.

I waited at home for A to call and say in that low raspy tone, "I'll pick you up on the scooter. There's more work."

But there was no call, and in the halls of the university there was no casual tap on the shoulder, nothing at all except these sightings in the café.

I grew frantic. Each night I spent hours standing by the window in my family's house, peering between the curtains. A dark Mercedes had been parked since supper under the street lamp. And the woman selling sweet buns at the corner — I had never seen her before. Could she be in communication with the driver of the Mercedes? What did I really know about this whole business?

The material of the curtain was a heavy decrepit brocade, taken from my grandfather's house on the peninsula. It smelled of wood smoke and stale pipe tobacco, aromas which penetrated memory, the old man's stiff grey suits and whispery Castillian accent, me perched on the carved bench sipping Ovaltine.

I jumped at every sound: the telephone, the crunch of a car door closing. If someone laughed, my heart would begin to jitter. The wail of distant sirens made every hair stiffen.

We all knew stories. In the streets, we would look away as the unmarked van careened through a red light. Perhaps I would be pitched into a cell and beaten, but not too badly. I would be left with picturesque bruises then dumped into the empty morning.

Then I would turn up at school, or at the café, and A would stride in as usual, heading towards his corner.

"My God, what happened to you?"

His face would register pain and sympathy and something else — respect.

The dark hair on his wrists is wiry and thick, so unlike a woman's wrists. He touches my wounded face, wincing, then he sits down, never taking his eyes off mine.

"What happened, Carlito?"

The light of the café hurts my eyes and he sees it.

"Come with me." It's an order, not a request.

I follow him across the plaza and through a zigzag of side streets where students live in dark rooms above restaurants and pharmacies.

"Here." He nods at the blue-painted door with a newspaper folded under the latch.

I mount the stairs after him to the third floor of the crumbling building with its exhausted light bulbs and skittering of cockroaches.

I have never been touched by a man, not that way. How does it begin?

He takes a final tug off his cigarette, tosses it on the floor, then moves his face towards mine. His hands remain at his sides, as if this kiss were a casual thing, instead of the beginning of a great longing.

None of this happens. No kiss, no beating, no cramp of desire. Instead, after a week of sleepless nights, where I'd lie on the mattress and count the beats between footfalls outside, I went up to A in the hallway at school. I'd seen him duck out of the lecture auditorium. I'd watched his head nod as the professor droned on about the Golden Era of Spanish Literature. The collar of A's shirt was heartbreakingly frayed. I fingered my own shirt, crisp Hong Kong cotton, pressed by Enedina and smelling of starch. Perhaps he could not bear boredom, not a millisecond. I followed his escape, and discovered him bent over the fountain, jerking the lever, attempting to pump the water a centimetre higher.

"My mouth is dry, too," I said.

"You won't get much out of here."

He made way for me.

When I was finished I saw he had already started down the hall, toward the library.

"Wait!" I had no idea what I was going to say.

Slowly he turned around. There was a small smile on his face.

I started to jabber. Not about anything important, just silly jokes about the professors and their alleged sexual habits. At first he looked impatient, and gave a pointed glance at his watch. But I touched his sleeve, making up some wild story about the Classics professor, a handsome man with white hair.

"He's making eyes at you, A," I steamed on. "It's so obvious."
Suddenly A laughed.

"Are you flirting with me, Carlos?" His voice and manner became instantly effeminate. "You want to know what it is we queers do, is that it? The trip to the barrio wasn't enough, you're getting greedy for real adventure." He tapped me on the chest with the back of his hand and growled, "Don't fuck with me, University Boy."

At that moment the doors to the lecture hall burst open and students began to pour out, chattering with released boredom.

I was at home, studying, while my family huddled in the back room watching the Three Tenors on television. The singers were making such a racket that I didn't hear the knock on the door. What I did hear was Enedina's clipped step as she approached my room, then her sarcastic voice, "A gentleman to see you, Master Carlo."

She always Italianized my name.

The man stood just inside our front door, erect, dressed in an olive green suit and grey tie. I knew immediately who, or what, he was.

We went into the solarium, a tiny space just off the kitchen where a great potted orange tree took up most of the floor.

"I am Jesús Zedillo." The man extended his hand and shook mine limply. He wore two rings which scratched my palm as he withdrew. I smelled heavy aftershave, which blended with the sweet orange fragrance into something sickly.

I indicated that he should sit in the chair on the other side of the mosaic table.

EXILE • ANN IRELAND

Zedillo crossed his legs and eyed me with good humour.

"So Carlos, tell me all about your little adventure into the colonia."

His manner was collegial: he was giving me the opportunity to be his equal.

I accepted a cigarette and tried to conceal my trembling hands. I confess to an intense excitement, as if I'd been unexpectedly pushed on stage to assume a leading role. From the back room Plácido Domingo and the boys were belting out "La donna è mobile" while Zedillo's polished shoe tapped lightly on the tile floor, keeping time.

Why should I protect A? Hadn't he humiliated me more than once?

Don't fuck with me, University Boy.

As if he were anything different! And whose fault was it that we'd hijacked the wrong goddamn truck?

Who would marry my sister if I landed in jail?

So I gave him the name he needed. It was surprisingly easy. He didn't even bother writing it down, nor did he express any surprise. Instead Zedillo stood, buttoned his jacket, and, without a word, left my house. I raced to the front room and watched from between my grandfather's curtains as he opened the door of his idling car and tore off down the street. It had all taken less than five minutes.

I went back to my studying, forcing myself to make sense of the words on the page: Economic Subsidies for Farm Communities. But all I could think of was A sitting in the café, body twisted in that awkward, tense way that I found so compelling. I imagined his rapid-fire speech suddenly dwindling as the man in the olive suit approached, and how in that second he would know what I had done.

It was a brisk clear morning, and the streets were filled with commuters and delivery trucks and jammed buses. For the first time in two weeks I marched buoyantly, waving greetings at the old man who tended the newsstand and a cluster of girls whom I knew to be friends of my sister. For once I wasn't glancing furtively over my shoulder. And for once my chest didn't tighten at every unexplained spark of interest from a stranger. Two policemen leaned over a food stand, devouring skewers of grilled meat, dripping juice onto their collars, and I felt nothing. All those days of wondering what would happen if I got caught, and here I was — found out, yet free!

My old gang at the café were pressing their bellies into the little table and whispering like crazy.

"A's been sent to La Isla," Luisa cried.

This was where they tossed enemies of the state. Cavernous jails from the last century, far enough from the mainland that no one could hear the prisoners' howls.

I sat down. When you discover a friend is ill, you know this saves you from the disease.

"No," someone said, "he's still in town. My brother spotted him coming from the courts."

Many versions. Many sightings.

"His landlady betrayed him!"

There was a chorus of assent. I felt myself lighten, so much so that I had to conceal my joy.

"An ex-lover turned him in."

"Which one!"

Raucous laughter.

They were fascinated by A, his boldness and unabashed decadence.

My fingers tightened around the handle of the heavy mug. So why had he rejected me? Was I so repulsive? The table cloth was littered with bread crumbs and spilled sugar.

"Are you flirting with me, Carlos?"

I pushed my chair away and rose, fed up with my friends' chatter. Next would be heroic tales of his missions, which would lead to intricate plots to free him, which would lead to more talk, more coffee, until it was time for afternoon classes to begin. I crossed the street, wending my way between the flower sellers and hurrying businessmen, until I reached the entrance to la Luna.

Journalists hung out at Café de la Luna on the west end of the plaza. Working journalists, not student-paper kids who had, as an audience, only themselves. This crowd wrote mainly for *La Voz*, considered to be a mildly liberal daily paper, though unadventurous. They sneered at the students, referring to us in editorials as "men without hats." Perhaps they remembered themselves not so many years ago.

I hovered over the table with its half-dozen familiar faces and clouds of cigar smoke: five portly men and one woman. They eyed me without surprise.

"Pull up a chair, kid."

The university barely noticed that I'd gone. I received a tuition notice in the mail which I ignored, because now I was no longer practising for life: I had entered it. La Luna and the newspaper became my new home, a jagged circle which effortlessly parted to make room for its new member. The men here all wore hats, Panamanian straw or canvas, and they carried battered leather portfolios instead of rucksacks. They expressed no interest in what I'd done on the other side of the square, or indeed anything about my scholarly background, and I understood that it was enough to listen attentively to their political gossip. They needed fresh blood, a new audience.

Before long I had been offered a part-time position, editing government press releases (I was allowed to change unimportant words) before they were printed in the paper as editorial content. An easy job, badly paid, which allowed plenty of time to hang out with my new cronies.

"Whose turn is it to praise the President on his foreign mission?"

This sardonic tone permeated our conversation.

I cut my hair and borrowed my father's sports jacket and learned to smoke Havana cigars. My old friends, when they bothered to notice me, cast looks of withering contempt. I would watch them scurry off to attend some impassioned speech by an earnest semi-radical thinker, and would feel not a shred of regret, or none that I admitted to.

"You've crossed the Square," Diego, the city editor of *La Voz*, and my new boss, said, slapping me on the back. "You're a pro now."

I often asked myself why I was so easily able to make the transition. What was so fluid in my nature that I could "cross the Square" without premeditation and instantly fit in?

I had been at my new job for less than two months and had finally been given a cubbyhole to work in. The paper was housed in the upper floors of an old bank, now turned into a hodgepodge of offices with a street level café no one went near. I was poring over the itinerary of our Minister of Finance as he travelled to speak to groups of potential investors in neighbouring countries. I was not sent to attend these meetings. It was an unnecessary expense and bother, since all I had to do was copy items from press releases and transform the language into the phrases our newspaper used with tedious frequency: It is anticipated that these high level negotiations will usher in a new era of economic prosperity…

Still new to the game, I had in mind that I would weave in subtle editorial comment, in the form of carefully inserted detail.

Diego drooped an arm over the flimsy divider and observed as I made copious notes on the stenographer's pad. Perhaps I looked up at him with a hint of despair, for he laughed and the divider shook, threatening to topple over. "Stop thinking," he said when he'd recovered. "Just do it."

I was shocked. At the time I still clung to scraps of idealism, a habit perhaps, not an actual longing. My fellow journalists were not fools: they knew which efforts were useless and a waste of breath, and exactly what sort of phrases annoyed which level of government, and precisely how much. They were experts at skipping through the labyrinth of censorship protocol.

As the days passed, I heard Diego's advice as a form of Buddhist incantation, which gave the work a certain honour. "Stop thinking, just do it." In less than a year I was promoted to the post of occasional arts columnist, to report favourably on the endless cycle of concerts and dances promoted by the Ministry of Culture, and to criticize visiting artists from less evolved cultures, such as the United States of America.

I had learned the most important aspect of my job, which was to understand very well what was required, and to enter, with a certain fervor, the language of the task.

At night I sipped brandy and scribbled, with my fountain pen, intense romantic odes, and line by line, achieved the balance that is so necessary to a healthy existence.

12

I POURED OUT A MUGFUL OF RASHID'S coffee, which had been sitting in the pot since six a.m., and took my hangover outside where the sun had finally cracked through the mist. My roommate hadn't spoken to me, merely performed an exaggerated sniff a few minutes earlier while I stumbled down the hall naked. He was mortally offended by the aroma of whisky clinging to my flesh.

I wondered if Rashid ever had sex, and with whom. I was certain that he would leap from bed and be standing under a pounding shower before his lover closed her legs. He would never have placed a hand on Rita's thigh, never inflicted his horny presence on some dewy co-ed. His cautious steps as he made his way through our house irritated me no end. The single black hair left in the sink was repulsive, his muffled farts and discreet coughs burrowed into my skull. My presence had been imposed on him and I was never to forget it.

How had we come to this? I can only say that when I first met the man I was available for friendship. I thought, in my naïveté, that here was a comrade and to each other we could whisper our secret lives and frustrations. Rashid had no patience with such sentimentality. The only way to survive here, he told me once in a rare exhibition of honesty, was to disappear. He'd left his real life behind. This new existence was merely survival, a period of waiting until it was possible to return. As he bicycled in place each day, so would he live without moving.

The children next door were jumping up and down on a plastic contraption fitted with a slide. Their dog, a grey mutt, was tied to a tree, yapping, and this is what had finally penetrated my sleep. The postman cut across the lawn, his navy rain cape flapping.

"Here you go, sir." He handed me the bundle of mail, held together with an elastic band.

I gazed at the elegant script and exotic stamps from Pakistan, India, Belgium, Italy… all addressed to Rashid. He was involved in an international committee of scientists-in-exile.

Why hadn't I heard from my own family? Loneliness sucks you dry, turns you grateful for the smallest attention. I popped open the front door and tossed his letters onto the chair, watching as one slid to the floor.

"Would you like this, Carlos?" It was the mother-professor from next door, standing just beneath my front steps, offering up a giant cut peony. "It must have broken off in the rain."

"Thank you." I took the shaggy-headed flower and held it while she peeled off her gardening gloves and scratched her cheek. I tried to remember her name.

"Yesterday was hellish," she said, "with the kids cooped up inside during the storm."

Yesterday.

I repeated the word to myself. The word should lead to a simple remembering, for all of us inhabit a "yesterday." What did I do then, and where was I when I did these things? A picture should come to mind without struggle. As she was trapped indoors with restless kids in the rain, I too must have been somewhere.

I could only gaze helplessly. Yesterday had vanished.

"You okay, Carlos?" She sensed something peculiar in my look. The quick sympathy in her face was unbearable, so I looked away, over her shoulder towards the children's climbing structure. This was being mounted by her youngest, a curly-haired boy in a diaper and T-shirt. When he reached the top rung of the ladder, instead of crawling onto the deck, the baby flung both arms skyward and began to teeter.

I was an animal, a gazelle this time, bounding across the grass. When the baby thumped against my chest, I felt a great shudder of elation. How simple this rescue had been. The mother spun, realized what had happened, then dashed across the lawn, hair flying. When I presented her with the gift of the squirming child, she hugged him to her breast and it was several moments before she remembered to look up.

"Thank you." Her smile was very small, because she understood that a rescue gives more pleasure to the hero than to anyone else.

I clipped the stem off the peony and floated the flower in a cereal bowl full of water. Even Rashid approved.

When A speaks, he draws his face so near that his beard may brush your cheek. But he never touches you with his hands. You feel that what he is telling you is so intimate and important, even dangerous, that no one else must hear.

Does an exile long for his old life and coat himself with memories, some true, some false? Who in this new country will know the difference? It is important to be interesting to those who have gone to so much trouble to help.

"Listen, my friend," A would say, and you knew you weren't really his friend, but you would listen. He was so easily bored, yet he himself was never boring.

A stayed in constant motion, seeking pleasure and fresh conquest. While the other students had respectable girlfriends or boyfriends, he had "affairs" and "catastrophes." These were spoken of in hushed, thrilled voices by the rest of us, who secretly hoped to be selected and made interesting.

I decided it would happen in the alley behind the ravaged stone walls of the Teatro Juárez, where I would suddenly press my knee between his thighs.

"You, Carlos, are the last one I would imagine…"

My column ran once a week in *La Voz*, and sometimes I wrote for the weekend edition: interviews with musicians, writers, and film stars, and social commentary. I became known for my cynical view toward the kids in their kerchiefs and berets who liked to play revolucionario between exams. I knew men at the highest level of government, and often received whispered phone calls at night from some high-placed councilman or lackey. I was the one who broke the news about the surgeon who was trafficking in body parts, selling corneas to rich Texans, and livers to the alcoholic wives of U.S. congressmen. For that I received the President's Special Medal. In my apartment I had a thirty-six-inch Sony Trinitron and on the roof was a satellite dish which received hundreds of channels from all over the continent. Of course I had to keep my soul alive, so I wrote my poems in red notebooks, and when I had enough, I published them. I wrote not of politics, but of love, and daily life in our city. I was despised by the leftists, who ridiculed my poetry as being "second-rate Yankee Beatnik," but they were jealous that I was able to be a poet and also live a comfortable life. At the Café de la Luna, where I stopped in most days, I was well known if not entirely loved. But we were all cynics and braggarts; it was the rule of entry to our society.

I was even, for a time, engaged to a girl called Leticia, the shy daughter of my mother's friend, but that didn't go well. She called me an exquisite lover but "without love," pleased with herself for such an original insight. There was always a moment when I hung over her naked body, breathing hard, verging into the infinite pleasure, when she would whisper, "Carlito, are you there?"

Several times a week I was invited to attend some diplomatic or artistic reception or other official function. Invitations poured through my mail slot, skimming across the tile floor below. I used to joke that as long as I had my position at the paper, I wouldn't have to spend a penny on food or whisky.

All this, and I blew it. One tiny mistake, because I'd made the greater mistake of believing I was safe.

The reception, Friday evening, was to welcome the new ambassador from Argentina, Javier-somebody, a tall man with huge hands. The 1960s concrete building hid a nineteenth-century landowner's plantation home within its sterile cladding. Dark wood coated the inner sanctum, plush green upholstery greeted the guests, who were obliged to endure a receiving line of diplomatic staff and a discreet bomb-sniffing dog. A uniformed butler took my hat and coat and disappeared into an immense cloak room. The string quartet, moonlighters from

EXILE • ANN IRELAND

our second-rate national symphony, played Schubert while platters of seafood were hoisted by a crew of very pretty girls. I spotted the new ambassador's wife leaning against one of the marble pillars, staring toward the walls lined with dour presidential portraits. Her dress, sleeveless blue velvet, clung to her slight figure.

Hovering in his customary position next to the bar was Tom Spicer, a stringer for a U.S. paper, in town to cover our election. He gave me a cordial wave.

"Carlos!" He grinned, revealing a chunk of cheese caught between his teeth. "Don't tell me they've let you off the leash."

I shrugged, feeling faintly annoyed. Everyone in town knew I'd been reprimanded for my column on the elections in our northern states. It had been easy to mock the ruling party's candidate, the owner of a discount appliance store who appeared on TV, shilling stoves and refrigerators in a mouselike squeak.

"And you, my friend, still on this undistinguished beat?"

Spicer's hand stroked the pocket where his miniature computer bulged discreetly. "Look who just walked in."

Following his gaze, I spotted the beefy men who surrounded a compact bald-headed figure in uniform. This new guest was greeting our hostess, his thin grey lips lowering to kiss her hand in a parody of the courtly manner. For this was no gentleman.

"Jesus, Son of God," the ambassador's press secretary whispered behind us. "It's the General."

As if choreographed, we took a step backwards. For it was the General who carried out our President's most notorious orders, and who was said to enjoy his responsibilities to an unseemly degree. I had never seen him close up, nor did I wish to get a single millimetre closer. In my country, when some fresh horror appears, an unexplained death or disappearance, or

164

even the closing of a popular restaurant or business, we blame the General.

When his head rose from the ambassador's wife's hand, his scowl was intact, his beady eyes already scanning the room. Every guest seemed to duck in unison, as if a bullet had whizzed over our heads.

"What's he doing here?" Spicer said, the only one who hadn't budged.

I waited until the room began to breathe normally before answering. "Remember that business with the Argentine miners?"

Spicer nodded: there had been a kidnapping, not a common activity in my country. The miners had been captured by some ragtag dissidents who claimed to be engaged in a war of conscience. Of course they seeked mainly to line their own threadbare pockets, yet someone had been killed. Diplomatic fence-mending was called for.

The General would only stay as long as necessary. Social occasions were known to be anathema to this small, middle-aged man from the campo.

Gradually the party resumed, but its tone had changed. There was a self-consciousness that hadn't been there before, a looming sense of dread. This, of course, was exciting. No one would leave early, not with the whiff of danger in the air. I chatted as always to my cronies on the other newspapers and journals, and we took turns boasting of our access to the highest sources in government and culture, and lightened each refreshment tray as it passed. Our voices lifted above the courteous mutterings of the diplomats. Yet always our gazes were seeking out the loathsome figure who seemed to slip from one corner to the next, leaving pockets of chilled air. I wondered what it would be like to create such a radius of power, so that each small gesture was met with a catalogue of possible interpretations. Did that raised paw mean silence? or was it merely a whisking at some passing insect? The tightening mouth was a response to an unfamiliar spice, or a sign of disapproval? Our bodies were held hostage to every nuance of his mood.

"And how are your verses, Carlos?" I was prodded by a colleague.

We were pretending that this was a normal party, acting out our accustomed roles.

Ignoring his hint of sarcasm, I informed this political commentator of my recent publication, *Insomnio*, a sequence of prose poems laced with romantic lyrics.

"Perhaps your book is a cure for the disease," he suggested.

They were jealous, of course. I was a real writer, not a mere scribbler, and they resented me for it. Perhaps I was too earnest in my response, for my journalist friends soon dwindled away. After a long moment of standing alone, which made me profoundly uneasy, I was approached by none other than Don Antonio, vice-president of the national petrol company.

"What do you hear of this new ambassador?" His expensive cologne filled my nostrils. He had approached me for this information, understanding that there was little that went on in Santa Clara that I didn't know.

"There was some difficulty with his service in the navy," I confided, sotta voce. "Rumours about stealing from the arms depot, making a killing. His brother is a rear-admiral."

"Of course." Don Antonio smiled and nodded. The information might prove useful.

Above us, caught in some slight draft, the pendants dangling from the chandelier twisted and shimmered, casting a fractured light over our faces. I didn't see the small man for a moment, despite my searching, a vertiginous experience as my eyes flitted over the room trying not to show alarm. I was the hunter pushing through underbrush, sensing the cougar's presence. The fruity drinks were strong and too sweet, and I wished that I'd stuck to the excellent Argentine wine, a gift from that government's cellars.

There he was, almost hidden by a cluster of fawning bureaucrats. I began to breathe evenly again, and tugged at my cuffs, filled with a sudden sense of well-being. In a minute the speeches would begin and then I would leave, perhaps scoop up Spicer and a few others for a late dinner by the wharf. I watched the ambassador's wife, so small and pretty. She looked exhausted and had drifted from the main party and was clinging again to one of the pillars, staring at nothing.

"You have met Mrs. de Silva?" Don Antonio asked, staring, as did I, at the enchanting vision. I'd forgotten he was still standing beside me.

"She and I will meet one day, but not here."

There was a quick intake of breath.

I couldn't stand these pious types who pretend never to have unseemly thoughts. Don Antonio's glass was filled with Perrier and a wedge of lime. When it came to women, he was our nation's upholder of virtue.

I leaned in and whispered in a confidential tone, "The last one, you must have heard, was stupendous in bed."

To my satisfaction, Don Antonio grimaced with distaste and hurriedly moved away. I had insulted the men of Santa Clara by my vulgarity. We are a nation that puts much store in manners. My father knew this better than most: a man does as he wishes, but never speaks of it.

A woman I hadn't noticed before was standing near the entrance to the room. She was almost a girl in her simple grey dress. Why was such a pretty creature standing alone? She held no food or drink in her hands, yet seemed not the least bit ill at ease. The rest of the room had planted itself into clumps of chatterers, a voice rising here and there, laughter sprinkling, always a little forced. Yet this woman stood by herself, undaunted by the obligatory pursuit of pleasure, or the need to pretend to be so engaged. Behind her, hanging from the wall, was a realistic painting of the bustling clip joints of Calle Florida in Buenos Aires, its cafés overflowing with happy tourists.

Buttoning my jacket, I introduced myself and she gave a nervous, childlike smile.

"I have heard of you," she said.

Perhaps it was those few artless words that caused me to reach for a drink off the passing tray, the extra jolt of alcohol which turns a man from being a harmless entertainment into an incautious fool.

"Why are you standing alone?" I whispered the phrase, to create a mood of intimacy.

She shrugged. "It's always like this."

"Why?" I leaned in too far, and inhaled her scent, a floral ambrosia. Her eyes were startling, large and wide-spaced in so small a face. She wore almost no makeup and there was nothing artificial or posed in the way she stood with the back of her head and shoulders touching the wall. This forced her chest outwards, yet her dress revealed none of the exaggerated cleavage so many of my clan prefer. It was almost a schoolgirl's uniform, though, up close, I could see that the material was a fine-woven silk.

"People are scared of me."

I laughed, perhaps a trifle too loudly. If I had not been so merry, I would have noticed the sudden silence which had blanketed the room.

"And what is your name, my terrifying friend?"

"I am called Cristina Graciela Hernández," she replied in her sweet measured tone. What was her accent? Argentine? I wasn't sure.

The name should have rung a bell, but the only bell in my head was the ring of my own beguiling genius.

"Perhaps you are the ambassador's daughter?"

She shook her head, clearly amused by this game. Then I touched her slim shoulder, a paternal gesture, and said with great seriousness, "Tell me then, you are a famous singer or actress in your country? '

Alcohol wobbled down my throat, unsure of its journey, a warning I did not heed.

Her head wagged again, tongue darting between her lips.

"You look bored," I went on. "Are these people so very dull? Let's cut loose. I know of an intimate café nearby." I spoke these words loudly for she had begun to laugh and made no move to escape my hand which had slipped on its own accord to the bare flesh of her upper arm. Of course I knew she wouldn't join me; this was an extension of the game we were inventing. Still, one could never be sure. She would certainly not be offended to receive an invitation from this man whose opinions and rhetoric graced page five of *La Voz*.

"I think," she said, "that you are about to have a surprise."

Cristina was looking past my head, her eyes bright with interest, and that's when the taste in my mouth turned gritty, as if I'd swallowed a chunk of agriculture, not liquor. I remembered, too late, her matter-of-fact words: it's always like this; people are scared of me. The slightly off-pitch music had stopped and all I heard was a swish of boots across thick diplomatic carpet and the seizure of blood in my brain.

I remembered then how and why I'd heard this appalling girl's name: she was the General's mistress, youngest daughter of an eminent Chilean émigré. My hand moved like a snake from her arm and hid in the pocket of my trousers, twitching. I made a half-turn, feeling cold breath snap across my back. Emerging shadowless from the party was the compact form of the General, medals flashing under the chandelier. His tiny piercing eyes immediately locked into mine with an expression of withering contempt. Military decorations took up so much space on his diminutive chest that his head seemed to sit directly on his shoulders, without benefit of neck. His jaw was tight and I could watch the seesaw motion of his molars grinding. As he drew closer, flanked by two hefty bodyguards in civilian clothes, I forced myself to meet his gaze, because if one is to die for love, it should be with open eyes. The General's celebrated left ear, which had been ripped off decades earlier by a madman, was shaped like a tiny letter *C* and powdered with faint hair. At this instant it was completely red, engorged with blood. The organ reattachment had evidently been a great success.

His gaze slowly dropped, its laser focus latching onto my name tag, and I felt my balls shrink.

"So," he said in a voice so thin and sharp it nicked my skin. "Tell us more about your 'intimate café'."

I began to sputter an apology, but of course it was futile. I should have said nothing, merely stood silent and with dignity, to show that I was would not be intimidated. There is nothing more disgusting to a powerful man than signs of weakness and fear.

None of this wisdom entered my brain.

Without thinking, I pushed my way through the mesh of guests until I reached a dark corner where I leaned against the wall, panting like a dog. The fruity alcohol threatened to rise from the dead while the string quartet bleated on again, filling the hall with a sentimental melody. Only Spicer dared look at me, his face contorted with barely stifled laughter. He would not lift a finger to help. Instead he was already composing the scandalous tale of the journalist who tried to seduce the executioner's mistress. Much more interesting to the people back home than tedious politics.

I understood that in those few seconds I'd lost my entire world.

Outside the official residence, a trail of black limousines was parked end to end, clear down to Independencia. Bored chauffeurs huddled in groups, smoking, barely glancing up as I stumbled down the sidewalk, expecting any second to feel a hand clamped over my shoulder.

What is it I see even now when the lights go out at night, and my eyelids flicker like tiny, relentless TV monitors?

The General's delicate pink ear. If you have seen a newborn mouse, you will know what I mean.

13

RITA WAS AFRAID THAT NOSTALGIA FOR MY own language and people would eat me up.

"Especially since you're a poet."

I would lose my way of thinking, and the habit of translation meant that nothing was ever itself: the poet would lose his authentic voice, "the way he speaks to himself," was how she put it. She wondered why I hadn't hooked up with the Latino community in Vancouver.

"People keep leaving their names with the departmental secretary. Why don't you call back?"

They were all members of solidarity groups, or volunteers for the Centre for Victims of Torture. The idea of meeting these people filled me with dread. The thought of entering one of those smoky dank cafés for disaffected refugees made my toes curl. What would they make of me with my cushy job and influential Anglo friends? And why did they want to talk to me? Who had relatives in Santa Clara or was perhaps himself a refugee from that angry town? My family is known. Every time a yellow message slip was tacked to my office door, I tore it into tiny pieces and stuffed the bits into my pocket. Couldn't they leave me alone, safe in my ghost life? I thought of Sharon's penetrating gaze in the darkness of the island cabin. "Are you afraid, Carlos?"

Fear, it seemed, was always a heartbeat away.

One morning I was a guest on a downtown radio program called "Vancouver A.M." It was taped at dawn and my groggy English made me sound sub-normal. The host was a man with rimless glasses who kept clearing his throat and supplying the missing words.

"When you first arrived here, Carlos, you must have felt —"

"Uh, I am feeling…"

"Bewildered?"

"Yes. Bewildered."

And bewildered still, I emerged from the massive steel and concrete building and found myself roaming the streets of Vancouver for two hours, just as the office workers were beginning to stream downtown. The city was like a giant beast waking up, flexing its limbs, yawning and twitching itself into the day.

I couldn't endure another of those wincing sympathetic smiles as I struggled with their language. I bought a hot dog and the vendor snapped, "Onions?"

"Yes, please."

And even in those two short words he heard that I was foreign, and his face braced, as if dreading that I might talk to him, and he wouldn't be able to understand. And he was himself a dark-skinned East Indian.

At the edge of Chinatown there was a rundown café which I had passed often. To one side was a boarded up storefront, and to the other, a drop-in centre for aboriginal mothers. "Café de Las Américas" was much less impressive than its name. The sign was hand painted and included a crudely drawn ocean wave and a grove of palm trees. It bore no resemblance to the cafés back home with their outdoor tables and uniformed waiters. Yet I hesitated. I'd been walking non-stop in my thin-soled sneakers, fuelled only by CBC coffee and the greasy hot dog.

"I know about you," a voice said in Spanish.

A young man was slouching in the doorway of the café, pool cue in hand.

"You're the poet at the university. I saw your picture in *El Diario*."

The crummy rag for the Hispanic community, full of ads for imported foods and seedy nightclubs. Editorial tirades spouted every leftist cliché you could think of.

"So you are coming to meet us at last," the punk said.

Then I had to. Besides, I was drawn inside by the familiar smell of real coffee. Not Starbucks sweetness, perfumed with cognac and amaretto and mint chocolate, but authentic, uncomplicated black coffee.

In the far corner there was a pool table covered with frayed felt. The walls, painted a bleak green, displayed sentimental landscapes of village life. Half a dozen men drank coffee and leafed through Spanish language magazines.

"This is the poet from UBC," the punk announced.

Everyone looked up, including the counterman. They seemed unsurprised and unimpressed, as if they'd been expecting me. We all end up here, in such a place, eventually. Pale overhead lighting shimmered from a 1950s-style chandelier that seemed too fancy for the rest of the place. As the men stared with their sleepy, familiar faces, I felt, for the first time in months, completely visible, a phantom whose body had suddenly slipped back into this world. It had been so long, filtering my voice through English, a pin pushing through many layers of cloth. So I sat down at the table where a man hunched over a chess board.

"I can play," I said.

He began setting up the pieces, giving himself the white men.

"This your regular hangout?"

No response, just the diligent setting up of pawns.

"Do you play often?"

Nada. Of course my questions were idiotic.

"Jaime's deaf," my young friend said. He was watching from the other side of the room. "Land mine."

Nicaragua? El Salvador? Peru? There were plenty of choices.

My opponent made his first move, and around us the café began to fill with customers. All men. No jobs, nothing to do but spend their days here and wait. Wait for what? Papers. Always the official papers, and then their real lives would begin.

My bishop skirted the board. I need always to move boldly, instinctively. A short man in a suit made his way to a table at the back of the café and several stoop-shouldered men began to form a ragged line. He carried a pile of file folders and a briefcase which he tossed onto the table. Immigration lawyer, I guessed. Or consultant. One hand pressed his cell phone to his ear while the other worked the zipper of his case.

After months of aching to speak my language I'd sat down with a deaf man.

Our chess pieces were made of molded plastic, the board was cardboard and ripping at the seam. Someone had attempted to mend it with Scotch Tape, which had dried out and curled, getting in the way. My opponent's cap was stamped with a B.C. Ferries insignia. His expressionless eyes suggested that the land mine had done more than make him deaf. While I moved quickly, relying on quick scans and the same manoeuvres I'd practised since I was a boy, Jaime took his time. His breath was wheezy, his belly spilled like dough over the top of his trousers.

I started talking in a quick, low voice, quiet enough so the punk couldn't hear.

"The women here are so cold."

When you speak your own language you are light, you are a dancer. When you love the sound of your own voice you forget what you are saying, like the conductor who forgets to direct his orchestra and just stands there, arms hanging in the air, rapt.

"They bore me entirely."

"Stop yammering," my father used to say when we played. "Concentrate on the game."

But chess is so boring and I hate waiting for my turn. The last time I played was after exams, second year university, because I wanted to impress A by my genius for strategy.

Yes, A.

"I don't want to speak his name," I whispered. "But you know the type, ragtag hair and clothes. He fucked with me and shouldn't have."

My opponent lifted a knight and planted it next to his queen. What was he up to? Defense or offense? I wanted to impress him, too, this stoic deaf man who smelled of mothballs.

"The cop came to my door, plainclothes. But I knew who he was. He wanted just a name, no details of the operation, just the name. Am I such a bad man?"

"Check," Jaime said. Deaf, but not dumb.

I stared at the board and saw that he'd nailed me.

"That's it." I rose and offered him my hand.

For the first time my opponent smiled and I suddenly thought, was the bastard really deaf?

Outside my office at the university, a girl was sprawled by the door, as if she'd been waiting there all morning.

"Who are you?"

"Felicia." She scrambled to her feet and went on, speaking in Spanish. "I've been trying to get in touch with you for weeks. Don't you ever answer your phone messages?"

"Sometimes."

I pushed the door open but didn't invite her in.

"I'm head of the Hispanic Students Association."

"Qué bueno."

She stared into my open office.

"I'm sorry," I said. "Not today."

She edged forward, half inside. "Mañana?"

"What do you want?"

"Just to talk, maybe interview you for *The Ubyssey*."

The student newspaper. Two doors down, Professor Millan was tacking a *New Yorker* cartoon to his office door. He chuckled to himself, anticipating the amusement of his colleagues.

"We'll see. Maybe," I said, then slipped into the neutrality of my own office and closed the door.

It was a setup. They were all in on it, the young punk at the café and Jaime the maybe-deaf chess player and, who knows, maybe this girl Felicia. She probably had an aunt who lived in Santa Clara and attended the same music club as my mother. The Students Association was a front for God knows what guerrilla group or cadre of government agents. They'd heard rumours ever since I arrived, and now I'd done no less than hand over my life, all because I couldn't keep my mouth shut in some seedy café. It was better, much safer, to be trapped in English, to sound stupid.

I looked out the window onto the parking lot where Felicia was crossing the asphalt, backpack sloping off one shoulder. A boy, dark-haired, joined her on the pathway leading towards the Student Union building. He carried one of those oversized art portfolios under one arm and flipped a skateboard under the other. They chattered, until suddenly she turned around, and pointed straight to the window where I stood.

"I will help you look for work." Rita had met me at the Graduate Centre lounge, a place full of bespectacled students hunched over tables, slurping espresso and discussing Chomsky. We sat on the beige sofa, knees bumping against the low table with its mess of newspapers and journals. The bar did not open until five. There was only coffee, tea, and cookies.

"I have work. My writing. My poetry."

"You need to earn a living once the Writer-in-Exile post is over."

"I have always earned a living."

She was becoming more and more uncomfortable. "Of course. But here it's different. The language difficulty…"

"People are interested in my poems. They have been translated and published in many magazines. I have given readings at both universities, at the International Authors Festival…"

"Yes, but if you added all those up, how much did you get paid?"

I looked at her. How much? How should I know how much? I am not an accountant.

"Less than two grand, I bet," she said gently. "And don't forget you're living rent-free this year and most of your food has been paid for. When you sail out on your own in a few months, you'll need to find a job. The Alliance will help; we have contacts. You could work in a restaurant, a factory." She helped herself to digestive biscuits on the lacquered tray.

"You are joking, yes?"

"How?"

"You expect me to work in a factory? Weld some piece of metal onto another piece of metal, like a robot?" I stared down at the sheet of paper she'd handed me. "And what is this? Planting trees? I don't plant trees, I plant seeds of knowledge, of truth." I tried to hand her back the paper but she wouldn't take it.

"Listen Carlos, you've got three more months, then your stint is up. You know what the deal is, we explained it to you carefully: you are our responsibility until then. But after…"

We both waited.

"I'm sorry Carlos, but we simply don't have the resources."

I was scrambling. "I am still writing my story, my memoir, for that important publisher."

Rita stared at her lap. "The thing is that you've been too slow. Political memoirs, well…"

"Yes?"

"They are no longer in demand."

"I do not understand."

"Publishing is a business. You have to strike while the iron is hot."

"I see. And this iron is now cold." Suddenly it hit me: she was completely serious. "But why can I not stay longer at the university. Through the summer?"

"Because…" Rita shuffled her handbag under one arm. "We have a Turkish dissident writer coming, with her family. She has spoken up for the Kurds; her life is in danger. Every day." Her eyes blazed. She was already thinking of it, the dramatic arrival, an olive-skinned woman and her children streaming dazedly through the airport gate where Rita would wait in her yellow slicker, lifting the CAFE sign, signaling greetings to the new, impossible life.

Sadness and unexpressed disappointments fell between us. My feet lifted onto the coffee table, pushing over the stack of old magazines, a mess which I made no attempt to repair. Maybe we could still speak as I'd spoken that night with Sharon. It wasn't too late to change. If there was intimacy, then that bureaucratic voice would disappear, and between friends there are always acts of forgiveness.

"I am disappointed," I said.

She held her hands cupped around the mug of coffee. "So am I, frankly."

"Then we are the same."

But we both knew this wasn't true. This was her home and I was the guest.

After a moment I rose to my feet, scooping my cap off the table, and waited for her to speak, to interfere with my leaving. But she did not.

14

I GREW UP SATURATED IN ANTIQUITY. MY FATHER, Jorge Silvano, wore beautifully tailored suits and his scraps of hair combed over his round bald head. He raised parakeets in ornate iron cages and I would watch — he was a short man — as he stood on his tiptoes to push a seed between the bars. The cages hung from the ceiling of the back sunroom because of Adolfo, our cat, who was, I believe, driven mad by the dangling squawking creatures. While Father cooed softly, poor Adolfo clawed at the air and meowed piteously.

While the rest of us ate bread and sweet rolls for breakfast, Father would ask the maid to bring him a single raw egg, and, standing in his shirtsleeves in the dining room, he would crack the egg on the edge of the sideboard, tilt his head back, and swallow it whole, like an oyster. That was his first meal of the day.

Each weekday evening, except Wednesdays, Father would call me into his study, which was a turn-of-the-century scholar's den with the cracked globe, dusty bookcases, and an array of fountain pens lined up neatly on his desk. This desk had belonged to a real sea captain, my maternal great-grandfather, who worked for a Venezuelan shipping company in the early part of the century.

"Come in, son," he would say, reeking of pipe tobacco and shoe polish. "Let's see how you're doing."

He didn't mean school work, because he had little respect for what passed for education in the convents of Santa Clara. He meant my readings.

"All right, where were we?" He flipped open the hefty tome titled simply *Romances*, which contained anonymous ballads of chivalry and legend that I was expected to memorize at a rate of one every three days. I was ten years old, clad in short pants, a clean white shirt, knee socks, and black oxfords, like an English school boy.

I began to recite: "Arriba, canes, arriba! Que rabia mala os mate," and came to my favourite line, trembly voice rising with chivalric vigour, "for my feet are unshod and my nails are oozing blood, I eat raw flesh and drink raw blood!"

He wasn't looking at me but at a photograph on his desk, sepia-toned in an oval frame with convex glass. It was a picture of Javier, sitting on an overstuffed chair, a boy of six when the photo was taken. He was my father's older brother who'd drowned in a well.

"I eat raw flesh and drink raw blood!" I repeated, too boisterously.

Alert, his eyes flickered back to the page, scanning the lines of raised print. He said nothing, but had noticed the repetition and knew that I'd forgotten what came next.

My voice fell silent. Late evening sun dusted the clay-red curtains and shimmered off the teak desktop. My father rarely became angry, at least not overtly. Instead, his lips would tighten into what someone less intimate might decide was a smile.

He handed me the book and said, "Come back when you are sure."

When is anyone ever sure! I should have told him this, sardonically, the way my sister spoke to him, and she was never dragged into tobacco-soaked rooms to recite the poems of long-dead clerics and anonymous balladeers.

"And what are you sure of, father?" I might have said, head cocked to one side. I would have loved to see those thin lips part in surprise. He thought no one knew, but I did. The leather-covered notebook in his top left-hand drawer, carefully hidden by a ledger, contained poems written in his own florid hand, archaic verses composed in ancient rhyme schemes full of thees and thous, unpublishable, unreadable.

Instead I crept back to the table where I did my homework in a small room next to the infernal din of the parakeets, and I mouthed the words of the *Romance* over and over until I was sure.

Father subscribed to all the scholarly journals, which he read, I suspect, while at the office. His ranking in the civil service was high enough that no one cared what he did. At any given time he was teaching himself a new foreign language: one year Russian, another year Italian or French. Words and short sentences would be printed on index cards and he would test himself, speaking the words aloud in a dramatic voice, mimicking the actors of the Comédie Française or Russian heads of state.

It was important that I receive a scholarship to the Instituto Secundario, a select prep school attached to the university and populated by the sons of professors. Not because we were short of money, but so that Father could say, "My son, Carlos, who was awarded a scholarship…" Others of his acquaintance were proud to spend the money, and to send their feckless boys to cram schools before the exam, but Father, exceptional in his milieu, was an intellectual snob.

He breathed over me as I studied, as I prepared and memorized and performed endless calculations, wrote essays on every conceivable topic, and ground my eyes to sand with my fists. I wasn't a bad student, just unexceptional. An elementary teacher once scrawled across my report card, "average ability" and my father had become enraged.

"There is no such animal as average. Damn fool!"

Who was the fool? Me, or my teacher?

The scholarship exams were held in the gymnasium of the Instituto. Over two hundred desks were jammed between the opposing basketball hoops. We were each assigned a desk — I was ninety-two, the same as Julio Berkman, the famous soccer player — and sat down amidst the lingering odour of sweat and dirty socks. We were handed out the booklets and instructed to write our number, not our name, on top of each sheet. As we scribbled, the assistant headmaster strolled the aisles, hands rattling deep in his pockets. He was a surprisingly young man, dressed casually in sports jacket, slacks, and open-necked shirt. The chairs creaked, tiny sighs of despair filled the air, and someone farted, seeping a bomb of sulfuric gas into the overheated room.

We were given a poem by Miguel de Unamuno to discuss, "with reference to his specific social and intellectual milieu." I wrote feverishly, unconsciously copying my father's speech, writing as he spoke, in a slightly archaic dialect. Then came the mathematical part of the exam. I hadn't a clue. Yes,

I had been taught all this, had frowned over the algebraic equations for the past weeks, had configured and reconfigured letters and numerals and dealt with the mysteries of different orders of infinity — but not after Miguel de Unamuno, never directly after poetry.

Desk number ninety-three, to my direct right, contained a young man with rigorous posture and bushy hair. I'd heard his quiet moans on the first part of the test, but now, deeply inside the numbers, he was flying. He wrote in a firm hand with a thick black pen, confident, nodding his head from time to time with pleasure and recognition.

I was sure that I had never spotted him in the halls of my convent school, and when I glanced downward, I noted that he was wearing heavy peasant sandals, no socks, and that his heels were coated with cracked brown skin, like a field worker. I even caught a faint whiff of the country, like Señor Perez, who came by our house each Thursday with eggs just dropped from his hens. There's a sweetness to country sweat; it was nothing like the athletic heat which permeated this gymnasium. It was the smell of a man who doesn't bathe often, because water must be carried half a kilometre in buckets over hard-baked hills from the river. I didn't know then that number ninety-three was just as urban as I was, but affected this earthy, campesino style and dialect.

The clock hands ground forward and I was growing increasingly desperate. The professor strolled the long aisles, hands clasped behind his back, humming under his breath some tuneless ditty. The frantic scratchings of pen on paper around the gym, a strange athleticism, sounded like a single machine, avid and efficient. The dust of equations blew through my vacant and exhausted skull, as and xs and meaningless signs, a language which was lost forever.

He'll kill me, I thought. No, Father was not in the least bit homicidal, but his disapproval was a long, slow instrument of torture. His silence could fill a room, drench it in tension. His carefully manicured hands fold over one another without a trace of nervousness, each nail sculpted to a half moon, the tufts of knuckle hair appearing at appropriate intervals. The only punctuation to this awful overbearing silence is a periodic clearing of the throat, which he manages to produce without parting his lips.

If I flubbed this exam... I could almost smell the sharp intakes of breath, followed by low steady breathing. Special tutors would be hired. The significant flaw in my character would be ferreted out, examined, prodded, and fixed.

I sat up very straight in my chair, yawned, stretched first one arm then the other, all the while keeping a close eye on the assistant headmaster, who was plodding up the aisle towards the front of the room, and I watched his back and his squirming hands seeking to scratch between his shoulder blades. He glanced at the clock exactly when I did, but for a different reason; he was bored, desperately bored. I was just desperate.

I pitched a look sideways towards the exam booklet of number ninety-three and, squinting hard, was able to read his confident strokes. Air filled my chest cavity and I was buoyant, as if I'd suddenly understood it all, how numbers and algebra unfold and cohere. It's like learning to read music, the written notes become sounds, a magical transformation. I worked hastily, as time was short, copying each answer, unconsciously matching my breath with that of number ninety-three, the rise and fall of his shoulders mimicked in mine. It never occurred to me that his answers might be wrong. He wrote easily, unhurried, with perfect confidence, and I'd already decided that a boy with such scabby sandals had to be there because he was brilliant. A prodigy from the altiplano, a musician of algebra. What magnificent joy filled me now that I'd divined a way out of the crisis. My daring and cleverness showed a force of character I'd never guessed in myself. We reached the bottom of the last page, and then ninety-three did something annoying. It was a question of geometry, a farmer's fields being sold off in chunks, but my neighbour placed his left elbow over the solution. I nearly whispered angrily, "Lift it, cabrón!" but already he was flipping through the pages of the booklet, reviewing his work and hunching sideways with his pen to make the odd snippet of correction. I didn't copy these, even the ones I could see. I knew that if my pen created identical corrections it might raise suspicion. This was better, I convinced myself; it ensured that our papers weren't exact duplicates. After all, we were now in cahoots, working to the same end: that I would get the damn scholarship and please my father, something that wouldn't harm this boy in the least with his rubber-tire sandals and cracked skin. I might even show gratitude later when we shared a classroom, nod "hello" while the other lads snubbed him. He could do worse.

I watched as he added a zero to an answer, peered at it, then crossed it out. For a moment, my confidence ebbed. I was so sure he was a genius, not given to second and third thoughts. Zero or not zero? Which was it, and did he know, really?

Suddenly number ninety-three dropped his pen and it skittered across the floor and ended up pressed against the leg of my desk. I stared dead ahead. Out of the corner of one eye I watched his hand pop up. The assistant headmaster frowned and walked over.

"What is it?"

Number ninety-three pointed to his pen.

The master waited until the pen was retrieved. The back of his linen jacket swept my hand and I felt my face redden. Then he walked back to the front of the room, humming as the clock sped ahead towards the hour, to the end of this wretched exam. And number ninety-three lifted one leg over the other and turned to face me. His eyebrows were raised and he glanced at my paper and nodded, mouth slightly upturned. He knew.

When we filed out ten minutes later, I was directly behind him, staring at the brown skin of his neck, smelling his hair oil, yet he didn't turn back or make any attempt to speak to me. I was mortified and scared, but already I was realizing something about this boy: he didn't care. My little transgression was noted, but meant absolutely nothing to him.

Number ninety-three was the boy I later knew as A.

Father slid the silver knife under the flap of the embossed envelope. My results, addressed to him, of course. I felt sick, a tight knot of dread between my ears. The sheet of paper was unfolded, read intently while I pretended to look out the window.

"We'll be celebrating tonight," Father declared.

The waiter, decked out in black vest and white shirt, poured coffee from a silver pot into tiny china cups. His hand shook. First day on the job, or perhaps he was rattled by my father, who had rearranged the cutlery and napkin until everything was just so, and seconds before had spun the cup thirty degrees so that the handle was lined up perfectly. We watched in horror as hot coffee splashed onto my father's lap. Rosario, home from boarding school for the holidays, placed a hand over her mouth while my mother sucked in a sharp breath. The waiter froze, but Father just closed his eyes and waved away all help. The wandering violin player launched into a sentimental folk song. Pain must never be acknowledged.

I hated every fucking minute of the Academy and got turfed out three times for obstreperous behaviour. My father would lift his palms and say, "Why, Carlos?" but already I was taller than him, and his diabetes made him weak, and his eyes weren't what they used to be. By the time I had the nerve to rebel he'd stopped caring.

It was eleven in the morning as I stood outside the principal's office and El Licenciado Jiménez looked up, groaning as he saw my hunkering form.

"Now what?"

I scanned the familiar yellowing diplomas behind his desk and the framed photo of our nation's President as he gesticulated from a platform.

"Now what?" the principal repeated.

"I have not eaten today." I hung my head in shame.

"Why have you not eaten?"

"Because there was no food in the house."

"Why was there no food in the house?"

I glanced behind me, sensing another presence. It was A, leaning against the doorframe, waiting his turn with the disciplinarian.

I turned back and said in a low tone. "Because my father..." Jiménez waited, eyes unblinking. "...has not been well."

This was true. Still, it was a reckless statement. All Jiménez had to do was pick up the phone, dial my home number, and talk to Graciela, the cook, who had overseen my breakfast of sweet rolls, coffee, and fruit.

The principal fooled with his fountain pen, an engraved gold instrument, and tapped it on a pad of memo sheets. Then, without looking at me, he reached into his pocket and pulled out two bills.

"Find yourself something to eat in the market."

I thanked him, my face pink with excitement, and brushed past A on my way out, hearing Jiménez growl to him, "Now what trouble, young man?"

A was suspended from classes for a week. He'd objected to the history master's interpretation of the upheavals in our northern states. It was not a happy time for our country or our school.

A disappeared for good during our senior year. There were two equally compelling stories which made the rounds. In the first, he had entered a delinquent centre for some violent act against a teacher. In the second, he'd made a girl pregnant and fled up the coast. The rest of us were children of officers, businessmen, and civil servants. A was different: he dressed shabbily, smelled rancid, his fingernails were caked with mysterious substances, and in our febrile imaginations, dirt equalled sex.

When I left the Academy I assumed I would never set eyes on the boy again.

I was wrong. Our national university, the public one, the only one that allowed me to enroll with my less-than-stellar marks, decided it would permit a certain number of intelligent but poor students to pass through its halls, tuition-free. And by then, kicked out of home by his family, A was genuinely poor.

15

DIEGO, CITY EDITOR OF *LA VOZ,* SLID the piece of paper across the desk. I glanced at the tissuey carbon copy, pounded out from an old-fashioned typewriter.

"Personal note to you, Carlos, from the supervising warden at La Fundacíon."

The notorious detention centre where prisoners who had caught the eye and ear of our leader would languish for years awaiting trial.

I read the two lines. "I am to go there at three o'clock? Why?"

"It seems that you, amongst all of us, have been selected to interview Mario H."

Diego, a heavy man who wore a wrinkled shirt with his tie undone, breathed raspily. A scrap of tobacco was stuck to his lower lip. I could hear the sound of his chest, a creaking noise like the frayed lines of a moored trawler.

"Shit." I was stunned, yet elated. "Really?"

Diego nodded and the bit of tobacco fell onto his shirtfront.

Why not me? At this point I wrote a weekly column of social commentary and the photo printed above my name had made me a minor celebrity in Santa Clara. Mario H. I knew, of course, by reputation, although in his photos he was never seen without a filthy bandanna swathing his face. He was a true revolutionary in our society of weary accommodators, a hero to the underclasses and a constant pest to the rest of us. He was a man I would love to meet.

It stank in La Fundacíon, an odour of piss and vomit mixed with the sting of despair. A stone building surrounded by barbed wire, La Fundacíon had a certain Victorian splendour in its turreted architecture; originally it had been built as a government tax collection agency. I was greeted by the usual rigamarole of steel doors, beefy guards, and then, quite unexpectedly, by a godawful racket. What a din! Devoid of rugs, curtains, upholstered furniture, or anything else to dampen noise, the men's voices filled and refilled the cavernous cell block, bouncing off the hard cement surfaces. I hesitated, stunned by the commotion. Somehow I'd anticipated a monastic silence, gaunt figures leaning over their tasks or staring through the space between their iron bars, but not this unearthly clanging and howling.

"In there," the guard mouthed, inaudible, then motioned towards a room with a steel door, not bars.

I pushed it open. Another guard was already in there, leaning casually against the wall, a shotgun nestled crossways against his chest. One hand fondled the barrel, and at first I thought he was half-asleep, until I saw his eyes, hard sapphire nuggets. The room smelled of fresh latex paint. The man I assumed to be Mario was slouched on a stool, his back to me, skull bristly with a quarter-inch of new hair, and marching across the revolutionary's head from one ear to the other was a squadron of small beetles.

The only other furniture in the room was a small wooden chair, like the ones in my elementary school classroom. When I sat on it, my knees nearly hit my chin. I stared at Mario, a gaunt face with violet bruises under his eyes, beard stubble, and cracked lips. It took a few seconds.

Then: " Jesus, it's…"

Mario, whom I knew as A, stopped me with a look. "We have eight minutes," he snapped. "They want me to tell my story, for you to print it in your paper."

He waited.

"Where is your notebook?"

I couldn't stop staring at him. Where was the bushy hair, the cocky sneer? Finally I patted my breast pocket and slipped out the stenographer's pad and a felt pen. He began to talk, but not in a voice I remembered. He spoke without intensity, as if the tale were something he'd memorized so well he'd forgotten the meaning of the words. I thought of my own recitations to my father of dreary antique poets, and scribbled in my journalist's shorthand, asking only the occasional, "what then?"

What he was telling me was utter bullshit and he knew I knew it. This was why he'd selected me, of all other journalists, as his medium of transmission. For in this story he cast himself as a misguided peasant, an illiterate campesino, who, with good intentions, had sought to better the lot of his people. Alas, the yearning for power was his downfall, and he'd managed to alienate the very people he was trying to help. All of this was uttered with no expression, without even the usual pauses for punctuation. Perhaps he was drugged. Meanwhile the guard shifted position, clearly bored, lit a cigarette without letting his index finger leave the trigger of his shotgun. It was hard to believe this scrawny man, this remnant of A, could be considered dangerous or violent.

Mario finished with this statement: "I am tired. I am happy that the newly created Commission to Investigate the Problems of the Urban Poor will take on this immense task and create solutions." Not the shadow of a smile crossed his face, nothing to indicate his true feelings.

"That's it?"

He nodded, and I packed away my pad. When I reached across to shake his hand the desultory guard suddenly sprang to action.

"Stop!" The barrel of the gun was at my temple, cold and metallic. Heart somersaulting, I retraced my steps through the half-dozen doors that led to the exit, past the barbed wire, the Jeep full of heavily armed militia, the final crunch of metal against metal as the barricades slammed shut behind me.

Back at my desk I laboured over the article for hours, changing my mind half a dozen times. What was A-slash-Mario hoping I would do? Did he want me to lay on the sarcasm, paint a picture for the readers of a warrior who was speaking one thing but clearly meaning another? Would I step on the sad helpless beetle that was the newly formed Commission? And most importantly — this made me wince — did he select me because he knew I wouldn't do any of this, that I could be counted on to toe the party line, to do as I was told so that whatever deal he'd made with the authorities wouldn't be jiggered by some self-important journalist?

As I pounded away on the keys I cursed him for putting me in this position. Every time I crossed his path I was made to feel diminished, half a man. The words that were eventually printed were his own, without editorial comment. Wandering home that night, rubbing my poor sore neck, I felt a pang for what might have been. What if I'd told the readers of *La Voz* of my connection with A-slash-Mario, and about that crazy ride in the meat truck delivering food to the women of the barrio? Would not my readers and colleagues, not to mention the new generation of bohemian intellectuals, look upon me with awe?

Thanks to my ability to lay ego aside, the column was printed, and A-slash-Mario, confessed and absolved, was released on parole a week later. He immediately fled for the hills, scooped up by comrades in a stolen army Jeep. The manifestos began arriving in all the news media, and proclamations in tedious revolutionary language were pasted up on hoardings during the dead of night. Mario was back on the job.

I had landed him in jail once, and I'd allowed him to be released. Yet who knew this, apart from the fugitive?

Do all young men believe they are lonely? The world of men is never enough, yet it's because you cannot expose your authentic self to a woman, and must disguise your yearning with endless rituals of courtship, that a great loneliness sweeps into your being. As a poet it is my duty to scratch away layers of pretense and false language and allow only what is true to exist. The women pretend that this is what they too want, that, like me, they crave what is real and authentic. All those hours in cafés, leaning into each other with total understanding: their eyes burn with it. A smell descends, an erotic perfume drenches the air.

And now I will kiss your tender skin in the glow of candlelight while your eyelids close and your soft breath fills the air. My hand slides up your thigh and I say the words, brutal, the way I feel them — and you jerk away, indignant, as if you have been invaded or raped, not seduced.

And so we turn to the world of men again.

I received another message while I was sitting with my colleagues at la Luna, about to bite into one of those figure-eight sweet buns. A man dressed in filthy jeans and a cardigan sauntered boldly up to our table, squinted at me from under his cap and said, "You are Carlos, the journalist?"

"I am."

My friends looked on, bemused but not surprised. We all have our informants and some, out of necessity, lurk in subterranean circles.

"You must come with me." He jerked his chin, indicating a direction: west.

"Must I?" I didn't hide my snap of irritation. Do manners count for so little?

The square was busy that day. Ringed by cafés, each with its regular crowd, the sweepers and cleaners were out in full force, preparing for a visit by the esteemed governor of our state, a landowner who had studied in some obscure American college and boasted of friends in Washington.

The messenger's eyes flashed back and forth, taking in the bulky forms of my comrades at *La Voz*, stark in contrast to his own emaciated body. He reached a gaunt brown hand out and dropped a note next to my coffee cup.

I uncurled it and read, while my pals made cracks about an illicit lover, possibly the governor's own wife.

"Come with Miguel to my camp." The words were written in a precise hand, in ballpoint pen on loose-leaf paper. It was signed Mario.

"It seems I have an appointment," I said casually, and refolded the paper. Gulping the last of my coffee and reluctantly leaving the remainder of my sweet bun, I rose to my feet.

I accompanied the filthy Miguel down a side street to an alley where a beat-up lorry was parked. Mario had sent such a rogue on purpose, to embarrass me in front of my colleagues — yet I never once questioned that I would go. My excitement was greater than any fear.

As we bumped along the country road, Miguel up front driving, and me alone in the rear crouched on an empty flour sack, I thought back to that other time, when I rode with the young men in the back of a truck on a crazy mission to feed the poor... corn chips. I laughed aloud. A familiar turn in the gut stopped the laugh, and it was as if I'd been swung back a dozen years to when I was nothing, a scrawny kid infatuated with danger yet scared to death to find myself in its presence.

Mario was over the first line of mountains. We lurched higher and higher, then, with a grinding of gears, began to rattle down the other side, and I could see nothing from the windowless box of the truck. Seeing nothing I imagined it all, the change in foliage as we climbed through pine forest, much depleted by grazing cattle and peasants desperate for firewood, then hurled down into tierra caliente. Heat beat through the steel sides of the truck and I tore off my jacket, snapped open the buttons of my shirt. Sweat was pouring down my temples, drenching my chest and back. At one point I heard shouts — an army checkpoint — and only then did the truck slow down, and I strained to hear the muffled exchange. Bills were passed, no doubt, and we rattled on.

Mario's camp was in the lowlands; the whole state knew that. From there he issued his manifestos and launched his small-time guerrilla manoeuvres: the occasional phone wire was clipped, and rich bankers and landowners were kidnapped from time to time to generate cash. He was no Subcomandante Marcos, from the great state of Chiapas in Mexico, though I suspected he had aspirations. Local boys were seduced to join up in exchange for guns, camouflage gear, and beans and rice twice a day. They would pose, lean lads in open shirts dangling cigarettes from their mouths, as foreign news photographers snapped their picture. Daring university students have been spotted in the Plaza back home wearing T-shirts with the grainy face of Che on one side, Mario on the other. We are a small country, but not without ambition.

I confess to a twinge of nostalgia for an earlier self, and crouched in the back of the rattletrap truck I decided it was not too late to become a warrior. Sure, I'd allowed myself to get sucked in by the easy cynicism of my brothers at the newspapers — and what is cynicism but a form of laziness and fear? Would Diego, the cigar-chomping city editor with psoriasis, be caught riding this truck on the way to a guerrilla camp? Fat chance. We may call ourselves newspapermen but we need our creature comforts more than we crave adventure.

"His manifestos are tedious enough," Diego would yawn. "I have no desire to meet their author."

He is afraid, of course, of fleas and dirt, and afraid that he might discover what's really happening in the countryside, not the government's sanitized version that we dutifully print under our bylines.

The truck bucked over a ridge of mud and I shot halfway to the ceiling. Fix the fucking suspension!

On CNN the most important journalists are not those air-brushed faces reading the news off the teleprompter: it is the men who stand in flak jackets in front of bombed-out buildings, yelling into the microphone over the racket of machine gun fire and artillery that we admire. All these years I'd been wasting my time at embassy cocktail parties cadging free drinks and tidbits of gossip. The same idiots turn up at every event, and I am one of them.

The lorry stopped with a squeal of tires and I pitched forward. When Miguel yanked open the panel I cautiously stepped down.

The light and heat were ferocious and it took several seconds before I could see anything other than a shimmering glare. My feet landed in mud. As my eyes adjusted, I saw murky puddles filling every indentation and crevice — the total yearly rainfall in these parts. We had pulled into one of those tiny villages way off the main road, the sort of godforsaken hole that makes you wonder how any form of human life can be maintained. There were half a dozen mud shacks and two cinderblock buildings. Laundry hung stiffly on a makeshift line between two trees while a rooster pranced across the muck, wattles flapping. Miguel scurried into the dark interior of one of the cinderblock buildings while I waited, shielding my eyes against the sun. There was a distinct stench of raw sewage and the tiny creek that trickled down the middle of the settlement was a milky blue-green colour. I fastened the buttons on my shirt and tossed my jacket over my shoulders.

There was not a single human in sight. Somehow I thought I'd be greeted by Mario himself, flanked by a couple of body-guards in camouflage gear. Man to man we would stand, look-ing into each other's eyes, unsmiling. After a beat of silence I would say, "What do you want?"

I would use his old name, the childhood name which so few people remember.

Instead I stood wilting under the midday sun, my mouth tasting of blood, for during the bumpy ride my teeth had drilled into my tongue. I spat, wiped my cracking lips, and waited, because there was nothing else to do. At last Miguel sauntered out of the building, accompanied by a boy of about ten. Both wore battered baseball caps with an Atlanta Braves insignia. Miguel swept his arm through the air, indicating I should follow. Jumping over puddles in my good Italian loafers, I trailed him across a makeshift bridge — two warped boards which spanned the creek — into the heart of the settlement, so-called. A yellow dog, nearly hairless, loped alongside, panti-ng and drooling heavily. My stomach tightened a notch. God knows what diseases swarmed in this sewer water. I resolved to eat or drink nothing. Glancing at my watch I noted that it had been nearly three hours since I'd been pulled from my com-fortable perch at la Luna.

He was sitting on a webbed garden chair flanked by two men in army fatigues. The chair, propped on uneven ground, tipped precipitously. He was skinnier than ever and had grown a thin beard flecked with grey. His pants were standard issue olive green, his shirt, open at the neck, was khaki coloured and ripped. Pulling a cigar from his mouth, he smiled at my

EXILE • ANN IRELAND

approach. The two men, perched cross-legged on the ground, glared at me from under straw hats. A huge radio seemed caught between stations, playing simultaneously a soccer game and Brazilian pop music.

I reached to shake his hand, although I was struck by the incongruity of the gesture out here, its pretense to salon manners. He didn't rise, ignored the hand and cuffed me on the side of the leg instead.

"Carlos, cabrón, you have finally come to visit me."

"So it seems."

"An important man like you…" He chomped the end of his cigar.

I felt a flash of anger.

Sensing this, he patted me again, this time on the hip, while eyeing me carefully.

"Sit down, old friend. Marco!" He barked an order to one of his men and Marco stumbled to his feet, crept inside the dark cement building behind and returned a moment later with a wooden stool.

A child's stool, something you place next to a sink so that a toddler can reach the faucet.

I straddled the thing, achieving dignity by not bothering to protest. "Journalists hold the real power in this nation," A pronounced. "The intelligentsia and government officials read your column over morning coffee, their bread crumbs sweep across your page. You are part of their lives. I am just a pest they think about only when they are forced to."

I shrugged modestly. His voice sounded weary rather than mocking. I liked his image, these important men brushing crumbs off my little photo, squinting down at the words as they munch their way through hangovers.

"What kind of shithole is this?" A went on, indicating the surrounding settlement. "We piss in our drinking water and crap on the open field. Who really cares, outside of a handful of spoiled university students and self-styled revolutionaries?" He sighed deeply.

I felt the stool pry into the clay beneath me. Marco batted the radio with his foot until it settled onto the soccer game.

"I want a comfortable bed, good food, good liquor, all the necessities. Why does anyone suppose I am different?"

"The governor hates your guts," I pointed out.

He nodded in agreement then lifted his eyes. "Yet here I am, the second camp this week, seventeen men sharing two scrawny chickens for dinner, my clothes stink..." He pulled at the collar of his shirt. "And I'm coughing my guts out."

As if to demonstrate, he began to cough, a godawful hacking, and I found myself leaning backwards, holding my breath.

"As you see, I am a sick man," he gasped finally. Neither of his flunkies paid any attention to the attack. "A sick man suffering in the tierra caliente while you are living your comfortable life in the cafés, then meeting the governor at the mayor's mansion."

I thought I was beginning to get it. "You want me to smuggle you into the reception?" I glanced at my watch. This could be amusing. "We don't have much time."

A chuckled. "But that is not what we are going to do today. Marco!"

He barked the order, although Marco was no more than a metre away.

"Get clothes for our friend!"

I began to protest but A interrupted. "Marco is Italian. His grandfather and father were fascists: it makes him very obedient."

Marco disappeared into the building again and I could see him rooting around a cardboard box while A continued to watch me, head cocked to one side.

"We had our little adventure together, didn't we."

I flushed. After all these years and all his skirmishes with authorities, he remembered that crazy trip.

"You never asked me again." I fought to sound casual.

He leaned forward and a dirt-encrusted finger prodded the air.

"That is because you were too much in love, Carlito."

He was looking right through me, into the man I'd been. To finally be truly known, to be seen through, is exhilarating. I could feel a wave of heat cross my face.

"Too much in love with the idea of your own heroic nature," he went on. "And that is extremely dangerous, not only to yourself but others. Ah, Marco." He looked up towards the panting man who approached. "A uniform for our famous writer friend."

He held up a pair of scruffy jeans and a black T-shirt from some rock and roll band's tour; the list of cities, printed on its front, included our very own Santa Clara.

"We have an appointment soon," A said.

"I have an appointment at five," I pointed out. "Reception at City Hall for Governor Gallardo."

"You will see your governor," A said with a mysterious smile.

Because of the mountains, we didn't hear the chopper until it was nearly upon us. Squeals of excitement rose from the village children as it hovered above the open land, drilling mud and dust in all directions. A deafening sound, like an invasion. And there were not one but two of the creatures, both painted in camouflage — military craft, one ancient, one shining new. We clutched our hats and ducked under the thatched canopy of the newly built soup kitchen. This was a simple structure, a propane stove which held an immense clay pot, shelves for storing food and bowls, and a couple of boards over barrels to make a counter.

The 'copters slowly lowered, like beasts from some other world. I looked like hell in these wrinkly clothes. Or perhaps not. Perhaps I looked like a man of the jungle, lacking only a rifle or machete slung over one shoulder. A had disappeared but I recognized some of his men slouching in the darkened doorways. Above, the freshly painted banner billowed wildly. "Bienvenido," it proclaimed in still-sticky paint, "al muy estimado Gobernador Sebastiano Gallardo Sánchez," who at that moment jumped clear of the blades of his shiny chopper, flanked by half a dozen men in military and civilian garb. One hand clutched the lapels of his magnificent suit, the other his cap. Gallardo affected a natty French-style beret in his trips to the countryside. It gave him a rakish air, suggesting long intense conversations abroad. He was a handsome man, thick-set and fiftyish, with plenty of grey hair poking beneath the beret.

His bodyguards followed as he stepped gingerly across the mud, then the second 'copter landed alongside. From this popped another bunch of men followed by — I gasped — two figures in jeans and khaki vests. Lupe, the news photographer from *La Voz*, and her lover, the kid reporter José, who freelanced, which meant he'd go any place, any shithole the rest of us had no intention of venturing into. Like this armpit of a village deep in the tierra caliente, featuring microbes of such complexity they have never been isolated. Lupe skipped over the mud, lugging an arrangement of cameras and lenses.

The soup kitchen had been erected the day before. The governor was using it as a photo opportunity, which meant Lupe would see her snapshot and credit stamped across the front pages of every paper in the nation. She could buy a fresh tank of gas for her moped.

I prayed that I was unrecognizable in these peasant clothes and straw hat pulled down low, I who never ventured forth without a clean shirt and pressed trousers. More to the point they would never expect to see me off my trapline of Santa Clara cafés, salons, and reception rooms.

Lupe screwed a filter over her lens and the two of them scanned the scene. Dozens of villagers were gradually filling the space, eager to get a glimpse of the governor.

There is a moment when you can make a choice whether to continue or walk away. What would prevent me from wandering into the shade of one of the buildings until this episode was over?

Maybe A was right about this infatuation with my heroic nature. What man does not wish to test his mettle, to prod the limits of the life he has built for himself? My hands trembled, my trousers sucked up into my asshole, and that's when it happened: I was summoned over to the steaming pot of stew by none other than the governor's own henchman. This was not a coincidence. I'd spotted the quick look pass between this man and one of A's undernourished thugs. Suddenly I felt as if I were in a movie, or dropped into one of those modern entertainments where the audience member is hauled on stage so that he might touch the rabbit and prove that it is alive.

I had no choice but to comply. Clad in the unfamiliar clothes, I strode forward, hat pulled low on my brow. At the same time, Gallardo stepped with dignity onto the platform, which had been constructed according to specification for this one-time use, lifted his arms to quell the imagined riot of applause, and began to speak in those plummy actor's tones which so entranced the populace.

"Compañeros…"

Sun poured onto the assembly of bare-footed children, weary mothers, and labourers hauled off the fields.

"This marvellous occasion brings me to your village…"

Kids picked lice out of each others' hair and eyed the pot hungrily. A rooster's comb bobbed to the surface of the quaking brew while beneath the great pot a bluish flame flickered. A huge wicker basket held bread. Flies were everywhere, enchanted by this rare opportunity to gorge.

I feared the worst: A and his men, in a blast of gunfire, bursting into the assembly and tearing through the governor's flesh, pumping his handsome body with bullets. What was I to be in all this — a recorder of the act? Is that why he'd brought me here? Yet A was not known to be a violent man, I thought desperately. His skirmishes were mainly acts of sabotage, a Robin Hoodesque rejigging of the social order, holes pricked in gas lines so that the locals could fill their cans, hydro poles toppled, and rich men kidnapped for outrageous ransoms. But he did not litter the landscape with corpses.

The crowd shifted. A flock of crows lifted off the roof of the building that I suspected A was waiting in, and at that same moment our governor paused in his speech and squeezed his eyes shut. A shadow had crossed the page that he was reading from, cast by the crows which hovered above, their huge wings spread, their oppressive cawing filling the air. The crowd spontaneously took half a dozen steps forward.

Our governor's eyes jerked open and after clearing his throat, he resumed his speech. The crowd froze.

Were they part of it, I wondered in a wave of nausea. They were A's people, trained to steal up on the governor, step by step, until they were on top of him — Mother may I take a giant step — so that he would be murdered, not by terrorists but by his own subjects.

"It is my pleasure and my great honour…"

I would be complicit, not as a reporter but as a member of the mob, summoned by A and to become part of his drama. An old man, nearly toothless, stood at my elbow, picking at the cloth of his shirt the way dying people tug at their sheets. Women wearing the wide-brimmed straw hats of the region trailed their colourful shawls in the mud. Babies were slung everywhere, off backs, hips, shoulders. And here in the valley, skin was browner, the people squat. Again I absorbed the impression that everyone was part of a performance, that they were standing on their marks like actors, waiting for the next cue. Was this just the oversensitivity of an urban poet? Despite the pounding heat, I was shivering inside my costume. Even the breeze which rolled through the valley was hot, tinged with the arid flavours of the mountains.

"Let us now taste this fine stew, prepared by the women of Jícama." The governor stepped down from the podium, buttoning his jacket, and made his way to the gurgling stew.

The crowd, no longer hesitant, streamed across the pitted ground to form a semicircle around the governor and his men. I made my way to the perimeter, hands deep in pockets of the baggy jeans, feeling my fingertips brush against a spent match. Lupe and José scurried to catch up, Lupe with her beautiful figure obscured by an ugly vest bulging with lenses and filters and extra rolls of film. I had to smile. She took herself so seriously. Yet she must know this was a setup to make our governor look noble, how the great father from the Capital would personally see that food entered the humming bellies of the peasants. But Lupe was still of an age to be impressed by her trip in the governor's helicopter brigade buzzing over the mountains of our troubled state.

Unless she had been alerted that more was going to happen than a gap-toothed child sucking from a soup ladle.

"You, my friend."

Heavenly Father!

That voice, that false grating smile, so familiar from a decade of speeches, was aimed my way.

The governor nodded towards the ladle.

"I would like to try this delicious stew." His eyes, hard brown nodules under furry brows, were unmistakably cast my way. A fat woman with no teeth pointed the ladle towards my sweat-slicked hand.

Why me?

Perhaps because I was the cleanest of the bunch. It was a brilliant move, to enjoy the first taste himself, proving that this food was suitable for any man, woman, or child. What a photo to plaster across the newspapers, our esteemed governor tilting his capped head forward to slurp the inaugural ladle of stew from the Jícama Village Soup Kitchen.

No time to think, merely to press forward and pick up the heavy ladle.

He muttered under his breath, "A small taste, idiot, and avoid the cockscomb or I'll have you shot."

Trembling, my hand pressed the scoop into the bubbling stew and wouldn't you know it, every time I began to lift, the cursed cockscomb would float into the ladle and I spent end-less seconds sifting back and forth in the murk. The steam rose and clouded my vision, making me sweat like a pig. Finally, like the fisherman in our polluted waters, I hauled it up for better or worse and saw, to my horror, a slug-like crea-ture coiled in the broth, its limpid green eye gazing straight at our governor.

Cameras clicked.

The man didn't flinch. Instead, smile intact, he tipped his head forward, fastened his mouth to the lip of the ladle which, due to my nervousness, began to jangle against his teeth, and gave a single long slurp. I gazed down, mesmerized, intent on gripping the ladle as firmly as possible. My whole being revolved around the task: I'd forgotten about the crowd, about Lupe, and any fear of being recognized. I had only to survive the next five seconds.

The governor used his teeth adeptly as a sieve. After his slurp, the broth had disappeared, yet all solid matter remained on the bowl of the ladle.

He muttered again, "Slide it back, imbecile!"

You can't recognize me in the photograph. That's because I was careful to slip the hat low over my forehead and keep my face in the shade. It is also because the photo centres around the gov-ernor's head, his eyes lifted just slightly so he is looking the cam-era eye straight-on. The ladle is set against his lips, steam rising from its nutritious broth.

My father preferred stories with morals and philosophical endings. He did not have much respect for journalists who crank out their columns in noisy rooms, without reflection. Their work lacked dimension and the patina of old books and yellowed pages, the history of mankind. My shadowy figure, dressed in wrinkled clothes and mercifully unidentifiable, was soon to be seen wrapping fish and meat at the marketplace, or carefully folded into paper airplanes or hats. Useful even when the words and images are forgotten. Which is more than I can say for his ancient books in their crumbling bindings.

My last picture of A was undramatic: he lounged by the path as the truck pulled away to take me back to Santa Clara. He said nothing, but a smile worked at his lips. He was anticipating the moment when I would be presented to the governor at the evening reception. Yet his elaborate plan to humiliate and endanger his old comrade failed. I would not be plucked from the receiving line as an impostor and possible insurgent, if that was his intention. For what A didn't understand was that a governor never sees, let alone memorizes, a peasant's face, and he would never remember me.

16

IT IS AN EXCELLENT WAY TO LEARN English, to watch television in the afternoon. The telenovelas display real people
in real situations, with the hospital, the jobs, babies. I was learning new vocabulary like "hydrocephalic" and "mediation."
Rashid tramped upstairs to his study with his computer. Tap-
tap. He wanted me to hear the sound of his working. I clicked
the remote, and the channel showed Jeeps bucking over desert
mounds and it was so boring, predictable. Ads for silly bour-
geois men in tan slacks who pretend they are driving through
parched Bedouin territory, not the leafy hills of North
Vancouver. Another showed an actor wearing a rubber mask
and I realized immediately that he was mimicking the Prime
Minister of Canada. Instinctively I gazed towards the window:
what if they saw me watching this? Would they think I was
mocking the government? I switched channels quickly. Who

was this beautiful woman? I leaned forward. A goddess! Her blonde hair tossed over her shoulders and she was wearing a sort of leotard, purple and blue with a V-neck that outlined every detail of her figure. Her chest rose and fell with her breathing, a hypnotic rhythm.

"One, two," she chanted. "And again. One, two."

Her hands pressed against her diaphragm as she sucked in a breath. A banner behind announced her name: Laura-Lynn. I placed my own hand above my belly and breathed with her, one, two, and immediately felt calm. She was demonstrating her invention, the deep-breathing way of losing weight and achieving vitality.

"Six minutes a day," she told us, moist lips and blue eyes facing the camera. Her skin glistened with health.

"If you want to feel better than you've ever felt before..."

Who doesn't?

I scratched down the information: a set of three videos for $49.95 plus tax. As her image faded from the screen my hand was already punching out the toll-free number.

Another day I flipped to the noon-hour news and found myself gazing at the Prime Minister of Canada perched in his hospital bed, wearing a dressing gown over his hospital pajamas. He was smiling, waving to the cameras, while the nurse backed away, making room for this regal gesture. Seconds later, a young doctor showed us diagrams of the inside of the leader's gut, and explained in bland, professional tones that a small piece of the patient's colon would be removed, the remainder sewn together.

I was astonished. At home, when our President was rumoured to be suffering from heart trouble, he was whisked away by jet to an American medical clinic where he stayed for several weeks. We were told he was vacationing in the Caribbean.

"I detest pigeons," Sydney Baskin announced as he stirred milk into his tea. "They are entirely without social benefit."

The window next to his dining table was swung open and the room filled with choral moaning. No one likes these ugly birds with their nondescript plumage and complaining song. They shamelessly drop their bacteria-infested crap on patio stones and encourage old ladies to feed them bread.

The CAFE members who sat around the table looked up as Rita dashed into the room, lifting her heavy rucksack off her shoulder with an audible sigh of relief.

"Am I late?" she said, staring at the half-empty tea cups and plates full of crumbs.

"Ah," said Syd, "our dancer pirouettes in."

I had arrived just moments earlier, thumping on the wrought-iron door knocker until I was summoned in for this important meeting, only to discover that they had been there at least an hour, deep in discussion, already yawning and pulling back their chairs to breathe freely.

Rita dropped onto a cane chair and helped herself to cold tea from the pot. Sandy Peeple, in her uniform of leggings and turtleneck, pushed her empty cup into the centre of the table, finished. Daniel and Sharon Rose played with crumbs of biscotti on antique plates. Seeing all this, Rita repeated her question.

"Am I late?"

"No Rita, you are not late," Syd assured her. "We asked you and Carlos to come at this time."

She flushed. "But you guys look well into it."

"I invited the executive to meet earlier."

She dropped a sugar cube into her cup and stirred. "I see," she said slowly.

I have observed this routine at the newspaper. Diego would call a meeting, but certain parties were invited half an hour early to make the real decision, which would then be imparted to the less important employees.

Lucy's arm curved to hide the paper where she'd been keeping the minutes. I wondered if I might ask for coffee, yet my nostrils picked up no encouraging smell. Rita had cut her hair and it looked brisk and professional, the few grey strands dyed dark. She posed at the edge of her chair with one with leg tightly crossed over the other, still breathing hard from her rushed arrival. She forced herself to sip the tea slowly, each gesture deliberate, well aware of our watching.

"We've been having a chat about CAFE concerns," Syd began mildly. "It seemed preferable to confer before you two came into the picture." He cleared his throat.

Rita tilted her chin, using her fingers as prop.

"There's been some boundary-crossing which isn't healthy for the program or the individuals involved." Sydney looked around the table. "Help me out here, fellow board members."

Sharon Rose took a deep breath. "There is no consensus on this issue, Syd."

Everyone stared at the centre of the table.

"What issue?" said Rita.

Sandy Peeple brushed back her tangle of hair. "We can't tell Carlos or you how to conduct your private life."

"Yet I hope you see how this compromises our work," Syd interrupted.

"I don't know what you are talking about," Rita said, while Lucy captured this interaction on her legal pad.

"It's a matter of board discipline," Syd continued. "We are a single body, and we must operate as such."

Sharon pushed her chair away from the table. "I don't want any part of this discussion." Her face was very pale.

Syd glared. "I understand your ambivalence, Sharon. This is not an easy subject to broach."

"Will someone please fill me in?" Rita said loudly.

For a long moment there was only silence, until at last Syd tapped his nose with his pen and said, "In any organization there are certain rules which must be respected."

"Your rules, Syd?" Daniel Rose spoke up for the first time.

He ignored this. "I realize that some of you feel, because we are a freedom of expression organization, that anything goes. Not so."

Lucy scratched this small speech on her pad.

"Do you not agree, Carlos?" He was looking at me now, they all were, Lucy's hand raised, waiting to trap my words for posterity.

I was rescued by my friend, Rita. "Are you saying what I think you're saying?"

Syd folded one hand neatly over the other. "I don't believe there is any need to spell it out."

Rita laughed, but there was no amusement in it. "Are you getting this, Carlos?"

I could only nod in confusion.

"Syd believes we have engaged in inappropriate behaviour." Then she stared at the president of CAFE. "How did you even know about this?"

There was a short but awkward pause.

"Rashid," I mouthed quietly.

Sharon stood up so suddenly that she jostled the table. "I vote we end this discussion now."

"I'm sure the point has been made." Syd pointed his pen at her. "No need for extravagant gestures. On to the next order of business."

Sharon sat down, reluctantly.

"We have arrived at a crisis point with you, Carlos," Sydney continued.

I smiled automatically at the sound of my name.

"We're not sure that you are happy here at the university."

Happy? I smiled to indicate my great happiness.

"For this we offer no explanation or blame, merely a possible solution."

I was instantly alert. A solution?

"As you know, the Exile Chair is an endowed position. You are given time to write, and opportunity to join the university community. The stipend is not merely a subsidy for your habits."

There were frowns all around the table but I wasn't sure — were they frowning at my many failings, or at Sydney's tone?

He tented his hands. "Sandy, perhaps you'd like to explain what we've come up with."

Sandy nodded and spoke in a rapid voice which I struggled to understand. "We will help you set up lodgings off-campus. There's a room in a house right downtown; it might suit you better, and there are all sorts of services we'll plug you into: welfare, Employment Canada, and free classes at the ESL clinic."

This dining table was oval shaped, very smooth on the sides, and I guessed that the wood was mahogany. It was held up beneath by heavy crossbeams which hit my knees every time I moved my legs or tried to cross them. The room was cramped with too much heavy furniture, which seemed to have come from a much larger house. Rita looked up at last and stared blankly at a print on the wall, some pink Impressionist masterpiece of a man and a woman in a boat, and said nothing.

I was remembering how I'd read my poems on their stage to a rapt audience, and how afterwards the interviewers crowded in asking questions, and how the most important publisher begged to publish my memoir, and how Rita had seized my elbow, her voice hoarse with emotion at my performance.

This time she set her hands on her knees, and said in a low, sad voice, "Maybe you're right. Maybe this is the way to go."

Sharon Rose looked at me with great apologetic sorrow, yet said nothing.

Rita waited outside the house, dangling her car keys.

"Need a ride?"

I nodded a formal "yes" and followed her to that little car which had driven me from the Vancouver airport into the promise of a new life. I was almost Canadian in my tersely contained silence.

"Hold on." She reached across the front seat and knocked a pile of junk to the floor before signalling me to get in. We drove towards my little house, passing cyclists and rollerbladers and skateboarders: so many healthy young people streaming down the streets with their smooth tanned faces and well-muscled legs. Cutting into campus she drove up to my house, braked, then turned to look at me.

"What can I say, Carlos?"

I set my hand on the door handle and flipped it up. Enough words had been spoken for one day.

"Do you feel I've betrayed you?" she said.

I slid one leg out of the car. I did not wish to discuss her guilt. *Now we will count to twelve / and we will all keep still.* The poet Neruda had once made the same wish.

"Wait." She reached out and grabbed my hand. "What choice did I have? Those guys had already decided."

I pulled away. "You have been kind to me. You let me stay in your apartment and eat your food and meet your son. You even let me..." I paused and saw her wince. "It is as you say." I got out and leaned over the open door. "You had no choice."

And I walked up the pathway to the house that was no longer mine.

17

"I AM SORRY, CARLOS, WE HAVE BEEN VERY patient." This is what Sydney said as I left his meeting.

I must leave my married students' quarters and I will no longer receive my salary as writer-in-exile, and will no longer have my tiny office in the tower.

What am I then? What will you call me in some rented room? Who is the exile when he has been demoted?

I was presented with a file of papers and pamphlets about the office of Welfare, Immigrant Services, and a government-sponsored school for English as a Second Language. There was nothing about being a writer, a poet.

The cliff, which takes you away from the campus, leads you to a dark and steep path that descends many metres to the beach below. First you must make your way through under-brush and there are so many trees that you have no idea where you are going. But you hear the muffled sound of the waves slapping to shore and the smell of the sea becomes stronger with each step. I had heard stories about this place, how people will lie naked on the sand for hours and I knew that this was one spot in this city where I might find an honest human. All costumes must be burnt. Back to skin and bones, water and blood.

I scrambled down the last few metres and stumbled onto the warm sand, peeled off only my shoes and socks, and looked around.

There were no women, only a dozen nude men lying on colourful towels, their skin baked bronze, glistening with oil. They were warriors, resting after battle, their hard muscles tinted by sun. Who knew what wrecked ship had cast them ashore?

I steamrollered through the sand, anger, or perhaps fear, buckling my knees. I liked this, their eyes scanning my body as I moved between the towels. There was no litter, no broken bottles or diapers fouling the stretch of paradise. The ocean trapped the shoreline, passed its long cold tongue over the sand. Then an old man rose to his feet and leaned over, his shriveled cock and balls dangling between his legs, and reached his hand inside a bag to pick up the shit of his tiny yapping dog.

If I had been born here, I could press my lips to the General's ear and tell him to fuck his ancient mother ten times over, and he could do nothing but flush deep red.

If I had been born here, there would be no General.

I spotted one other man on the beach who wore clothes, and he approached from the opposite direction as I strode along, my skull tight as I wrestled the equation: the exile of the exile, two negatives which did not create a positive. What branch of modern physics had I fallen through?

Of course the men were homosexual. These bodies anointed with oil were gods of sensuality in a world without women. Someone played hip hop music on the radio, a pulse which seemed too fast and hard. Nothing is censored in this country, and yet they walk around as if sealed in plastic wrap, their faces shiny, buffed masks.

The clothed man was so near that I heard him clear his throat and so I stopped, brushed sand off a log and sat on it, stretching my legs, burrowing feet deep into the warmth. I knew he would join me there, that he would be drawn to my feigned indifference.

Out in the water the sailboats veered to starboard with a gust of wind.

Many people in Vancouver had promised me trips in their boats, but none occurred. The suggestion is made, fuelled by enthusiasm and generosity, and the speaker imagines my joy and gratitude as I perch in his boat, hair tossed by breezes, and best of all he experiences his own elation for thinking of it. I am the same; I require only the concept of generosity to feel alive.

The man lowered himself onto the other end of my log. I cast a furtive glance his way, hot with self-consciousness. He wore a pair of chinos and a denim shirt with the sleeves rolled up, and no shoes or socks. Clean shaven, he was perhaps half a dozen years older than me. Tanned, sparse hair, a little chunky.

"You like to suck cock?" His voice was pitched low.

Finally, after all these months, a direct question, without layers of meaning, a pure expression of desire! Then I watched in amazement as the front of my trousers lifted. No translation required. Within seconds I'd been transformed into a man. He got up, and I felt the log sink at my end. Was it possible that I misunderstood? In that second of uncertainty I was tossed by a rogue wave of nausea. But he nodded, and I saw that I was to follow him into the ridge of bushes behind the path.

I didn't hesitate. I craved sensation, I needed to be touched by this man who had no idea who I was. I could feel myself coming to life, and each step made me bolder. His hips swayed as he strode ahead of me, clutching the sand with his feet. He kept his hands in his pockets, tugging the thin cloth of his pants tightly across his ass. I thought I heard him whistling to himself, but it could have been a bird, or wind coasting between hydro wires. A tang of seaweed caught my nostrils, and I inhaled deeply, saturated with pleasure.

He held back the branches and I walked into the cleared area inside, a boys' secret place, a tree stump to sit on, cigarette butts scattered on the sand.

The clubhouse. No girls allowed.

The man, who had a square face, betrayed no emotion as he made room for me in the shade. Above us, a distant jet clipped the sky, but we were invisible to all but the birds.

Quietly, deftly, he unzipped his trousers and pushed them over his hips.

I began to shake.

His hips were lean, and the crotch was a dark thicket, the hair much bushier and blacker than the remaining hair on his head. His cock was purple as it stood straight up, and he stroked it lightly with one hand, his knees slightly bent.

What could be more natural than for a man to take another man in his mouth? Who else would know better how to create the intense jolts of pleasure?

So I knelt in the sand, smelling his clean heat, pausing with my lips a centimetre from his cock until he moaned, "Please…"

So polite are these Canadians.

My world became the basement room of Mrs. Chin's rooming house off Granville Street. A maroon carpet coated the cement floor and there was a bed, a small table, a shelf for my few clothes and books, and the cassette player that Rita had given me.

Daniel Rose in his van had gathered my things from the house I shared with Rashid, and hauled them to this place downtown. He stared at the subterranean room and said, "It isn't so bad. God knows I stayed in much worse as a student," and then he placed a foil-covered serving dish in my arms. "Sharon made this. Some sort of casserole. She says keep the container; it's oven-proof."

And then he fled. As they all had fled.

I shared a kitchen at the end of the hall with Mrs. Chin's two nephews, who lived in another room. They spoke only Mandarin and worked in the family's grocery warehouse in Richmond. For this they wore uniforms of bright orange jumpsuits. We nodded politely, when it was necessary.

The toilet, also shared, had no tub, only a corroded shower cubicle, and a laundry line strung from one end to the other, which frequently held the dripping jockey shorts of my flatmates.

This was the gauntlet I had to pass every time I entered the building: first their cavern-like bedroom, then past the toilet with its smell of drains, then through the narrow kitchen, which was really a segment of the hallway. Everywhere the ceiling pressed in, the walls tunnelled forward, and every fart and fried onion smell lingered for days. My skin became cast with a grey pallor, and I couldn't avoid thinking that I'd been rescued from one basement cell only to land in another.

I discovered that I could slide open the window in my room and heave myself outside onto the cement walkway. So this is how I would enter and exit, nimble as a thief.

The notebook, my writer's diary, baked on the window ledge, paper curling in the humidity. I thought of it as a sort of plant, a cactus which needed months of dry sunshine and was suffering in this fetid climate.

I kept my appointment with the social worker. Mr. Benedict had white skin, thick glasses, and a chipped front tooth. He never looked me in the face, only scanned the papers in his folder which set out the sorry tale of one Carlos Romero Estévez. As he scribbled notes I watched, in fascination, the jerky movements of his pen. This was a bulky plastic concoction, with three nibs: gold, green, and blue, the colours of my national flag. At the countless state dinners I attended as eminent columnist for *La Voz*, the head table would be draped with a cloth in these patriotic colours, and each smaller table would contain a miniature flag in its centrepiece.

I was case number NC-560-1001.

If I ever forgot who I was, I could look in this olive green file and remember.

"You will receive payments while you attend ESL classes and the weekly sessions of employment counselling," Mr. Benedict told me. Then he gave a pinched smile and slid the file onto a cart with hundreds of others.

I sneaked a peek at the photo on his desk: it showed a log cabin perched near a cliff face above the sea, and I was instantly swept back to that weekend on Daniel Rose's Gulf Island with the graduate student seminar. How they'd listened to my stories with such compassion and interest! Unlike Mr. Benedict, who said with an ill-concealed yawn, "We all have a story," when I tried to explain what had brought me to his cubicle in this featureless concrete building.

I attended the intermediate level ESL class at a converted senior public school a dozen blocks from my room. Nobody in the class had white skin, not even the instructor, Miss Tanin. She was a large, cheerful Caribbean woman, dressed in a stretchy skirt and a crisp pink blouse. Her bosom was immense and a string of wooden beads rolled over her chest whenever she moved.

I found a seat near the back, folding my body into a combined chair and desk which reminded me of my old preparatory school in Santa Clara. In the math room of that institution, my father's initials could be spotted dug into the desk at the end of row ten, and I'd always been amazed by this, that my stern father had once been a restless boy with a pen knife.

Here, at the Duke of York Senior Public School, a band of fluorescent lights flickered overhead as we inhaled the familiar pong of old sandwiches.

"Good morning, class!"

"Good morning," we chorused back, grinning with embarrassment. We were to write our names with felt pen on the stickers found on each desk. I glanced around: no surnames in this room. Only Dexter, Winston, Ursula, Maria, Ling, Ashok, Beatriz...

The adult students sat shyly, binders on desks, their hands playing with loose-leaf paper. Directly in front of me was the dandruff-speckled hair of a man in a multi-coloured vest. But most of the students were female.

"Today we are shopping for food," Miss Tanin announced in a sing-song voice. "We will be reviewing numbers, names of vegetables and fruit, units of measurement, and direction comprehension." She turned her back to us and set on the ledge of the blackboard a card containing a picture of an apple.

As her arm moved, we could see the wide strap of her bra and I wondered about her sigh of relief when she returned to her home, tore off the damp blouse, and released her fleshy breasts from the elastic confines. Would she hold them in her hands, allowing them to expand into the air, to breathe after their long day of imprisonment?

"What is our first item of produce? Please use a full sentence in your response."

Obediently we opened our binders and selected a blank page. My hand moved laboriously, as if forming letters was too great a chore. It had been so long since I'd written that I had to carve out each letter individually, like a craftsman chipping names on a cemetery monument. Words may appear on wood, marble, paper, parchment, neon tubing — any surface in the world, including your own name pissed in the sand. The poet is flexible, he can write with a brick of coal on the walls of a cave. But first he must have something urgent to say. The first book that I owned was a floppy vinyl volume of a half-dozen pages, each illustrated with a common household image and the corresponding word: Apple, Car, Mother, Father, and finally, House. This special book could go in the bathtub without injury.

Many of my fellow students had brought cups of takeout coffee or other drinks. This was never permitted in the classrooms of my youth. One small-boned woman was eating spiced peanuts out of a bag, licking her fingers constantly. I smelled lime and chili and salt. And something else: cleaning fluid.

Perhaps she had come directly from pushing a mop down some endless office corridor. At home, wherever home was, she'd be directing her maid to prepare dinner.

When our teacher asked a question, we all stared at our desks.

"Come on, people, you going to hide the rest of your lives?" Miss Tanin chortled. "You'll starve to death!"

Gradually hands went up, but only from the women. The few men remained glumly silent.

"I-am-seeking-to-purchase-a-red-apple," a woman in a sari read aloud from her foolscap. Then she beamed, pleased with herself.

"Excellent!" Miss Tanin declared.

I walked out at coffee break. I do not learn a country's language in order to go shopping for groceries. You speak because you must speak, because what you are thinking is too volatile to contain. And you speak because there is a man or a woman who waits for your words.

It had been raining while we'd been trapped in the classroom and I scanned the still deserted sidewalks, trying to locate the bus stop. This area had modest wooden houses with small front yards, many of them growing vegetable gardens. Eavestroughs dripped water and the gullies sloshed with dead leaves and sticks.

"Are you enjoying the class?" It was the woman in the sari. Up close I saw she was older than I'd thought, at least forty.

"No," I said. "And I will not return."

"It is difficult for men," she informed me, tilting her head. She wore a dark bindi mark on her forehead.

"What do you mean?"

She smiled. "Because you do not like to show foolishness. My husband, too." Her thick eyebrows rose. "He is afraid."

"I am not afraid."

She turned away and inhaled the freshly watered streets and city soil.

"So you say. I must go back now and learn."

Suddenly I wanted her to linger. "Please," I said. "Why do you talk to me?"

And why did she think I was afraid? I wondered where she'd come from, what embattled corner of Asia. Did her husband lounge at home in front of the television set, locked in some depression, while she set forth into the new life?

The woman lifted her hand, decorated with many rings and bangles, and waved lightly. "I say anything that comes to my mind," she laughed before disappearing inside the school.

I almost followed her. Instead I snuck around the old brick building, passing by the windows of Miss Tanin's classroom where I hesitated and looked in. There she was, my new friend, leaning over the shoulder of another woman, this one perhaps African.

"Hurry up, people," our teacher cried above the din of scraping chairs and desks. "There is no time to lose." But she was having trouble settling them down, as if during that ten-minute break her students had found each other to be more interesting than the studies.

Returning home, I sat on my bed and punched "play" on the cassette machine and listened to Neil Young sing of the harvest moon. Both machine and tapes were from Rita so every song I heard in my room had once been chosen by her. I wondered if she missed them.

It's not as if I didn't have plenty to do. It is a good thing to have regular exercise, and so each morning I would roam the streets of Chinatown and buy one of those steamed buns full of barbecued meat, and continue further west to Gastown where I would sit on a bench and watch the tourist families in their T-shirts decorated with slogans. I liked the fact that I was losing weight. I was becoming a gaunt man with a haunted look. One day I snatched a look at myself in the drugstore mirror and it was a shock — not to discover that my skin had grown pale and without lustre and my lips were dry from a lack of crucial vitamins — this was not what caused me to gasp. The face that stared at me under the merciless fluorescent lights was A's face, as I'd seen him in that concrete bunker, the interrogation room at the Santa Clara jail. We could have been brothers! I grabbed my thatch of hair and vowed to cut it all off, shave my skull so that the shape of my head was undisguised, authentic. I had the idea of walking so lightly across the ground that no one would ever hear.

18

THE BARBER SAID, "BEAN SHAVE, EH?" AND I told him, "Yes, make me look like a bean."

I thought of those blanched garbanzo beans, which turn up in every soup back home, and I sank my head into the care of his precise hands. The scissors clipped for many minutes and then he drew a razor across the freshly exposed skin. A splash of something citric made me gasp.

Leaving the shop I ran my hand over my slick wounded scalp and it was as if it wasn't my head at all. So tender, the brain pulsing just beneath the flap of skin. I thought of the line of lice marching across A's skull when I stood behind him, and how he didn't seem to notice or feel their small feet.

That night I tried to write. Blowing dust off the notebook was the easy part. I crouched on my bed, pen in hand, and began to move my hand over the seamed pages, but my brain had become too quiet. There was no clamour in there which demanded expression: this was the still mind that spiritualists seek, spending years in isolated caves. What I felt was a sort of tarpaulin spread over my nerves, a heaviness that was not unwelcome.

I was an unintentional monk, living my simple existence. Yet still, memory lurked in the shadows, ready to ambush any time I let down my guard. I would have to become entirely disciplined, learn to bite off each image at the neck, no past, no future, and, with perseverance, no present. It was so easy to be transformed by memory, to be whisked away to another place and time, to become again a dreamy, self-centred child perched on a pillow at the long oak dining table, sucking lemonade out of a mottled glass.

I hung an orange "danger" sign in my mind, like you see on the highway warning of rough road ahead. Every thought must pass by this sign before it was allowed in. Sentimental memories were cut off immediately, without a hint of compassion.

It was meaningless to remember that for years I had appeared every Tuesday and Thursday in the finest newspaper in Santa Clara. Pointless to fret over who might have taken my place: that rat's ass Gómez with his oversized teeth and slicked-down hair who was always chewing around the desk of the managing editor. The idea made me sick. Equally foolish was to remember pressing lips to the nicked coffee cup at Café de la Luna for the first luxurious sip of the day while street sweepers bid a cheery "Buenas días."

I told Mr. Benedict, my case worker, that ESL classes were going very well, that I was becoming an accomplished food shopper and soon would learn to go to the dentist and ask for the strongest possible anesthetic. He popped his red nib and underlined something in my file. I made my rounds most days:

a trip to the smoke shop on Cambie, stop for coffee at Donut World, and sometimes, if the weather was good, I'd cross the Burrard Street bridge early in the morning on foot and stop at the mid-point, smoking and watching the city awaken.

I took a bus to Kitsilano because I wanted to see the students parade down the streets, the boys in their oversized jeans, the girls in scouting shorts and tight tops. They rollerbladed or skateboarded into juice bars and ordered up healthful concoctions from the row of whirring blenders, then sped down the sidewalk sucking wheatgrass from plastic cups. From a distance I spotted Daniel Rose striding between two Amazonian girls, sweating from the effort of keeping up to their long-legged gait. His lips moved non-stop, engaged in some persuasive lecture.

On the way home the bus was nearly empty. A man got on at MacDonald, heaving himself up the steps while he grabbed the railing. He was stout, middle-aged, and dressed in a shabby suit and a felt hat. After fumbling for his transit ticket, he plunked himself down with a wheeze onto the seat directly ahead of mine and twisted his legs so he was facing the aisle.

"You live around here?" he asked with his chipmunk face.

"Not too near," I said politely.

"What's your name?"

I told him. But I was nervous: who was this man and why had he sat here? I sensed the driver, a woman with a ponytail, was leaning back on her webbed seat to listen.

"My name is Charles," he said. "I live just over the bridge." His eyes flitted over mine. His skin was mottled purple yet his teeth were perfect. "Will you come back to my place for awhile?" This was spoken not in a whisper but in an ordinary conversational tone.

My polite smile froze. The driver slowed for the next stop, yanking the shift as she manoeuvred into the right lane. The man drummed his knees and waited for my answer.

I panicked. "Excuse me," I muttered, and the moment the bus stopped I raced out the exit, darting looks backward to see if he'd followed.

Through the tinted window I watched him raise his hand in a wave and realized I was breathing heavily, as if I'd just escaped from some terrible fate. This was nothing like being approached by one of the men at the beach, where the mood was celebratory and purposeful. There we were Adonises, escapees from the tedium of convention. This encounter was entirely different, tainted with despair and loneliness. What had Charles seen when he spotted me?

I stood in the sun and realized I had no money in my pocket, no way of returning to my basement room but to walk. It would take at least an hour. I could have told him a simple "no" rather than scurry out of the bus as if I were guilty of a crime. The city sloped towards the ocean and I began to follow its long tilt into the heart of downtown. I would stop in the art gallery and use their washroom, splash cold water over my face and chest. My life measured itself out in pit stops, like some nomad traversing a desert.

One afternoon I received a message from Rita. It was the first contact from CAFE since moving day and it came in the form of a pink Post-it note stuck to my door by my landlady, Mrs. Chin, who owned the only telephone in the house.

Lunch, Grad Centre, Tuesday — Rita, the note said, written out in Mrs. Chin's careful hand.

Tuesday was tomorrow, according to my radio announcer who added that it was also the birthday of an important historical figure, a Polish nun who had saved many children from the holocaust. Lunch less than twenty-four hours away! I had not anticipated this and I confess that I was so excited I couldn't sleep. The cellar rat who didn't speak to anyone for days on end, who existed on shrimp-flavoured ramen noodles, who fought to forget everything, was being snapped back into life.

Rita had been thinking of me. I had not disappeared from the world. I still had my friend, an important contact at the university. She was, no doubt, feeling that my situation was not the best and that I must come back to my office at UBC, which was above ground and healthy.

I would even happily return to that cramped house with Rashid, and endure without complaint the squeak of his stationary bicycle and his eye-watering curry smells. The thought made me buoyant, and like a fool, I forgot my pledge to eliminate all images of past and future.

I would become again the Poet-in-Exile with my faculty membership and library card, the running tab at the student pub, my professor friends and confidantes.

In the morning, after not sleeping a minute, I rolled out of bed to the familiar wheaty smell of Red River cereal, which the Chin brothers boiled at dawn each day. I showered, shaved, and dressed carefully, wishing I'd had time to launder my shirt. My hair had grown in a quarter-inch, filling in a shadowy "V" to my forehead and again I thought of A and his dull voice when he dictated to me his ridiculous story in the Santa Clara jail. We all do what we must to be set free. I smeared Vaseline on my ragged lips until they shone.

For the first time in weeks, I felt a surge of my old energy and optimism. A man's life, after all, was not a straight line. I was a warrior hiding out in the forest, subsisting on berries and grubs, waiting to be summoned again for the noble war. Soon I would be invited once more to parties in large houses crammed full of intellectuals and high-placed businessmen. Cold beer would be pressed into my waiting hands, beautiful women would smile with that heady mixture of sympathy and passion, and all of them would yearn to hear my story.

I arrived at the Graduate Centre fifteen minutes early and waited in the lounge with its neat stacks of newspapers and magazines. A giant urn of coffee stood on a table, surrounded by mugs and a small printed sign: Help Yourself. I didn't touch the thing, knowing that my anxious hands would send coffee spraying all over. It was a beautiful room, decorated with prints of totem poles and Aboriginal folklore.

An African student sprawled at a table in the corner, studying. Long corkscrew braids spread over his peacock blue shirt, his black skin glowed with health. He chewed on the tip of a ballpoint pen, brow furrowed as he pored over his chemistry text, legs jiggling in oversized jeans. When he looked up and saw me grinning like an idiot, he smiled back.

Light streamed in from three sides of the modern building and my eyes burned from the unaccustomed sun. Delicate retinal tissue sizzled, and I could hardly contain my excitement. Self-pity vamoosed, and I wondered how it had all happened, those dank underground weeks, and worse, my troglodyte psyche. Somewhere outside a machine was cutting grass, and inside, the black man hummed to himself as he worked at his chemistry. Inside and outside should always be a porous membrane; this was a poem, this was the world waking up to itself.

"Your hair!" Rita strode into the lounge, her gauzy skirt billowing behind her.

I rose to my feet.

"And you've lost so much weight." She gave me two feathery kisses, one on each cheek.

I thought of my diet of crinkly noodles and steamed buns, the way MSG makes your teeth sing. A monk should subsist happily on thin gruel, but frankly, I was bored with such dour asceticism. It didn't suit my nature.

She looked me up and down. "Let's have lunch," she said, then made a theatrical gesture towards the staircase that led downstairs to the cafeteria.

I felt a pang of disappointment. Upstairs was the smaller dining room, where one may eat at round tables with vases of fresh flowers and where there are menus and young servers who seek to please.

I followed Rita, padding down the stairway, sliding my hand along the banister as her heels clipped the worn broadloom. The smell of meat and overcooked vegetables and gravy greeted our arrival and the racket of spilled cutlery was a familiar music. I had eaten many times before in this cafeteria with its serious students who had come from all over the globe to become engineers and doctors. Many sat alone flipping pages of texts, rapidly making notes between bites of Country Stew or Pasta of the Day.

We grabbed trays, still warm from the dryer, and skimmed them along the metal rack. Rita knew everyone and exchanged greetings with the boy ladling potato salad from a bucket and the student who was fastening the top of a green garbage bag.

She slid a salad and orange juice off the glass shelf, without thinking, as if this were an act she performed every day, which, I suppose, she did.

"Anything you want." She smiled at me, reaching for her staff credit card in her purse.

The student server was waiting with spatula in hand, the tubs of lasagna and stew steaming into her dark face. I wondered if she was from one of those small islands overrun with tourists, and what she was studying here: astrophysics? If Canada is a stew of nationalities then my country is a creamy pudding: simple, classic, yet undeniably rich.

Rita nibbled on a carrot stick, waiting for me to make up my mind. Suddenly I was ashamed of my appetite. An important man does not eat like a peasant, heaping piles of potato and meat and bread. I thought of the governor glaring into the ladle that I proffered, the cockscomb floating insolently in the state-ordered soup. His long careful slurp was an act of public relations. In this country, to demonstrate power, you must understand that food is merely necessary fuel, and pleasure comes in forgoing temptation and pleasure.

Reluctantly, I tipped a chicken sandwich onto my tray, hoping that Rita would protest, urge me to take more, but she had already slipped along to the cash register, and I knew that my gesture was lost, that what I had done was so normal in her world that it was invisible.

We settled into a table by the window. The gardens beyond the glass spread lushly towards the cliff, great beds of red and white impatiens surrounded by grass so green it looked like an architect's rendering.

"How have you been doing, Carlos?" She'd peeled the wrapping off her salad and was squeezing dressing out of a tiny envelope. I waited to see if she would look at me, but she was too intent on her small activity. Rita's neck was long and thin, ringed with white lines where the sun had missed, and her hair had grown again since I'd last seen her. At one time I would have reached over and touched the silky nest where it met her shoulders.

How have I been doing? That, my friend, was a complicated question. Should I tell her of the hemorrhoids that made me weep when I shit?

"I am very well." My hands fumbled with the sticky plastic wrap, trying to liberate my chicken sandwich.

"I confess that surprises me, Carlos."

My hands stopped moving and I dreaded what might come next. I did not want to hear that I was unwell, that I had not flourished in my independent life.

"Your son and you are happy?" I asked politely.

Her lips tightened. "Andreas is still interested in reptiles and amphibians." When I smiled and nodded, she took a deep breath, "I'm not going to beat around the bush, Carlos. We've been hearing some disturbing news about you."

We? CAFE, of course. This was a voice that belonged to someone else, the emissary, not Rita the artist, Rita the mother. Or Rita my one-time lover.

"You haven't been showing up for ESL class, for starters."

That was all? I laughed, and finally succeeded in releasing my sandwich, which was icy, the bread half-frozen.

"The classes are not intelligent," I told her. "The teacher had no understanding."

"No understanding of what, Carlos?"

"Language or ideas or how we must speak to each other." I hesitated. "And the class was full of ladies."

"I would think you'd love that."

I must be very patient, I told myself, but I was sweating and I felt myself shrinking inside my clothes, like an old man.

"This teacher, she only talks of shopping." I waited for her to laugh, but Rita did not laugh.

"And I am not interested in shopping." Now do you see, my eyes pleaded.

She finally spoke very slowly, underlining each word, as if I were deaf or an idiot.

"The classes are a prerequisite to receiving social assistance. They have informed us that they will cut you off, Carlos. That means no money."

Mr. Benedict had warned me of this in his brittle voice, but what are they going to do, let me starve?

"No money, Carlos, and CAFE cannot bail you out. Do you understand?"

A fetid smell rose from the floor and I realized it was my sneakered feet. Mortified, I pushed them far under the table.

"How do you expect to get a decent job without a better command of the language? Do you want to be sloshing a mop around some hospital hallway? We want to help, Carlos, but you make it so hard."

This was what Sharon had confided in me that long-ago night in the magical cabin: "You make it so hard for yourself, Carlos."

I could have become angry or indignant, but I realized that it was not my friend's voice that I heard, it was the official tone of CAFE that she was designated to deliver. This was not the Rita who had buried her face in my shoulder when she returned from seeing her ex-husband, nor was it the Rita who once slowly unbuttoned her cardigan sweater as I watched, and guided my hand to her pale skin.

"I have a job," I said, mimicking her slow speech. "I am a poet, a writer."

This provoked an exasperated sigh."You still don't get it, do you, Carlos? You refuse to accept the reality of life here."

I had to laugh. "Reality? Let me tell you something which is reality."

She leaned back in her chair, pushing hair away from her face. Finally a gesture that I recognized.

"Do you want to know who I really am?" The intensity in my voice alarmed even me.

This dancer, so natural in her grace, had dropped her lean arms to her sides, vaccination mark gleaming. All around us graduate students were chattering in accented English while maids cleared the tables of plates and cutlery. Only here you do not say maid. You say "bus person" or "wait staff."

You do not say poet. You say hospital cleaner.

"I am not the man you think I am." My face was burning, yet I didn't care.

"Please, Carlos —"

"Listen to me." I leaned forward, and in response she flattened against the back of her chair. "I cannot be what you are wanting. I cannot be —"

"Carlos, please." Freckles seemed to spread across her nose, beckoned by the sunlight that stole into this underground restaurant. "My own life is hard. What more do you need from me?"

We stared at each other. So, this was it, two injured people clogged by their own misery. Instead of making me feel less alone, I felt sideswiped by sadness, not only mine now, but hers.

"How have we come to this?" she said after a moment.

I could only shake my head. The look on her face was not one of compassion, but pity, and something else had crept in: boredom. She'd heard my stories a dozen times, felt sympathy once for my heroic excursions into the barrio, but now she had re-entered her own life. The gap had closed.

When Rita excused herself to go to the toilet, I scooped up several sugar packets and a shiny envelope of mustard and slipped them into my pocket. I would no longer invade her life with my disturbing presence.

19

I WOULD BECOME THE MOST DISCIPLINED MAN in the world. By shutting down my own mind, that quarrelsome kennel of yelping mutts, I would shut down memory. And without memory, there is no regret.

My basement room in Mrs. Chin's house was the perfect place to practise this art: I could live in absolute simplicity with the maroon carpet, bamboo blinds, the cot with its thin mattress, and the poster of the Great Wall of China above my bed.

Nothing from my earlier life must be allowed to infect this haven. No smells that might remind me of the panadería on Avenida Raúl de Madeira would enter my nostrils. If this meant crossing the street to avoid the bakery on the corner, then I would take the extra steps. I would enter no café, avoid gas stations with their magnificent stench of spilled gasoline and diesel fuel, and I would avoid, especially, women.

The trick was not to become lost in some reverie of Santa Clara, anticipating the sound of a friend's greeting or our maid's aimless chatter. Once such a dream swam past the barricades, I was lost. For example, there was a certain sewer opening near the store where I bought my noodles whose odoriferous vent was so reminiscent of the night air near my family's home that I held my breath while passing.

Maestro Neruda, so beloved by romantic temperaments, writes of the poor exile: "We breathe air through a wound." That is when we remember to breathe at all.

Memory is stereophonic: it engorges both sides of the head. When this happened I would stop immediately, wherever I was, press my fingers to my temples, breathe deeply and count, uno, dos, tres, until my brain went blank. After this had happened several times in the street, I decided it was safer to stay in my room.

I also discovered that abstract counting was less successful than the numbering of actual things. Instead of being irritated by the line of ants that marched down my window ledge and scurried along the baseboard to the door, I was elated. On my knees I watched them for hours, choosing a set point on the floor to count them off, as if they were Olympic sprinters. Later, I lay on my cot and stared at the white tiles on the ceiling, each one pitted with tiny perforations, so many I counted them over and over, never achieving the same result twice.

The loose fibres of the maroon rug wove in and out of a lucid pattern of circles, and first I counted the circles, then the fibres themselves, an exhausting process that took days. When I was done, I fell asleep for eighteen hours and fourteen minutes.

Awakening, I panicked, for my eyes couldn't focus properly. The holes in the ceiling tiles blurred into a swatch of grey. Worst of all, I felt my entire past crowd in, a million stories clamouring to be heard. Then I heard it, the distinct dit-dit of a tap dripping. The brothers down the hall had neglected to crank the kitchen faucet shut.

Filled with ecstasy and relief, I fell back onto my bed.

… tres, cuatro, cinco, seis, seite, ocho …

The dripping tap would last as long as the reservoirs of Vancouver collected rainwater.

I chanted the numbers, sang them for variety, and it took several seconds to realize that another sound had intruded, a fugue-like accompaniment to the tapping faucet.

Someone was knocking at my door.

Astonished, I rolled off the bed, crossed the room in two steps, and unlatched it.

My landlady, Mrs. Chin, stood surrounded by a dim glow from the underpowered hall light.

"Is second day of month," she said. "Where is money?"

I stared, uncomprehending. For days I'd lived inside my counting, and this strange utterance came from another universe.

"You give cash." Mrs. Chin rubbed her fingers and thumb together, that universal symbol. "Today," she added for good measure.

I then realized that no welfare cheque had arrived. I must have been cut off, just as they'd warned me.

So I had no money, no food, and soon, no place to live.

I smiled at Mrs. Chin, thinking how much prettier she'd look if she let her hair grow, and I calmly buttoned my shirt. A strange euphoria had seized hold of me. Let's see what corner of the world would cast its net. I would become a wandering monk, launched into the streets with nothing but his begging bowl.

Emerging from my basement room, I was chased by an insistent Mrs. Chin. "You come with money. Four hundred dollar! You come back soon or I take other tenant — pensioner!"

I hatched a plan. In my travels around the city, I had watched people of all ages play musical instruments on street corners to collect money. A girl often stood in front of the Scotiabank with her cello case laid out, digging into the strings of her instrument with her bow, creating music amongst the shrieking traffic.

I would recite my poems in Spanish and they would pay, as they should, for this small moment of cultural aggression.

20

SHE SPOTTED ME, AS I KNEW SHE would. I was leaning
against the outside wall of the department store declaiming
my poems while pedestrians buzzed by. Some dropped a dollar
coin in my straw hat. Most didn't bother. I didn't shout; I wasn't
a crazy person. Last week a girl with a fiddle had been playing
here, Celtic dance tunes with her open case drizzling coins.
There is not so much interest in this city for poetry. At times I
would be offered jobs. Usually this came from middle-aged
women, who would stop and listen, then say, "My lawn needs
mowing." Or windows needed washing, eavestroughs required
leaves to be dislodged. There was no end to these domestic tasks.
But I always refused because I wanted to be here on this street
corner when Rita, inevitably, walked by.

She would see what her exile had become. This was the man
who had stood on the great stages in this city and recited his

poems to the most important people in business and cultural circles. For months money had been raised to bring me here, to help me escape the dire circumstances of my life.

Now I recited before the window of mannequins dressed in summer sportswear. Molded plastic men and women who wore sharply geometric dresses, deliberately frayed shorts and painted-on haircuts were my most avid audience. At lunch hour the sidewalks filled with workers dashing to the bank and restaurants, with their faces buried in pita bread sandwiches, a passing smell of fried onions so tempting I nearly snatched the food out of their hands. Cell phones rang inane sequences and for awhile the sound of chatter was even louder than the traffic noise. Everyone knew everyone. It was a city of friends and colleagues.

She was alone, carrying a small canvas shopping bag. She spotted me from several metres away, and for a moment she hesitated. Perhaps she was thinking of making her escape. I continued my recitation, raising my voice just a little. Rita would not flee, she was too curious a woman, and behind her nervousness she knew that we had a link that went back many months to the moment she first set eyes on me in the airport. I was not what she expected then. It was the guilt of that first disappointment that pursued her even now.

"Carlos, is that you?" She set her bag down on the sidewalk.

"I hope you remember me."

"I tried to call," she said, "but Mrs. Chin said you were gone."

"It is true. I am gone."

"Where are you staying?"

For eleven nights I had been bunking at the men's hostel established by the Salvation Army, hot meal at breakfast, the smell of dirty feet, but I did not tell her this. Instead I waited a beat, then smiled. "I am nowhere: I am a free man."

A woman with a phone pressed to her ear marched between us, trailing heavy floral perfume. A police cruiser wailed by, threading in and out of the stopped cars.

"You look terrible," she said above the noise, and I could see that she had made a decision. "Come with me, Carlos."

I thought that she was going to lead me to a coffee shop where I would be fed something nutritious and quizzed on the progress of my existence. I picked up my straw hat, tipped its few coins into my pocket, and followed as she crossed through traffic, heading east.

"Your hair's grown back," she said as we deked up a side street. "I like it."

The lunch restaurants were gearing down, waitresses swabbing down the tables, pushing chairs aside to sweep up crumbs. Yet we paused in front of none of these and it was clear that Rita had somewhere specific in mind.

"Where are we going?" I said at last, as she turned onto a residential street in the heart of Chinatown, only a few blocks from my old room in the basement. The honking sounds were abruptly muffled and the murk of exhaust fumes disappeared. Now we could hear our own footsteps on the concrete walk, Rita skittering just ahead of me. She didn't answer my question at first and I was breathless from this athletic march. Embarrassed by my wheezing, I made an effort to mask it with small coughs and throat clearings. The houses were small with front yard gardens where speckled melons nestled amongst the wide leaves. It was very good to be self-sufficient. I resolved that if I were to live again in a house of my own, I would grow food and never worry about hunger again.

Rita stopped in front of a tiny two-storey stucco house with no vegetables in the yard, only wild roses crawling up a trellis.

"Home," she said, and gave me a quick look. "Just long enough to get you cleaned up and fed."

"But this is not your apartment."

"You're not the only one whose life changes. Andreas and I moved a couple weeks ago." She searched for her keys and pushed the front door open. "I'm afraid it's a terrible mess."

When she'd dropped her bag she followed my gaze from the small front room down to the back of the house, a distance of perhaps thirty feet. The hallway was filled with boxes, each labeled carefully: kitchen, bathroom, bedroom, etc.

"My aunt died. At first I was so excited. I mean, a house in downtown Vancouver. I'd never be able to afford one." Her voice sounded tentative, almost girlish. "What do you think?"

The plaster on the walls was cracked right to the ceiling. Tiles were missing from the linoleum and there were patches of wall which had fallen away, exposing wires. Yet Rita's familiar furniture filled the space, in exactly the same configurations as in her apartment. The boy's foam blocks spilled from a plastic box in the centre of the floor.

What did I think? I recognized her tone: a woman who is seeking help suddenly defers to the man's innate nature. He will miraculously produce a hammer, a box of nails, a plan. A distinct smell of mouse permeated the place.

I knocked on the wall that ran down the length of the house, cutting its small width into rooms and hallway. "You must demolish this, make everything big, open, breathing."

"It's a load-bearing wall, that's what the last guy said."

I snorted, then tapped with my knuckles and heard the hollow sound. "It is not difficult."

"It's not?"

The boy had grown. His head was now in perfect proportion to his small body, and he wore a pair of faded bib overalls and red sneakers.

"I remember you." He didn't sound pleased.

"And I remember you."

He hopped alongside his mother as she fetched plates and spread them on the dining table, and he carried the wooden chopsticks, a pair for each of us, and laid them at our places. And so we were suddenly a family, diving into the cardboard boxes of steaming rice and chicken and noodles. A chunk of plaster dropped onto the floor beside us, spitting dust.

"I guess you could stay in the spare bedroom," Rita said. "For a few days."

I tore down the wall when she was at work and the boy was at nursery school. Dust entered every orifice of my body so that I thought my blood would become clogged with it. When I spat, the mucous was grey. When I blew my nose it was the same sludge. My new hair was an eager nest for it, until I learned to wear a bandanna, but the room, even with the bits of plaster still clinging to the old outline, was wide and stunning and filled with unblocked sun.

When she came home she gasped, "It's brilliant!" then quickly frowned. "The ceiling is starting to dip."

"This is normal. It will settle very soon." I imitated the confident voice of my rancher uncle.

Yet doubt had crossed her face, a shadow which grew deeper and more complex as she swept up, filling plastic bags with rubble and dust. The boy fell into an overstuffed chair, thumb planted between his lips, and stared at his favourite cartoon on the television.

"I hope you know what you are doing."

The house seemed frail, but I didn't tell her that. Perhaps it was used to the old auntie tiptoeing around in her soft slippers. The bounding leaps of a small boy as he took the stairs two at a time made it shudder to the core. When a toilet was flushed, the water rose to the lip of the bowl and hovered there, unsure of its next move.

"Do you think he will always be sad?" Rita stared at her son as he listlessly flipped the pages of his rabbit book.

I reached out with my toe and tickled the boy's belly and he pulled away, his face stony. His father left more than a year ago and he would not be appeased. Months of living up my own asshole made me as sensitive as a newborn. If I could pull down a wall I could break through this small boy's reserve. So I sank onto the floor with Andreas and together we upended the box of tiny army figures. For a moment his sadness fell away as we arranged the men into strategic formations. Miniature Crimean warriors overwhelmed British paratroopers from a century later. We used the rubble from the renovations to create fortresses and battlefields.

When I drew myself back to the land of adults, rising, after a bolt of dizziness, to my feet, the boy scowled. He began to kick at the cuffs of my pants, at first with a sense of mischief, bicycling his legs in the air, and I was a good sport, gently thwacking him back while his mother watched.

When you are a guest there is a question that lurks around every corner, infesting every pleasurable moment: how long will you be permitted to stay? I would never ask directly, for such a question demands an answer. Each day without the dreaded conversation was a triumph. Soon there were seven such days.

"Are you still writing?" Rita said one morning.

"I am always writing," I lied. She was leaving for work and had dropped twenty dollars on the table for me to buy groceries for dinner. I was to pick up the boy from his nursery school promptly at 3:15, a job formerly designated to a woman down the street. Just last night Rita had confessed, "it's a relief to have two adults in the house." I didn't dare respond. She was in the midst of listening to her own mind.

I slept on a pull-out couch in the spare bedroom upstairs. The house was constructed as a simple box with stairs running up the side, zigzagging once to reach the second storey. One of the three small bedrooms was still full of the aunt's sewing things, an old-fashioned Singer treadle machine, and bolts of cloth. Indian wicker baskets were loaded with buttons and spools of thread, and a dressmaker's dummy leaned in the corner, headless and naked, its torso marked out in white stitches. This is the room where I slept. An old lady smell issued from the floral wallpaper, not unpleasant, reminding me of my own aunties, well-upholstered women, a trio of sisters sheathed in widows' black although none had ever married. Perhaps they mourned their own claustrophobic lives. There was even a sink in the corner by the sewing machine cabinet, and its faucets, when pried open, produced a brackish water. I could live entirely in this room, if I wished, when Rita and her son grew tired of me. I could piss in the sink, wash, shave, and gaze out the window into the patchwork of tiny backyards below, each a sculpted masterpiece of cement squares and foliage. Women in baseball caps stooped over the gardens in the late afternoon, plucking vegetables for dinner.

Everything in a house leads to another like an infinitely complicated knot: the light bulb is screwed to the lamp, the lamp is fixed to a wire, the wire leads to a socket, the socket is attached to the wall, and inside the wall is a tangle of wires and plumbing and heating ducts. It is a pulsing organism and I was a surgeon diving in with fearless hands. The torn-away wall had revealed a rodent's nest containing artifacts from the past, shredded paper and bits of wool and string, all carefully bound together. These creatures had no need of money or paid labour; they were foragers, hunters and gatherers, like our own ancestors, and in this lay their freedom.

I left the nest inside the wall, its droppings petrified by now, the ghosts of the builders released.

Rita rose early, bathed and applied makeup, dressed in sleek suits and drove out to the university to enter her tedious job.

"Why do you do it?" I asked.

She looked at me fiercely. "Money doesn't grow on trees."

In the evenings, if she wasn't too tired or dispirited, Rita would unroll the yoga mat and perform her stretches, letting out long relieved exhalations of breath while her son and I watched television.

The rodents' nest made me into a writer again. I dissected the nest carefully, using a screwdriver to gently pry it apart, and discovered, woven inside, a much-gnawed wooden toggle button and a child's toothbrush. Between its bristles were slivers of human toenails.

There are poets who try to contain the entire world in a poem. Others seek to frame tiny moments and cause a surge of revelation, but always it is the presence of the unexpected that thrills. Those chips of human nails, convex, yellowed, and encrusted with ancient toe crud trapped in the child's toothbrush were an authentic poem. Memory, craft, and heart, hidden all these years. These mice had no need of the applauding audience. They selected the objects they needed, and under the cover of night created their masterpiece.

I began by tearing a page out of *Insomnio*, and stuck it behind one of the battens. But this was not good enough. I would write something new, and hide it inside the walls, a gesture of liberation, like tossing a bottle into the ocean. It was the first time I was excited by imagining a home for my poetry. The scribbled words were just an excuse for the final implantation. So intent was I that it was nearly three o'clock when I realized that Andreas would soon be waiting for me at his school.

How long it had been since I'd hurried for anyone! As I raced out of the house, dressed in one of Rita's oversized shirts with my jeans, I liked the way I looked, a man who is expected, a man whose presence is required.

I collected Andreas at his playschool where everything was miniature. I loved to fetch him in the bright room with its low tables and tiny chairs, and the damp smell of Play-Doh and poster paints, a place for everything, the children trotting around like monks in a cloister, with long painting robes tied at the back. It was the earnest diligence of Canadian children that I watched as they replaced each puzzle and plastic tool in its proper shelf.

"What is this called?" The teacher, Miss Miller, held up a picture of New York City. Her finger pointed to the tall building, the very symbol of this noble skyline. Hands tossed into the air.

"Andreas, do you know?"

I clenched my fists until his solemn, confident voice answered, "The Umpire State Building!"

The day's artwork was being rolled up, bits of cotton fluff untacking from the construction paper.

"Tell Daddy it's your turn to bring snack on Tuesday," Miss Miller said, and she was speaking to Andreas, but nodding in my direction. I crested with pride and scooped the boy up before he could protest.

I, who have never cooked, became a chef. Mostly there were Asian people in this district so we got by in the market with gesticulations. The old men in the barbeque shops with their wispy beards and spattered aprons raised ancient cleavers and hacked off chunks of pig meat. The wooden carving block sagged in the middle like an old mattress, far from its beginning as one of the noble fir trees stalking the coastline. Chinese pop music blared out of a stereo.

Rita stared at her plate with the meat and bread. "Ever heard of scurvy, Carlos?"

On Friday evening she drove the boy with his Flintstones rucksack across the city to Jane's townhouse. This was where Peter lived with his girlfriend, Jane, a woman whom Rita described as being "terminally nice." She returned, face pale, and sat in the darkness of the middle room with a glass of wine, staring at the flickering television.

This was a familiar posture. When Father left each Wednesday evening to make love to his mistress, my mother sat gravely in the dark and waited for his return, drinking and playing her wretched piano. Rita aimed the remote and punched buttons because every show bored her. Instead of the marching piano keys I listened to hysterical laugh tracks of a dozen comedies. I stood at the door, frightened by her loneliness. As a child I had huddled under my quilt and prayed for my father's return.

In the morning Rita was bravely normal, covering her naked body with a towel as she emerged from the bathroom and made her way down the hallway. I was on the way to the toilet, wearing only shorts. I smelled strawberry shampoo and saw the wet footprints on the dusty linoleum floor. With her wet hair combed back she looked so young, like an adolescent girl. I flattened myself against the corridor wall, so that she might pass without touching.

She laughed, poked me in the chest with her finger, and said, "Good morning!"

I had set up a corner of the dining table with my writing things and this excited her.

"What are you working on?"

"Erotic poems."

She flushed, but merely said, "Lucky you."

I sat at the table in the middle of the front room, the newly demolished wall now swept up so that I was surrounded by open space. Outside the window, children paraded up and down the street on bicycles and scooters, and the adult voices that blew through the opened pane spoke a high-pitched Cantonese that in no way disturbed my thinking. I didn't use a typewriter or computer, only my own hand and the hardcover notebook that Rita had bought me so long ago. I liked imagining her at the office, her confident well-modulated voice making arrangements as her sheathed legs crossed with a whisking sound. I wrote line after line in that room, and because of the heat I was clad only in a pair of army shorts. I could feel my hard-on press against the metal zipper, which felt like teeth, anyone's teeth. Later I would roam the streets in search of supper materials, the bulge in my pants not embarrassing, but a signal that I was alive.

"Quit looking at me." Rita smacked at the air, as if my looking were a bothersome insect.

"You think it is strange that I want to watch an attractive woman?"

"I feel self-conscious."

So I backed off, just a little.

Each day I waited for her return. After collecting the boy from school, I slipped the meat in the oven, pushed my writing tools to one side, and laid out plates and forks and knives. If she was late I became anxious. What mood would she be in when she finally strode through the doorway? Perhaps she would go directly to the shower, peel off her clothes, and scrub away the frustrations of the day. Twenty minutes later she would emerge, pink-faced and refreshed, and I will have poured a glass of chilled wine, calculating the precise moment when her hand would reach for it.

We were both dancers now, enacting a daily pas de deux, and even when she was gone, I stayed in it, shifting my weight to contain her absence.

"Don't stare, Carlos. It's unnerving."

My mother, a stately woman who wore her hair tied into a bun, was called Puga. She dressed in teal-coloured silks and linen, never black, as her own widowed mother had worn after the death of her husband, an engineer on the Panama Canal.

I saw her naked once, that I remember, but only for a second. I was twelve years old, wandering into the bathroom as she was rising from the tub, her dark hair wet and trailing past her shoulders. My shock was at how massive she was, flesh spilling all over, breasts and belly and hips, and I retreated hastily, blushing to the sound of her soft laugh. A few days later I pushed against the door again, forgetting to knock, and something prevented my entrance. A latch had been fastened.

"Who's there?" she called out.

I hastened away without replying, grateful I'd been stopped, but also uneasy. What must I be stopped from seeing?

Rita showered with her son, snuggled in bed with him, his tousled head set between her breasts. I ached with jealousy, but was never sure: did I want to be the young boy, or did I want to be myself as a man pressed against her?

This is not my house.

This is not my house.

I have crumpled up my poems and pressed them deep into the hollows and covered them with drywall and that is my body in there, my dripping, stiff body, the hidden juices of a man who must never misbehave.

The boy's skin is so smooth and his breath so pure, yet I am not permitted to caress him as a father would. He tells me to "bug off." Each time I reach for his hand, he flinches. He feels my sentimental need for intimacy and it disgusts him.

I think again of my mother, deserted by her philandering husband, tiptoeing down the hallway to my bedroom, so full of her own yearning and theatrical tragedy. And how I would huddle under the quilt in dread of her approach, because I knew it was not really me that she was seeking.

I thought of my life in the men's shelter where I'd gone after being kicked out of Mrs. Chin's basement, where phlegmy geezers would stick their hands in your pocket to fondle your prick.

It was evening, and I'd been at Rita's house for nearly ten days in this strange state of constant arousal and formal politeness. Never had I touched her. I was the model guest, handy with meals and child care, hammering nails when needed, then climbing onto my own bed behind the closed door. There, alone, I would slide my hand between my legs and after a single stroke, moan in such a low tone that no one was disturbed.

This evening seemed like any other. She had just put Andreas to bed, after one of those awkward moments that infected our life together.

"Say good night to Carlos."

"Why?"

Her voice, very patient, "Didn't he play with you for a long time, and pick you up from school, and make you a snack?"

This list of achievements only made the boy more suspicious. He stood in his striped pajamas, tousled hair, wearing the most sullen look available to mankind.

"I don't want to say good night."

"Please," I said, "let him go."

After reading to him, Rita joined me on the couch downstairs, her face troubled, and she drew her legs up, pressing the material of her robe into a tent. "He doesn't want to go to his dad's this weekend. I wonder why."

"He is afraid," I said.

"Of what?"

I lounged next to her wearing only jeans unbuttoned at the waist, my bare chest glistening with sweat. At night I was always so tired, muscles aching from hunching over my notebook for hours, eyes smarting from the dust, which never seemed to disappear.

"He doesn't want to leave us alone together."

"But that's ridiculous!" Her hand reached for the neck of her robe.

"Is it?"

My legs sprawled, heels digging into the floor, and the bump in my jeans was so obvious that she couldn't pretend not to see.

She opened her mouth to speak, then didn't, for her eyes had begun to coast down the length of my body, a silken cloth rippling against skin.

Still I would not touch her. I would wait, as I had waited for so long. I tilted my head back and let my hands remain at my sides. She unhinged her legs then stretched one out, the blue and white patterned gown slipping off so that we were both admiring her perfectly formed calf. She was a dancer again. Not a mother, not an administrator, and not an ex-wife. Music pulsed through the window from the karaoke joint down the street.

Rita touched my hair, slipping her fingers from the front of my head to the back, a slow tender raking, and I closed my eyes. When I opened them again, I saw that the belt which held her kimono together had slipped over her hips and the robe had fallen open. Her body was almost entirely exposed and yet she just gazed at me, her hand now moving to my ear, then my neck, dusting my skin.

"I'm tired of hiding from you," she said.

When a woman removes her clothes you know what you must do; her body is an invitation that must be honoured. This was what I'd been dreaming of those long hours at my desk, each poem heated anticipation, her body breaking open in every corner of the house. I'd had her on the floor, in the bathtub, standing up in the kitchen, I'd had her every time I lifted a demanding finger, had her begging for it, tearing off her blouse the moment she entered the house. All of this activity had been conducted in complete silence, in the church of the deserted rooms.

My legs splayed open and I allowed her to tug my jeans over my hips, and only then did I lift a hand to remove her kimono, slowly slipping it off, as if there were no urgency. I even folded the garment, set it neatly on the arm of the couch, making her wait, as I had waited. She was exquisite, like a model from a magazine, her posture erect, letting me savour every delicious inch of her. She smiled, then leaned over and nuzzled her mouth against my belly. Then she was tonguing my navel, small cat licks which made my prick throb against her cheek. A dancer is trained to meet the flow of energy from her partner. Rita knew what my next move would be before I did; a shifting of the hips or lifting of a leg: she was there to match it with gentle pressure. Even her breathing became calibrated against mine. Her spine was a supple snake, no position too awkward. I had been swept into a virtuoso performance of lust, and this was when I knew why her husband had left.

I felt like a piece of her choreography.

"What's wrong?" She stared at the sad sight between my legs.

"I don't know." I pulled up my jeans.

"But you seemed so…"

I should have stroked her head and told her that it wasn't her fault, that I was tired, or overeager.

I want you too much, I could have said.

She stretched her arms until there was a cracking sound. "Maybe it's just too late for us, Carlos."

I was grateful for this solution which allowed us to make our separate ways to bed.

I dared not sleep, even if I were able. Perhaps if I didn't sleep, the next day would be nothing special or different, coffee and scrambled eggs for breakfast. I thought not of Rita, but of the man on the beach and how I'd followed him into the clearing, where he'd pulled out his stiff cock and waited for me to sink to the sand with my open mouth. My mouth licked and sucked his salt and it was part of the landscape. I remembered with complete accuracy the smell of sea and sweat mixed with coconut oil. He wasn't faintly interested in who I was, only what I could do for him.

In the morning we did not speak of it. She only said, "Syd's coming over later."

"Professor Baskin?" I was astonished.

Rita stood at the counter constructing a tuna fish sandwich for her son, spreading the mixture across a slice of twelve grain bread. His lunch box was one she'd had in her own childhood, decorated with characters from some television show.

"What does he want?"

"He will tell you." She didn't meet my eyes. She was already bathed and dressed, and she moved quickly, sliding the sandwich into a plastic bag then rinsing the cutting board and knife, showing me that there was much to do on these hurried mornings.

"Baby? Put on your slicker. It's going to rain." She tossed the hooded raincoat to her son who fought with it, fastening his arms to his sides in rebellion.

"Please," she said, crouching now, her voice low and patient.

"What were you guys talking about last night?" the boy said, refusing to look at me.

Just the faintest twinge of fear crossed his mother's face. She reached over and lifted one of his stiff arms to slip into a sleeve. "Nothing much, sweetie."

"You were whispering." This was an accusation.

"That's not against the law." His mother glanced at her watch. "Hurry up, kiddo, I'm already late."

"My stomach hurts. Can't we stay home today?"

I pretended not to be listening, working with the remaining breakfast dishes in the sink, dying for a smoke. They would be gone soon and I would step onto the front porch and take my first breath of the day.

Rita rose to her feet and tossed the raincoat over the boy's head.

"Get your goddamn coat on and let's go!"

A dish fell out of my hand and disappeared into the suds. I was crumpled with dismay, realizing this anger was meant for me, not the boy. When they left moments later, Rita was pale and the boy was whimpering. The door slammed with neither of them saying a word of farewell, and the lunch pail remained on the counter, forgotten.

I went into the front room, plucked her kimono from the arm of the couch, took it upstairs and dropped it on her bed. I'd never set foot in her bedroom, only caught glimpses when I walked by. She made a point of keeping the door closed, but today she had forgotten. The walls were painted yellow, the quilt was a geometric black and white pattern, the bed a simple mattress on a box spring. There were no photographs on the wooden bureau, no silver brushes or combs, just a Japanese fan lying open showing a scene of travellers crossing an arched bridge, and beside it a hinged mirror and a jar of cold cream. The paper blind was pulled down, seeping morning sun. I stood there only a few seconds before fleeing downstairs, hands grabbing the packet of Camels from my shirt pocket.

This is not my house.

No es de ningún modo mi casa.

21

"**R**ITA TELLS ME YOU'VE BEEN WRITING." SYDNEY Baskin stood at the door, an odd figure in this neighbourhood in his neat blazer and chinos. "May I come in?"

"Of course."

He stepped over the various perils, paint cans and jars of soaking brushes, the CD player blasting American blues music.

"Can we turn this thing down?" he mouthed, his whole body cringing.

I obliged, and he immediately relaxed.

"Beer?" I nodded to a cold one I was working on.

"Not this early in the day."

Of course.

He perched gingerly on the window ledge and glanced towards the dining table where my notebook lay open with an arrangement of pencils.

"I am delighted to see you making good use of yourself." Syd folded his white hands on his lap. "You've been quite a challenge to our little group, my friend."

I bowed my head, then took a quick jolt of beer.

"Let me tell you why I'm here." He pulled a letter from the inside pocket of his jacket and handed it to me. "Our parent organization is holding a major conference early next month. They've invited you to participate." He watched me take the letter and spread it open.

As I scanned the letterhead and my own name in the salutation, spelled correctly, the professor rose from the window ledge.

"They have no idea of the difficulty you've had here. We've seen fit to keep it to ourselves."

"That is good." Of course they would not want their failure broadcast. I continued to read.

"Our funding comes, in part, from them. As you can imagine we want to keep the channels open and running smoothly. May I tell them your answer is yes?"

I plowed through the formal paragraphs but only isolated words and phrases stood out: global economy, organized resistance, impunity…

"What am I to do at this conference?"

"Just speak of your experience in your homeland. There will be the usual panels and seminars. I'm confident that you will do well." Then he smiled, an odd arrangement of face, and added, "You will be paid, of course."

I brightened. "Then you must tell them my answer is yes."

Sydney smiled and looked around the room and its disarray. "A work in progress," he noted. "But then our Rita is drawn to big projects." He turned his attention back to me. "How long have you been living here?"

"Not very long." I sensed he would not approve of my lingering, and of her allowing it.

"I assume you'll be getting a place of your own soon."

"It will be necessary," I agreed.

We both understood that this exchange was obligatory, and continued to stand a metre apart, two men of approximately the same size, but I had not shaved and Sydney's neck and face were pink and smooth. Each hair on his head was pressed down in place, the sides scored with grey. He seemed uneasy in this dishevelled house, kicking aside Andreas's foam blocks, slipping his hands into his pockets then pulling them out again. A small-featured man, he was nearly handsome, yet his lips were too thin, lacking sensuality.

Why was he not leaving? My beer was almost done and I wanted another.

He cleared his throat. "You're a curious fellow, Carlos."

"I am like any other man."

"Are you?" Then, to my surprise, he took a step closer, so that his chin was level with mine. "When I came here today," he said, "I had a simple purpose: to deliver this invitation. You know that."

"Yes."

"Don't look so frightened."

"I'm not."

"Good." He smiled his thin smile. "Thank you." His forehead was very pink now, the temples throbbing. Then I saw that it was he who was frightened, not of me, but of himself. I stood before him in his colleague's house, the exiled writer who had caused so much grief, wearing my old black shirt, worn jeans… and he couldn't leave. So I became very calm, yet also cautious, because I knew that whatever happened here, he would never forgive me.

I stuck my thumbs into the back pockets of my jeans and my shirt fell open. He allowed himself a quick glance at my chest.

"You understand why our organization has made certain decisions in the past. It is sometimes necessary to…"

Then he simply stopped speaking.

I took a step backwards until I felt my ass press into the writing table, then heaved myself up so I was perching on its rim. A pencil rolled to the floor and landed under the radiator. Now, my friend, it is you who must act, who must reveal yourself. I spoke these words to myself and watched, in the same state of calm, as he slipped his arms out of his linen blazer and tossed it onto the window ledge.

"I might have one of those beers, after all." There was something choked in his voice.

Nodding towards the kitchen at the back of the house I said, "Help yourself."

He moved, not towards the refrigerator but towards me. I stared without smiling, watching his three cautious steps across the linoleum. At the same time I heard the sputter of Rita's ancient car as she pulled up outside the house. I knew it was she, but of course Sydney had no idea. He lifted a hand and caressed my cheek with his fingers and, with his other hand, loosened his tie. He could hardly breathe. When he began to probe one finger between my lips into my wet mouth, he shivered violently, and then I touched his fingertip with my tongue. This pleasure was almost too sublime, and he let out a moan.

The door pushed open, letting in a scurry of dead leaves.

"What was going on between you two?" Rita had seen our

guest to the door and stood staring as he clipped down the sidewalk towards his parked car.

I had never seen Sydney so fretful as he was just a few moments before, picking up his jacket, the contents of its pockets falling out, a too-hearty laugh, then the panicky grab for keys, spare coins.

"What do you think?" I said.

"I don't know what the hell to think." She finally closed the door and turned back into the room. She unhitched her blouse from the waist of her skirt and let it float free. "But I know what it looked like."

I was still perched on the edge of the table, serene.

"Was that a seduction scene?"

I waited a beat. "Perhaps that is exactly what it was."

"I can't deal with this!" She flipped her hair. "Who was seducing whom?"

"What do you think?"

"Don't answer my question with another question. Just tell me — are you queer, Carlos?"

"Certainly not."

"Because Sydney is." Her voice dropped a notch. "Did you feel you had to, because of his position?"

"Perhaps I wanted to see."

"See what?"

Good question, but I thought I knew the answer. "I wanted to see what would happen."

She was standing precisely where Syd had stood moments ago, except she was taller and more dramatic. Her tension was alive, the breath coming too hard and fast. The dancer's perfect control had vanished.

I lifted my legs and trapped her, scissor-like. "Come here."

She obeyed, until her belly was pressed to my groin.

"Are you still wanting to see?" she said.

I lifted her skirt and peeled down her panties, which were paper thin, to her thighs. With my other hand I wrenched my own jeans over my ass. Just far enough. My cock was hard.

"What if I hadn't turned up?" she whispered. "How far would you have gone?"

"Who knows?" I slid my fingers between her legs. Soon the image of Sydney would go away, and with it, my courage. Rita, excuse me, but I am so calm now, neither of us need worry.

I didn't want to see anything, only to feel.

22

THE PROGRAMME COVER WAS BLUE WITH AN engraving of
a pen, a gold tipped fountain pen like my father's, writing
across a piece of paper which was engulfed in flames. The topic of
the conference was "Writers Under Fire" and I was in it, on page
three, with a small photograph. I was to appear on a panel with
two men and one woman whose names I couldn't pronounce. We
would be discussing our personal experiences with "The Cost Of
Silence" and every time I thought of it I felt sick.

Participants streamed in from all corners of the world.
Volunteers staked out airport lounges, on the lookout for men
and women dressed in sarongs or dashiki. Since it was early June,
most of the students had gone home and the university resi-
dences were commandeered, the foreign visitors put up on student cots, except the most distinguished ones, who received
hotel rooms. The keynote address was given by an eminent

judge who had presided over the South African Truth and Reconciliation trials. In his photograph I saw a cadaverously thin man with a mane of white hair and thick round glasses. I was amongst the elite, the top people of this earth.

Jack Kerouac, the beatnik writer, said: Try never to get drunk outside your own house.

He made me laugh, because I knew it was the reason why everything had gone so wrong for me here. Because my own house is not these walls and staircases and warped doors; it is not this city with its neat curbs and shiny new buildings and whirl of traffic. My house is the country where I was raised and where, if I drank, I was safe, or so I thought. The General's ear bent towards me like a cup waiting for my words, my idiot words.

I brushed my teeth and hair, scrounged a new jacket from Rita's pals, and announced to myself, "I will not shame her." I really meant, "I will not shame myself."

The judge told the audience terrible stories, chilling tales of the suffering of the South African people under apartheid, and as the details spilled forth in his crisp unsentimental voice, the audience sat rapt.

"I spoke to one child who'd been dumped, bleeding and helpless, by the side of the road..."

I sat thinking I would kill anyone who laid a hand on Andreas. To hurt a child goes beyond the normal crimes committed between men — it is a crime against all of humanity. After his horrifying speech there was a moment of stunned silence, followed by a boisterous performance by an Aboriginal dance group. Music blasted through the speakers from pre-recorded tapes while the men shook rattles and beat drums and chanted wildly. We saw many such events at home in the Teatro

Folklórico on the main square. The Indians' clothing here in Canada was colourful and brand new, with not a speck of dirt. The colours were too bright, almost fluorescent, plastic beads sewn to animal hides and moccasins. At home there is a drearier panorama. Ancient ribbons and bells and feathers and animal hides toss around the stage. But the music is always live with hand-carved flutes and drums. Our President loves such shows. You would see him standing at his box seat on the first balcony, applauding while his bodyguards pressed in.

I wore my special certification, a name tag dangling from my neck which allowed me to attend all conference events for free. There were three rows of seats at the front reserved for us, the participants. People watched as I made my way down the aisle just as the lights were dimming. Who was I, and where was I from? What unspeakable offense had I suffered or witnessed?

After the opening ceremony, delegates crossed the campus to the hospitality suite, which was in a new building, funded by a millionaire businessman and named after his mother. The day was clear and windy, and as we crossed the parking lot we watched a group of summer students flying kites, the long paper snakes straining at their lines, aching to escape. There was a large group of us, name tags flapping, and we were from all nations, chattering in many languages. I found myself trotting alongside a beautiful woman from Pakistan who wore a sari and spoke in such a soft voice I had to strain to hear.

"Where are you from?" she asked, hand closing the material at her neck.

I told her.

She smiled. "I am not sure where that is. Near the coast?"

"Exactly on the coast."

"It must be very beautiful."

Yes, Santa Clara is very beautiful, and hearing her say this made my heart kick with longing. What if I never got back? I had never allowed myself to think this, but now I was surrounded by men and women, many who called themselves "exiles," and for them it was not a poem. It was their reality.

The hospitality suite was decorated with paintings by the Haida and furnished with beige chairs and a leather couch that hinged in two directions. Someone had placed vibrantly blue irises in cut-glass vases that reflected the blooms over and over. A huge window looked out onto the water and distant mountains. All of us paused to stare at the peaks, one of which was still dusted with snow. I thought of the times I'd been promised ski trips, visits to chalets which didn't materialize.

"Wine, sir?"

I accepted a drink and realized that my hand was shaking. A few sips and it was as if my body filled with pure oxygen. It wasn't just me: I could tell everyone in the room felt the same way. The judge asked for whisky. I hadn't known that you could, and now I wished I'd thought of it. As he drank, standing just a few feet away from me, his eyes darted around the room. A woman was speaking to him but he was hardly listening. She seemed intense, too eager for his attention, and perhaps he was thinking, "I have listened too long."

His eyes stopped on mine and I felt a twinge of terror. This man knew who you were and what you had done.

I gave him a short, dignified smile and suddenly he was right in front of me, his tall form bending over. Up close I could see he was older than I'd thought, yet stern cheekbones held up any sagging flesh and his eyes were charcoal beads, as if they'd soaked up all available light in the world. The white hair was brushed back, comb marks visible, and touched the collar of his cashmere jacket.

"How many political prisoners in your country?"

He'd glanced at my name tag. When I didn't answer immediately he snapped the next question.

"And how many are writers?"

My mouth opened, fishlike, but no words emerged.

I knew nothing; I had no statistics, no facts, nothing useful. The pretty waitress approached with a tray of hors d'oeuvres and I smiled with such a gust of gratitude that she must have felt it, for she smiled. "Something to eat, gentlemen?"

Simultaneously, the judge and I reached for the cheese pies.

"How active are human rights groups in your country?"

I clutched the little pie and frowned while the judge prepared to eat. I was, of course, assumed to be an expert in these matters, yet I wasn't sure I could even name two such groups, and what if he were to ask for details, dates and names, objects of aggression? His mouth reached for the food, his jaw opening, chin tilted, a sense of urgency in the gesture. Then something shocking happened: the pie exploded. A piñata-blast of sizzling hot cheese spurted out his mouth, over his hand, and down the front of his shirt.

"Shit!" the eminent judge cried, and napkins were produced from all corners of the room. A cup of cold water was offered to cool the burning mouth, a flurry of women worked to mop up his clothing while he stood very simply and solemnly. If possible he seemed more dignified as result of this small catastrophe.

"I'm so sorry," the waitress said, dabbing at his chin with a wet cloth.

"I've seen worse," he said.

My presence and any lingering questions had been erased.

"The cost is in the body."

The Iranian writer was sitting at the edge of his seat, pressing his hand to his chest. He was a young guy, maybe thirty, with nicotine-stained fingers. The lights were so intense that when we, who were sitting on stage, stared into the audience, we saw only a black breathing curtain.

"The body can never be silent," he intoned in heavily accented English that I worked to interpret during the silences which fell between each statement. My fellow panelists, the Pakistani woman and a Kurd, looked down at the table, frowning as they listened. I poured water from the pitcher into my glass and slurped noisily. This terrible thirst... I couldn't get rid of it. My lips were parched, my throat felt like it was closing. My turn was next. The Pakistani journalist had spoken of the cost to society of censorship and how lies and rumours grow in the place of facts. I thought she said "farts." The Iranian spoke of his five years in prison as a renegade poet who'd dared to dance against the clerics.

"I am lucky to be alive," he whispered into the microphone. "And I know exactly how much my death is worth." The sum of his fatwah, he modestly declared, was a fraction of Rushdie's. "I will paint you a picture of my cell," he said and began to swing an imaginary brush through the air. "The cot is here, the bucket here..." He interrupted himself. "It is a funny thing when I remember this place. You might think I would feel sick and want to wipe it away, but it is the opposite."

Yes, if memory goes you have lost your life, even the parts you may think should be lost forever. I crossed my legs. All the water made me have to piss, but there was no time: I was up next. I could hardly skitter off stage while the Iranian poet wound up his heroic tale. What would they think? That poor sucker is nervous, or else he can't hold in his piss after so many kicks to the kidney. Just when I was sure the Iranian was done, he began to speak poetically of the tiny cell window which cast an ever-shifting noodle of light across his bed, and how this was the only visible mark of time passing, "that and the beard on my chin and the hair on my head." He paused. "I've always thought that without this light-clock I would have gone mad. It reminded me that there was a world outside."

I could feel the audience's coiled sympathy, the intense breathing darkness across the stage lights, like the hum of crickets outside a country cabin at night.

"I was one of the lucky ones," he said.

Lucky? Because the bars had become an after-image burned into the retina, always visible, even now, a grid that marks out his vision into neat quadrants.

I will swallow now, I instructed myself, and relax the throat.

"We welcome next, Carlos Romero Estévez, poet and journalist in exile."

My hand played with the empty drinking glass. The Pakistani woman in her emerald coloured sari moved the microphone across the table in front of me and a loud scratching noise echoed through the auditorium. I blinked into the ghastly lights.

"Thank you ladies and gentlemen."

The silence pleaded for more. My heart was hammering wildly. They really wanted to know, what was, in my experience, the Cost of Silence, and did I not know as well as anyone the cost of having to hide who you really are so they will not back off in disgust? The cost of being the court fool, the wandering man who, as Homer wrote, "tells lies for a night's lodging, for fresh clothing."

But you, kind Canadians, do you want to know all this?

I could perform when I was called upon. Dear Rita, I would not disappoint you.

"Excuse my English," I began and there was a murmur of sympathy.

And so I read my famous poems, and this time I felt like a carpenter tearing down a dead wall to make the space larger. I wrote these words when I thought I was a free man, but I was an idiot. The audience thought I was making something beautiful, but I knew better. This was demolition. This was peeling off everything you think you know. I was naked, but they saw only my badly fitting clothes and sad story. I moved into Spanish, without apology, my voice filling the room while people grabbed for their headsets. I was again a small boy standing in my father's study with its antique desk and dark bookcases and windows smothered with curtains, reciting the poem I had memorized: Arriba, canes, arriba!

When I was finished I told them, "In silence we have to find our voices again and again, even if no one is listening. Muchísimas gracias."

I had never sat down to dine with so many dark-skinned people, all exiles, like me. What immense pride I dared feel to be part of such a gathering, and as we entered the Greek restaurant, the other clients stopped talking and looked at us. They had read of this conference in the newspapers and heard interviews on the radio. Our group clustered around a long table surrounded by the plaster fountains and taverna lanterns while waiters busied themselves with menus and wine bottles. A belly dancer shimmied past, trailing the gauzy cloth of her shawl over our heads. We were a miniature United Nations, all men except for Rita and the Pakistani journalist. We gladly soaked in the smells of garlic and retsina, and the trills of laughter and mournful Middle Eastern music. Our work at the conference was almost done and our appetites were huge. The Bosnian novelist sat opposite me and spoke in rapid-fire English, punctuating the air with his fork. To my left was the Iranian poet, twisting on the chair as he spoke to Rita.

"I owe my life to people like you," he was saying. "And it is good to live." His hand held her wrist and she stared intently at it. "But I tell you the truth, I am disappointed in my visit here to Canada. No one asks me about my writing, my books. They ask only about my experiences in prison."

His thin shoulders pressed against the cloth of his wrinkled corduroy shirt. Smoke filled the air from all sides, and I am a man who enjoys smoke, yet it was too much, too thick, too urgent, as if these men couldn't breathe without the cigarette to tell them how and when.

A pair of tiny birds were set on a platter before me, surrounded by lemon-tinted potatoes and beans.

"No no!" The Bosnian reached across the table as I attempted to pry meat off the miniature bones. "You must put it in your mouth and eat it entirely."

I watched as he picked up his own quail and began to munch vigorously through its delicate ribs.

"I have become, it seems, a professional exile," the Iranian poet said as he pushed aside his plate of eggplant, untouched, and continued drawing on his cigarette. Rita topped off his glass of retsina.

"But you must not think of yourself as an exile after three years have passed." The Pakistani woman spoke for the first time.

The Bosnian agreed. "You must enter your new life fully." He patted at his beard with his napkin and all traces of the quail were gone. He was a thin man with a recent belly and his clothes hadn't adjusted. The cloth of his shirt splayed open, and he kept reaching down to tug it shut. "You make a place for yourself in the new land."

He spoke with such confidence, yet I'd heard him earlier on a panel speaking of his time in Stockholm, where he'd been flown by an international agency, plucked from the raging streets of Sarajevo, and how he'd cowered in his new apartment for months, afraid of the streets, of the people, of the grey looming skies.

To my right was a Nigerian who lived in Frankfurt, or was it Munich, and worked for some refugee organization. He was a playwright, famous in his homeland yet banned there, and penniless now, for the refugee organization was volunteer-run. He was elegant, middle aged, with skeletal wrists and long fingers, dark brown on one side and pink on the other.

"We would pull the blinds and play cards," he'd told his audience earlier that day. "If the police swarmed in, our meetings would appear innocent."

Apparently the ruse stopped working for he'd spent half the decade in a series of deteriorating prison compounds. He had a way of smiling even as he described the most atrocious events. Perhaps he felt apologetic at bearing such news of the human race.

The Iranian finally let go of Rita's wrist and swung himself back to face the table.

"When you first arrive in the new country you are a kind of hero," he told us. "Someone gives you a nice apartment, a TV, clothes, and used clothes in bags."

The others laughed.

"Big plastic bags full of old suits and sweaters," the Bosnian commiserated.

"And there are invitations, two, three times a week, for dinner or to make speeches or interviews, to visit the national parks."

We were all nodding now, remembering those early weeks of celebrity.

"Your dance card is full and you think this is how it is going to be here. You go from your cell, hauled out in the middle of the night without explanation, pushed onto a cargo plane at dawn. You don't know where you are going or why. They force a pill between your lips and you wake up in Sweden!"

Or Frankfurt, or Vancouver. There was Rita in her yellow slicker holding up a sign saying CAFE, and under it, in smaller letters, the words that I recognized as belonging to me: Carlos Romero Estévez. Your name is a sort of star or constellation which is the same everywhere in the hemisphere.

"But how long does it last?" The Iranian thumped his hand on the table top. "How long do the phone calls last, the invitations for dinner, to country homes and ski holidays?"

I was staring at Rita, whose face flushed, perhaps with anger at our lack of gratitude, for were we not so much better off now?

The Pakistani woman toyed with her food. "How many times have I told my stories: the book burnings, the angry mob at my door?"

The Iranian smiled. "Our stories are too much the same."

A trio of heads nodded. Behind us, leaning against the wall, was his lone bodyguard, a bulky RCMP officer fitted with a tiny headset.

"And how many books were burned in your streets?" the Pakistani went on in the same implacable voice. "Ten thousand? Fifty thousand?"

"Six books," the Bosnian interjected. "Because this is only how many the publisher printed."

There was much raucous laughter, as if we were aging pop stars sharing memories of days and nights on the road. We had to laugh at our miseries, because everyone else made them holy. The quails, I decided, were delicious, bones and all. I thought of Beatriz, my father's parrot, found with her talons coiled stiffly around her roost one morning.

The dancer rippled her muscled belly in celebration of our visit, and shimmied alongside, earrings dancing, eyes half shut, mesmerized by her own movement. Her skin smelled of cinnamon.

"And what of you?" The Iranian turned his attention to me. "How many of your poetry books have accumulated in the bonfires of Santa Clara?"

He was making a sort of joke, and I knew that, but I could not mimic his easy tone in response. Maybe it was Rita's face cocked to one side, lips slightly parted, expectant, hoping that Carlos would measure up in this band of international exiles. I began to speak in a too-earnest voice.

"I woke up one morning just after Christmas. Normally this is a quiet time in my city. Everyone is fatigued from the holiday celebrations and the children are indoors with their toys. There is only a street sweeper out on the plaza, shovelling rubbish into his burlap bag." As I spoke I could smell the sizzling stews from the marketplace because even on this day people had to eat. The women with their long metal spoons were wrapped in blankets and wool sweaters and wore gloves with the ends of the fingers cut out. Their breath created cones of smoke in the morning air.

"As I awoke I could hear the sounds of a crowd gathering and because this was unusual I crawled over to my window and opened the shutter." At this point I cast a quick glance at Rita. What had I told her of my house? Only that the Romero Estévez family live high up on the hill at the edge of town, because my father hated noise and confusion.

"Young men were shouting and shaking their fists and there were barrels, half a dozen barrels full of cloths that had been soaked in kerosene."

All of this could have happened and none of my listeners seemed surprised. The Iranian was reaching into his mouth to dislodge a piece of food. The Bosnian journalist leaned over to splash retsina in my glass.

"I saw they had copies of my books and they were tossing these into the barrels…"

"Ka-boom!" The Iranian spread his arms wide. "It makes very good heat, does it not. Where is the dessert here? I am tired of these vegetables."

Dinner continued, thick coffee, then pastry soaked in honey, and I felt their disdain for me leach into the air. I had told my story without humour or grace, as if I were the only one.

Over orange-flavoured liqueur, the exiles began to talk of my country.

"It's your turn, mate," the Bosnian said, clamping a hand over mine. "Have you seen the news lately?" He looked around at the others. "Our friend should be front and centre, telling the world of his country's skirmishes."

"Why have they not given you a keynote speech?" the African said, forming the words carefully. He wasn't drinking alcohol, I noticed, only glass after glass of fizzy water.

"My English…" I shrugged.

"This is unimportant," the African said. "There are excellent translators."

I didn't dare look at Rita: she'd pushed so hard to have me included at all.

"Who is this guy in the jungle we hear about?" the Bosnian said. "With his ragtag army."

"Mario."

"You know him?"

"Of course."

Suddenly all eyes were on me. Even the Pakistani woman stopped picking at her dessert.

"What sort of man is he?"

I pretended to think. "Brave. A bit crazy."

The Bosnian sloshed more liqueur into my glass. "So you have worked with him?"

"Many times. Many missions. And we went to the same preparatory school. Our lives have followed parallel courses." I sipped slowly, letting the glow fill my chest, and turned to Rita. "It is with Mario that I took the food trucks."

She looked even more surprised than I expected.

"Mario?"

"Of course."

She gave a little laugh. "Then you must tell your friends how you and the famous Mario stole food for the poor people."

I shrugged modestly. "It is a long story."

"No, it isn't," she insisted, and I heard her breath quicken. When I didn't respond, she turned to the others and said, "They'd hijack trucks bound for the supermarkets and drive them into the barrios."

I stared at the tablecloth. Such heavy cutlery in this restaurant, such huge linen napkins.

"They could have been killed," she went on, and I felt her hand touch my knee.

"This man, Mario," the Bosnian said. "I would like to meet him."

"Perhaps you will." Rita gazed at a scene painted on the wall. A group of fishermen pushed their dinghies into the Aegean sea.

The closing gala was a festive occasion. Drinks were served in the lobby before the show while young people circulated with petitions and sold buttons which spelled CAFE in green and blue, a dollar apiece. A brand new sailboat sat amongst waves of aquamarine gauze, luring audience members to buy tickets and drop them into a cylinder, from which a lucky mariner would be plucked. You could spot the exiles — each was the centre of a group, shaking hands, smoking and dropping ashes onto the carpet despite the prominently placed No Smoking signs. Our palms were hot and sticky from so much goodwill. Flashbulbs filled the air. Two men with heavy television cameras moved through the crowd, trailing slim female newscasters, and I waited my turn to be interviewed. Then softly persistent "dings" announced that the show was ready to begin and we reluctantly slid into the beige auditorium.

A man in a dark suit stood in the centre of the stage, his arms flat to his sides, grey hair slicked back. He began to sing, unaccompanied, some folk song in a language I didn't recognize. It was a plaintive tune, sung without flourish, but I imagined simple people living off the land, fishing, farming, loving. After, Rita leaned over and whispered in my ear, "We're so lucky to get Viktor." There was a subdued hush before applause broke out.

Then a lectern was dragged to the centre by two stagehands, and a woman in a white gown marched on stage, the material of her dress floating with the breeze of her own journey, and she began to read from a piece of paper names of men and women who had been arrested this very month for violations. But I could not listen because the Grecian food had laid a sudden bomb in my belly. After the woman, a young man strode on wearing a bow tie and suspenders and began to deliver some speech which at first caused much laughter. As it went on the laughter turned into chuckles then a long uneasy silence. I pressed my hand to my stomach and hoped for the best.

Rita leaned over again to whisper into my ear, "Bring on the hook."

Even this man finally disappeared into the darkness to tepid applause while a movie screen was being lowered slowly from the ceiling.

A woman's voice filled the speakers. "He was born in the mountains," she began in the falsely intimate style of a professional actor.

On the screen there was a mountain scene, grainy, badly photographed. A village of mud huts and concrete. Yes yes, we have such places in my country. And as I watched the children standing barefoot in the door of their pathetic hut I felt a surge of irritation. These were my people. Even here, with my conference name tag, thousands of miles away, I was not safe from their pleading eyes. One of the kids was holding something up towards the camera — a doll? a gun? Let's hope it's a gun.

"From the mountains to the city, and now back to the shimmering heat of the jungle…" the voice intoned.

The screen showed a man hunched against a tree, smoking. The tree had huge floppy leaves and the man was thin and grizzled, with a scrappy beard, wearing military fatigues.

I sat up straight.

Christ.

No mistaking that sardonic look, unintimidated by the photographer.

"Jailed on April 20 and sentenced to death for crimes against the State…"

The image stayed up there, huge, each pore on his face enlarged, the whiskers greying — how had he gotten so old? Sentenced to death? I hadn't known.

The voice faded, then finally the image on the screen dissolved and darkness returned to the auditorium. We watched as a spotlight searched a corner of the curtain at stage left and a slight figure appeared, dressed in tan shirt and chinos, and began to walk with a pronounced limp to the centre, light spraying over his face. And A, you were so young now with the beard cut off, you looked as you did when we were students, hardly like a warrior as you smiled into the fog of audience. Who were now all on their feet applauding furiously.

Rita clutched my elbow and bellowed into my ear. "You must introduce me to your friend." I could only nod my head. The sick feeling had spread from my gut through my whole body.

"You knew this," I managed to say.

She was beaming. "Of course. But I was sworn to secrecy."

A lifted his arm in an oddly tentative gesture and said into the microphone, "Excuse me for my English."

Do not apologize, my friend. I winced against the frailty of his voice as he continued. "I give many thanks to be here today."

He knew what to do, I assured myself. He'd orchestrated this whole event, he was in charge, as always.

"Our life is difficult, those of us who resist…"

I became excited: soon he would see me, he would point into the audience, dead centre, and he would smile, and all the others would follow his gaze and I would be lifted into his world again. I found myself sitting erect in my chair, chin raised, willing him to pierce through the glare of spotlight and find my waiting face. But he scanned the unseen audience, blinded by stage lights, and he saw nothing and no one.

"I do not wish to speak of my suffering, for it is common, an ordinary sensation. Let me tell you, instead, a brief story."

Yes, tell us a story, A, and we will listen, for you have always been the master storyteller. Back in university when you dashed into the café between adventures, we stopped our banal chatter and lifted our heads to witness your entrance. You brought news from the outside world, and we were desperate to be entranced.

"The small bird, he lifted his wing and try to cover the massive crow, but he is too small."

My ears strained, a great effort to untangle his laboured accent. I glanced at Rita and saw only her tilted chin and eyes filled with tears. The story was some allegory, a mode unfamiliar to A, and he struggled through it, hands jumping in and out of his pockets. "He attempts to help his friend, but the friend is sick and unable to fly, and so, you see, the small bird must disappear in the wind."

There was a pause while A bent his head, signalling the end of the impenetrable tale. Spotlights crisscrossed his hunched figure in the middle of the empty stage, and for the second time the audience rose and their applause swelled like an railway engine roaring into some deserted station. I joined them and it was as if I was applauding my own arrival a year earlier.

23

TINY LANTERNS SEEPED WHITE LIGHT AMONGST THE ferns and grasses of Professor Baskin's back yard. How different it looked at night, full of shadows and unidentified shapes, the fish pool gurgling sanitized water to the orange carp within. Its own lights were recessed and cast a blue shimmer as if the pool were a flying saucer docked in this sprawling yard. Fifty-six people from the conference were at the party, hand-picked from the participants by Sydney himself. There were important directors of CAFE from Toronto and Ottawa, and I spotted the eminent judge himself, now shed of his cashmere coat, looking almost informal in rolled-up sleeves, puffing on a fat cigar.

"Not Cuban," I heard him say in a raised voice.

Not while the bearded dictator clings to power.

Where was A? There was something wrong with my throat; I kept clearing it, then it would close again. Drinks helped. He had not spotted me in the crowd back at the theatre, nor in the foyer afterward, where he'd stood surrounded by press cameras.

I received a slap on the back from my old CAFE friend, Daniel Rose.

"You were good up there yesterday," he said. "Held your own." His curly hair was uncombed and he wore a collarless shirt under his jacket.

"Thank you." I gave one of those quick bows that I'd invented the instant I set foot on this soil. "And how is your beautiful wife?"

His face tightened. "Sharon has left me." Then, when I did not quickly respond, he said, "Are you surprised?"

Of course he wanted me to tell him I was astonished, that surely no woman could leave such an accomplished and passionate man, but this was not a night for polite lies.

"No," I said, "I am not surprised."

He laughed, more like a bark. "Seems no one but me was."

He'd been drinking. It was apparent in his hooded eyes and the way he bobbed sideways as if searching for his centre of gravity. Next he'd be wanting to pull me to some back end of the garden and talk long hours about his great sorrow, because I, Carlos, the exile who had suffered so much, would understand his crushing loneliness. Yet I could think only of his wife who had finally managed to break free.

"Excuse me," I said. "I am searching for my old friend."

"Mario?"

I'd just spotted him at the side of the cobblestone patio with our host, Sydney, their heads tilted towards each other.

"Yes, Mario."

Daniel lifted his arm and made an arc through the air and declaimed, "Then you must go to him."

My hands were shaking so hard that my glass splashed its contents to the patio floor, but I was not distressed by this awkwardness. This was not some examination hall or guerrilla camp in the back country: I knew this place better than A did. The nervousness was even welcome, a sign that I was fully alive, and that everything I remembered from my old life was about to pounce like a cat into the middle of this polite gathering.

While A listened to Sydney he leaned over, frowning, his chest concave as he attempted to understand what was being said. I was drifting back to the examination hall in Santa Clara, scrabbling to answer mathematical questions and watching the boy with stapled huaraches and calloused heels, the whiff of country in his hair. I could enumerate his shoes through the years, beginning with peasant sandals, on to American sneakers while at university, then the cheap prison-issue thongs, followed by the scuffed combat boots of his days in the camp. And what did he wear now? A pair of brown loafers, excellent leather.

I crossed the patio, waiting for him to look up so that I could relish the moment of astonishment as it transformed his face.

"You must introduce me." Rita, who had disappeared into the crowd the moment we arrived, was suddenly at my side. "Now's our chance."

I felt myself being propelled across the yard, Rita's step secure in her high-heeled sandals, her hand pressed into my back. This was too fast, the approach was all wrong. I should be alone, backlit, face in shadows, walking a steady pace, not this pell-mell march. Rita, of all people, should understand this. We passed a journalist whom I recognized, a short man who called after us, "You're going to Mario?"

"I have known this man for nearly twenty years," I cried over my shoulder.

And how long since I'd seen him? Four years at least.

We barrelled past the musical entertainment, a woman dressed in a long skirt and shawl who daintily plucked the strings of a harp.

"Oh no," Rita moaned. "'Greensleeves.'"

Melting wax gathered on the tablecloth beneath silver candelabra and the dancing flames lit up an arrangement of food, but I was not hungry. The cobblestone was uneven under my feet, each placed in a careful random pattern, edge to edge. We were Eskimos hopping across ice floes, approaching our prey. The journalist had pulled out his notebook and was trailing in our wake to be witness to the historic meeting. I was not even faintly drunk, despite my best efforts. Syd looked up, smiling from some amusement, his hand sliding off A's shoulder. Seeing me about to interrupt his tête à tête did not give the professor any pleasure. The slim body, which had teetered with forbidden longing just two weeks earlier, had found a new object of affection.

Rita chattered at my side, "Poor guy must be sacked after the long flight."

A glanced up, alerted by the sound of Rita's heels, and up close I could see his eyes were red, and he was squinting as if trying to see properly.

I spoke too hurriedly the words I'd selected, "The world shrinks, my friend. Who could have foreseen this moment?" I waited for the anticipated moue of astonishment but he merely stared at me politely. I was thinner perhaps, or it was a shock, this sudden intrusion from home. I'd spoken in Spanish, in the accent of our state, but he merely continued his steady stare. I felt my gut twist. The group around us waited for the historic moment to unfold. Why were these old comrades not embracing?

So I called him by his real name, not Mario, but A, which only a fellow citizen would know. I spoke it tenderly, aware that I was possibly the only man in this city, even this country, who would remember.

He started, shoulders bracing, and a look of alarm crossed his face. "I am sorry," he said in a tight voice, "but I have forgotten your name."

Lantern light flitted over his forehead like the beating wings of a moth. His expression was incurious as he spoke, and I saw the way he looked at Rita, his eyes darting sideways as if seeking a mode of escape.

"Carlos," I said with an effort at tranquility. "Carlos Romero Estévez."

Rita's fingers dug into my waist.

He waited a long, eternal beat then said, "I do not understand why you are here."

I reddened, then quickly recovered. "I live here now." The words surprised me by their simplicity. At last his hand reached out and I quickly moved to shake it, remembering that it would be a limp clasp, not the earnest pumping that is fashionable amongst the men of this country. Instead he gave my cheek a pat.

"So you too have been rescued."

We could only wonder at the sequence of events that had brought us both to this manicured yard in the middle of a city we'd barely heard of.

"Tell me where I know you from," he said.

Was it possible he had forgotten our shared history? Citronella fragrance sifted through the air, mixing with the barbeque fumes. I cleared my throat.

"We were schoolmates," I began, then stalled. Where to begin? I stared harder and wondered if he was mocking me again. But there was no laughter in his eyes, only a hunted look, and his jaw was so tight that his lips were colourless. And so I remarked on the preparatory school we had both attended, his disobedience there, and as I spoke his expression grew even more uneasy and I got the impression I was saying too much, that all of this was a past that had swum away from him, overlaid by more important enterprises.

I glanced at our host sipping at his spritzer, a wedge of lemon clinging to the rim of his glass.

"You will live here now?" I said, reverting to English.

"No. I am in Frankfurt. A post at the national university."

How odd this was, this suddenly banal exchange, as if we were tourists meeting in an airport lounge.

"Writer-in-Exile chair?"

"You know it?" He seemed surprised, eyes locked in a permanent squint, and I was shocked by wrinkles pleating his skin. His lips were frayed, and his teeth, never the best, were a mess.

"Of course."

Sydney coughed discreetly. "Perhaps you should introduce Rita. She's been waiting."

"Of course," I said again. "My friend, Rita Falcon."

"Like the noble bird." A smiled his old warrior's smile.

"Thank you for speaking to us at the conference," Rita said in a low voice. "We need to hear your story."

A nodded, almost a bow, yes, the very bow I had first assumed a year ago.

The reporter was scribbling something in his note pad.

At this moment a tray was presented with drinks and I selected a martini and glanced at the waiter to thank him. I recognized the handsome boy who'd been lounging in the second-floor bedroom of this house more than twelve months earlier. Rita dropped her arm from my waist and was now pressing forward to listen to the revolutionary hero.

"Frankfurt is excellent," he was telling the group of avid listeners. "I am giving speeches and they have arranged translations in several European languages."

He was so thin, bony as a bird. Soon he must learn to digest northern food, or he would fade away. His gestures were heated and insistent, as if he were afraid of the possibility of his own disappearance. Suddenly he clutched his knee, swearing, and began to hobble back and forth as if to shake off some terrible pain. The slight gimp I'd noticed as he crossed the conference stage was now a definite lurch. We all stared and wondered what ghastly wound was concealed by his ill-fitting trousers.

A waved off their help, and tried to smile. But there was no hint of amusement in his face, only a bewildered exhaustion.

I lifted a bottle of vodka off the table and took it to the far end of Sydney's yard. With the darkness came a muted clamour, as if the party had been draped in flannel. I heaved myself onto a decorative rock. The air back here was saturated with lilac scent, a smell which whisked me back to my family's home high on the hill above Santa Clara. Each spring our maid would snip the branches of the flowering bush on the patio and bring a bouquet inside to use as a centrepiece at the table.

Sydney was reaching for A and Rita, pulling them into a huddle, then he pressed his mouth toward the new exile's ear, no doubt speaking slow clear phrases of instruction.

I do not get stupid when I drink, only more alert. A looked up once and I am sure he was searching for me in the darkness. The rock was cool against my body, and the moss growing in its crevices, which I stroked now with my fingers, was as coarse and damp as pubic hair. No one could see me, but I could see all of them.

ACKNOWLEDGEMENTS

I AM INDEBTED TO SEVERAL CLEVER AND sympathetic people for reading this book in its mutating forms along the way. For editorial assistance and overall support I would like to thank: Tim Deverell, Bill and Tekla Deverell, Cynthia Holz, Jenny Munro, Sarah Sheard, and finally, Barry Jowett at Dundurn.

For timely financial assistance I gratefully acknowledge the Canada Council for the Arts, the Ontario Arts Council, and the Toronto Arts Council.